It was then that it occurred to him, a possible way to rid himself of her assistance and distracting presence.

"Miss Mabson, it has occurred to me that we never set the parameters of our wager," he said.

"Param——— sounding breathless.

He grin——— when I win?"

"Is it not ——— ow you are a winner?" she shrugge——— a loser? Whatever the case may be."

He watched her mouth enunciate each syllable. So precise. So perfect.

"Then it is nothing more than a race. But a wager, a wager has consequences. You either win something or you lose something," he said. "It raises the stakes, provides more impetus for success."

"I'm beginning to think, Inspector, that you have given this much thought. What is it you want from me?" Then she smiled. "*If* I lose?"

"A kiss."

Other AVON ROMANCES

A DANGEROUS BEAUTY *by Sophia Nash*
THE DEVIL'S TEMPTATION *by Kimberly Logan*
THE HIGHLANDER'S BRIDE *by Donna Fletcher*
THE TEMPLAR'S SEDUCTION *by Mary Reed McCall*
A WARRIOR'S TAKING *by Margo Maguire*
WHAT ISABELLA DESIRES *by Anne Mallory*
WILD SWEET LOVE *by Beverly Jenkins*

Coming Soon

BRIDE ENCHANTED *by Edith Layton*
TOO SCANDALOUS TO WED *by Alexandra Benedict*

And Don't Miss These
ROMANTIC TREASURES
from Avon Books

BEWITCHING THE HIGHLANDER *by Lois Greiman*
HOW TO ENGAGE AN EARL *by Kathryn Caskie*
THE VISCOUNT IN HER BEDROOM *by Gayle Callen*

Tempted At Every Turn

Robyn DeHart

AVON

An Imprint of HarperCollinsPublishers

AVON BOOKS
An Imprint of HarperCollins*Publishers*
10 East 53rd Street
New York, New York 10022-5299

Copyright © 2007 by Robyn DeHart
ISBN: 978-0-06-112753-3
ISBN-10: 0-06-112753-1
www.avonromance.com

First Avon Books paperback printing: August 2007

Avon Trademark Reg. U.S. Pat. Off. and in Other Countries,
Marca Registrada, Hecho en U.S.A.
HarperCollins® is a registered trademark of HarperCollins Publishers.

Printed in the U.S.A.

10 9 8 7 6 5 4 3 2 1

To Mom, who never said no when I asked for a book. You are the reason I love words.

To Paul—I don't know how I wrote happy endings before you.

And to Cordelia—you will be forever loved and missed.

Tempted
At Every Turn

Chapter 1

London, 1893

"Well, well, well, if it isn't a letter from 'Anonymous,'" Finch said, handing the envelope to James. "You haven't received one of these in a while."

Inspector James Sterling grabbed the parchment and sat behind his desk. The old chair creaked under his weight. He carefully unfolded the note and read through the flourishing words. A smile curled his lips. "It's been over a month since I've heard from her. Perhaps two."

Finch leaned over his own desk to try to peek at the letter, but James covered the paper with his hand. "Still convinced it's a woman?"

"Look at this penmanship." James flipped it around to show his fellow inspector, but gave him no time to read it before he dropped it again. "No man can write like that, with all the precision and elegance. Not to mention the vocabulary that she uses. She's educated."

"You can wipe that grin off your face, I don't think she's exactly an admirer." Finch stood and stretched.

James tucked the letter into his side pocket. Finch was right; the woman was no admirer, but the fact that he could annoy her so without even knowing her amused him greatly.

"We've got work to do." Finch pulled his tweed coat on. "The carriage house is sending a rig out front. You coming?"

"Right. We have to finish up the Clemmons case." He grabbed his own coat and followed Finch out of the Scotland Yard offices.

His mood sank. He hated having a keeper, having to report in to someone. And Finch had been his equal a few months ago, until Superintendent Randolph put him on suspension. Now James was stuck working under Finch as punishment.

It wasn't working with Finch that irritated him. Finch was a good detective; James respected him. But the fact that James had worked tireless hours and solved more cases than almost anyone and then had it stripped away was beyond frustrating.

Now it was like working backward. He'd asked Randolph just yesterday how much longer this grueling penance would last, but the boss had just grunted and shrugged his shoulders.

Randolph was disciplining him for allegedly breaking the rules, yet he, himself, wasn't following any specific rulebook on James' punishment. The bastard was making things up as he went along. Something James knew all too well. It was how he lived his life.

Tomorrow, James would visit him again. If nothing else, if he pestered Randolph enough, perhaps he'd give in and give James back his team.

"You off to the Spotted Duck tonight with the rest of us?" Finch asked as they stepped into one of the Metropolitan Police issued carriages.

"No. I'm having dinner with Colin and his wife tonight."

"Oh, tell the old chum I said hello. Any chance he'll come back to the Yard?"

"Doubtful. Maybe I'll join him on his own. It would beat working for Randolph."

Finch chuckled. "You'd miss the glory."

"Oh, right, the glory," James said dryly.

"It won't be too much longer," Amelia Brindley said. She glanced at her husband. "I'm certain dinner will be ready momentarily." She smiled warmly at Willow.

Willow Mabson nodded politely. Amelia was her best friend and she loved her, but she should have declined the invitation to dinner tonight. She needed to be home caring for her mother, instead of leaving poor Edmond to do so. Her brother had much more important things to do than watching over their irascible mother. However, she'd been in such a state this past week that someone had to sit with her at all times. Thankfully, Edmond wouldn't have to handle things alone for too long as their father was returning from his short trip tonight.

Forcing herself to focus on the present, she noted the parlor was ornate but tasteful, decorated in soft golds and yellows. She should have felt calm and relaxed, yet she couldn't shake her feeling of unease. Willow plucked a wayward string off her blue satin skirt. She didn't have many evening dresses and it seemed silly to don one for a simple dinner with her friends. But propriety was quite clear on that matter. Besides, she had no idea who else was invited tonight; Amelia had been quite mum about the details.

Willow glanced around the room and noted Amelia and Colin exchanging knowing looks. Colin glanced at his pocket watch and nodded to his wife. The air was charged; something was amiss. Amelia and Colin were far too suspicious.

"Precisely what are you two about?" she asked.

Amelia jumped slightly. Her hand flew to her neck, where she fiddled with a necklace. "I haven't the faintest notion to what you're referring." She smiled brightly at Colin, who stood by the piano swirling the drink in his hand.

"Nothing at all," he said stiffly.

Willow resisted the urge to roll her eyes. They were up to something. She was no fool.

There was a quiet knock on the door, and then the Brindley butler, Westin, appeared. He cleared his throat. "An Inspector James Sterling has arrived. He said he would be in momentarily." He bowed heavily and stepped out of the room.

Willow came to her feet. *Sterling*? She shot Amelia a pointed glance as her heart inexplicably skipped a beat.

So this is what they were doing.

Amelia had offered to introduce them on several occasions, all of which Willow had declined. She hadn't wanted to meet him. Hadn't wanted to make a fool of herself. Because she knew that once they met, she would end up opening her mouth and chiding him for his flagrant lack of regard when it came to the rules and regulations of being an inspector with the Metropolitan Police.

She'd had opportunity to view those very guidelines once, while visiting her cousin, who worked as a clerk in the Yard offices. She'd only read through them as a matter of curiosity, but the instructions were clear and had been created to benefit both the people of London and the investigators. At the time she'd thought very highly of the head of the police for instituting such requirements. Without rules it was quite likely that the men working London's streets would abuse their power, become corrupt, and end up as criminals themselves.

Her cousin had told her that many of the investigators were disgruntled over the new rules. In fact, several of them had already voiced their disapproval of the system. Primarily one by the name of James Sterling.

She'd nearly forgotten his name and the regulations she'd read until one day while reading the paper, a small article had caught her attention. So, over the past two years, she'd followed his cases in the *Times*, and on more than one occasion—well, if she was honest, on several occasions—she had sent him a letter, anonymously of course, detailing all of the areas where he neglected to follow the rules. She'd gathered some of the information from her cousin, so she was privy to a few details that the average *Times* reader was not.

At first, she'd merely sent harmless inquiries into how he'd solved this case, or how he'd uncovered this bit of evidence. If she was honest, she knew it was none of her concern, that she was simply being nosy—although it seemed to her that as a citizen of London, she had the right to know how the police managed their investigations. Besides, her cousin had been more than willing to fill her in on any gossip from his work and had informed her that Inspector Sterling often had complaints filed against him. She'd created a way for him to respond, all the while keeping her identity a secret, but all of her inquiries went unanswered, which, frankly, had annoyed her, so she'd altered her tactic.

She'd foolishly believed he'd find her suggestions instructive. However, it had become increasingly clear the inspector had either failed to receive her letters or was blatantly ignoring them. Willow had a great deal of confidence in Her Majesty's postal service; therefore, one could only assume Mr. Sterling felt himself above helpful criticism.

It was Amelia's fault, really. If it were not for her insistence that they start the Ladies' Amateur Sleuth Society, Willow would never have bothered reading those bits in the newspapers. . .

Good gracious.

James Sterling swaggered in as if he, himself, had invented arrogance. It dripped off him and made her palms itch. He wasn't at all how she'd envisioned him. And she *had* envisioned him—only she'd wanted him to be short and fat and wrinkled, not tall and athletic and positively dashing.

Willow shot Amelia an annoyed look that her friend sweetly ignored.

"James," Amelia said with a smile. She walked toward him and he graciously bent his head over her hand.

"Amelia, you look as lovely as always." The

deep timbre of his voice feathered across Willow's skin and she had to remind herself to keep her mouth closed. She took a deep breath in a vain effort to try to ease the chaos that had erupted in her stomach.

The two men exchanged pleasantries and Amelia met Willow's gaze and winced slightly. Were Amelia not full of good intentions, Willow might be angry. It was awfully hard to be angry with someone as kind as Amelia, but this really was testing Willow's patience and good will.

"James, might I introduce you to my dear friend." Amelia led him over to stand in front of Willow. "Miss Wilhelmina Mabson, Inspector James Sterling."

She put her hand out as respectability demanded, but he when nodded absently over it, she snatched it back before was customary. He raised his eyes to meet hers and cocked his left eyebrow.

"Most intrigued, Miss Mabson," he said.

Dismissed again. Just as he'd done with her letters.

He was far more foppish than she would have imagined. His suit was at the pinnacle of fashion, making her all too aware of the faded fabric of her own dress. She grabbed a handful of her skirt and now wished it were a much larger dinner party so that she could shrink into the background.

His clothes were certainly well tailored, but he was no dandy—far from it. For one, his hair was too long; it brushed the tops of his shoulders and had not a drip of smoothing cream in it. He did not look like a dandy. He looked . . . dangerous. Well dressed but dangerous. Willow swallowed.

She turned to Amelia. "Might I have a word with you?" she said, her voice coming out much softer than usual. "In private," she added.

Amelia practically beamed. "Of course." She linked arms with Willow and led her out into the hall. And then her dear friend had the audacity to blink at her with innocent eyes. "What?" she asked sweetly.

Willow frowned. "What? What do you mean, *what*? You know very well what."

"James?" She waved a hand in front of her. "Oh, he's harmless. I thought it would be best for the two of you to meet. Clear the air, so to speak."

Her lip curled unconsciously. "Honestly, Amelia." She would have to concentrate to keep her mouth shut tonight else say something she would really regret. She fully acknowledged that she should never have started sending those letters, but things had gotten out of hand. Her pride had been wounded. She was certainly used to people ignoring her based on her appearance, as she wasn't considered handsome by today's standards, but when it came to her mind, she did not like to be dismissed.

Amelia held one finger up. "He is handsome, don't you agree?"

"I most certainly do not agree." She tugged on the hem of her jacket. Yes, he was handsome. Outrageously so. Which, frankly, made the entire situation all the more humiliating. Had she ever thought meeting him was an actual possibility, she never would have sent that first letter. But at the time Amelia had not met Colin, and James Sterling was just a name to her.

"I know he's arrogant, Willow."

"And reckless," Willow pointed out.

"Yes, reckless. But he's a decent man, not the devil you believe him to be." Amelia tilted her head. "If you wish to leave, you may, I shall make up an acceptable excuse so to not embarrass you."

Willow couldn't do that. Her friend had gone to all this trouble, and Willow had already been unkind. Sure, she had no wish to befriend the inspector, but she refused to be any more inconsiderate to Amelia than she already had been. She needed to be kind, keep her mouth shut, and get through the evening without embarrassing herself or Amelia.

"I'm not leaving. I should like to see what the cook has prepared." She smiled at her friend. "Shall we?"

"Yes." Amelia took a step forward. "Oh, and Willow—"

Willow held up a hand. "I shall endeavor to be kind to the man."

It was quite evident that Amelia was suppressing a smile, but she merely nodded and opened the parlor door.

"My dear," Colin said. "Dinner is ready."

"Very good." Amelia stepped to her husband's side and linked her arm with his, an action that left Willow awkwardly standing in the doorway as if she were a frail wallflower waiting for an escort.

Far be it from her to play the pretty maiden, she turned and followed her friend.

But Inspector Sterling was quick to find his way to her side. "Miss Mabson, please allow me to escort you to the table."

Willow forced a nervous smile. "I don't believe I'll lose my way, but thank you."

He chuckled at her response and linked her hand into the crook of his elbow, then draped his hand lightly over hers.

They said nothing else as he led her to her seat, and Willow concentrated on her steps so that she would not stumble.

Several quiet moments passed after they were all seated as they waited for the first course to be served. Willow was quite aware that a particular set of eyes was on her, but she refused to look in his direction. She pushed her spectacles farther up her nose and examined her empty plate.

"Thank you both for coming. Our two dearest friends," Amelia said, glass high in hand. "To each of us."

Willow quickly raised her glass and nodded. Finally the hot food was served and Willow was relieved to have somewhere to focus her attention. The aroma of pork and potatoes reached her nose and her stomach grumbled in response.

"So tell me, James, how fairs it at the Yard these days?" Colin asked.

Willow kept her head down. If she paid no attention to the discussion, she could keep her mouth shut, not say anything she would regret. Not say anything about her anonymous letters, or why he refused to acknowledge them.

James gave his friend a scowl. What were these two about tonight? And who was the less-than-charming Miss Mabson? Certainly not a vain attempt to match him with one of Amelia's spinster friends. James released a deep breath. As if his life weren't complicated enough.

"Randolph is still on my back," he finally answered.

"So you're still working with Finch, I gather?" Colin asked.

"Working under him," James corrected. No reason to pretend the situation was anything other than that.

"How much longer for your probation?" Amelia asked.

"As long as Randolph decides, I suppose. I've asked repeatedly and I never get a clear answer. I've decided my next plan is to ask him on a daily basis. Perhaps if I annoy him enough he'll come to his senses and give me my old post back," James said.

It was then that Miss Mabson looked up from her plate and locked gazes with him. Even behind her spectacles he could see the chocolaty depths of her intelligent eyes. She wasn't smiling, precisely, but he detected a slight movement of her lips. Was she smirking? Before he could be certain, she looked away.

What was this woman about, with her mysterious expressions and dismissive attitude? He'd never before had a woman dismiss him so coolly, so unaffectedly as she'd done when he'd offered to escort her into the room. It was as if . . . as if she were immune to his charm. He hated to boast, but he had yet to meet a woman who could resist him. It wasn't vanity; it was simply experience that had taught him that women found him engaging, charming, and appealing. Clearly, this woman was unbalanced in some fashion. Perhaps she couldn't see well, thus the spectacles, and could not see his features clearly.

He pulled his gaze off her and focused on Colin. "I suppose he could have paired me with someone other than Finch. At least Finch recognizes my abilities and doesn't treat me like a dolt. Just the same, I much prefer working on my own."

Colin held up his drink in a salute. "Precisely the reason I left the Yard."

"No, you left the Yard because you don't like people in general," James corrected. He leaned back in his seat. "I simply don't want anyone to tell me what to do. They can work with me so long as they allow me to use my own techniques."

A small choking sound erupted across from him.

"Willow, are you quite all right?" Amelia asked.

"Quite," she said tightly.

Willow wasn't an unattractive female, although he'd certainly seen finer specimens. She had a pleasing figure, as best he could tell in her excessively modest evening gown. It wasn't cut low enough to reveal any hint of cleavage, as was customary, but he could see enough to recognize a sizeable chest. She wasn't overly thin or particularly plump, but she looked soft in those places where a woman ought to be soft.

He'd never met a woman who wore spectacles, but they seemed to fit her. He could appreciate a well-shaped mouth, which, were it on any other woman in the world, he would have assumed was made for sin. On Miss Mabson, he imagined she clucked her tongue in disapproval on more than one occasion. A pity.

"We're finishing up a counterfeiting case right now," James said. "Not very interesting, I'm afraid. Nothing more than a bloke who took advantage of one of the abandoned buildings down on the docks and figured he'd print his own currency."

"Inspector?"

He looked up at Miss Mabson.

"I was merely curious as to whether or not it is appropriate for you to discuss active investigations with regular citizens?" Her lips pursed. "Would not such behavior be frowned upon?"

He was beginning to wonder if this entire evening was some sort of jest. He glanced at Colin and Amelia, who looked as confused as he felt. "I'm speaking to a former Yard detective; I don't suppose that matters much."

"Amelia and I are also in the room. Surely that is against the rules," she countered.

He gave the lady one of his lazy smiles. "I'm not overly concerned with the rules."

"Clearly not, since your supervisor saw fit to put you on probation." Her tone was still even, sweet-sounding, but James sensed there was more fire lurking below.

"My supervisor doesn't know what he's talking about," James said.

"Surely he has some elevated skills, else he would not have been given his position with that rank."

"I think, madam, that you speak of much that you know very little about," he said through tight teeth.

"You would be surprised what I know." She tossed her napkin onto the table and her eyes blazed. "You disregard propriety as if the rules were nothing more than guidelines developed on a whim of boredom," she said. "Were it not for these rules, much of our civilization would be in chaos."

His stomach jolted. He'd heard those words before. "What did you say?"

She had the grace to look slightly guilty. "Chaos," she repeated. "I believe that without structure chaos would surround us."

"No, not that—the other thing you said."

She folded her arms over her chest.

He knew those words. That exact phrase about disregarding propriety. He'd seen it only that morning, in that bloody letter. This small scrap of a woman who hid behind her tongue and a pair of spectacles. She was responsible for all of those anonymous letters.

Well, that was simply too good to be true. He chuckled at first, but then released a full-fledged laugh. Slowly, he stretched his legs out in front of him, not caring if he kicked her foot with his own. "I knew you'd be a woman," he said with a smile.

The crease between her brows deepened. "I beg your pardon." Her speech was so refined, so crisp.

"The letters, Miss Mabson. Do you think me dense?"

She opened her mouth, but he cut her off. "Don't answer that. I received your most recent one just this morning."

"You said you'd stopped, Willow," Amelia whispered.

"I did," Willow said softly. "It was just this once."

"You knew?" James asked Amelia.

She smiled sheepishly.

"What the devil is everyone talking about?" Colin asked.

James didn't take his eyes off Willow. "Do you want to explain it, or shall I?" He didn't wait for her to answer. "I think I will. I wouldn't want you to leave out any details. The lovely Miss Mabson has been sending me anonymous letters for some time now. Letters that criticize everything from my technique at solving cases to my record keeping. I'm rather surprised she's never commented on my choice in clothing."

"Well, had I known," Willow blurted out. "I

don't suppose any of the other inspectors dress in such a fancy manner."

He said nothing, merely eyed her steadily.

"Had you responded to my first letter . . ." she stammered. "I did not criticize, at least not originally. I merely had some questions. But you," — she pointed at him— "ignored me. You don't answer to your supervisor, and evidently, you don't answer to the good people of London."

So that was what lit her ire. Well, he wasn't ignoring her now. "As you mentioned before, it really isn't appropriate for me to discuss investigations with people who do not work for the Yard." He loved tossing her words back at her.

Her eyes flared.

He chuckled. He'd love to see that passion, that fire, put to something more pleasurable and productive. "There is one thing I've been curious about. How do you get all your details? You know things about the investigations that are not printed in the papers."

Her lips tightened into more of a line, if that were possible. "I will not tell you that." She shifted in her seat as if uncomfortable. "Perhaps you did not owe me an explanation, but you could have, at the very least, acknowledged my letters. It is the polite thing to do. Be that as it may, your disregard for proper procedure is flagrant, at best," Willow pointed out.

"I appreciate your concern, but I can assure you that regardless of my methods, I am quite capable of solving my assigned cases. Some might even say I'm rather accomplished at my job."

"Were I to have the same resources the Metropolitan Police offers you . . ." her sentence trailed off without her completing it.

He leaned forward and scraped at the day's growth on his chin. She was bold, but he could beat her at her own game. "I do believe you're making quite a daring assumption, Miss Mabson. You seem to imply that you might be better than I at solving these dastardly crimes and catching criminals," he said.

"I did not say that," she said.

"Oh, but you seem to have been insinuating precisely that. Or were you simply boasting?"

She stiffened.

He'd hit a nerve. He smiled.

"No, I was not boasting," she said, her voice lined with defiance.

"Then you believe you could solve a case?"

She eyed him for several moments before she finally nodded, almost begrudgingly. "Yes, I do."

"Very well," James said.

She actually smiled then, and her white, even teeth stopped the words of his response. With a true smile in place, she was actually pretty. Very pretty. It was unfortunate she was so opinionated.

Whatever happened to the demure young miss who did nothing more than smile sweetly and nod? Apparently, women like that were in short-age. Not that he'd actually be interested in such a creature. Far too boring.

She was quite pleased with herself—that much he could tell. But it was time to challenge her hand. It was time to call her bluff. He reached into his pocket and pulled out the gloves he'd stashed there earlier and tossed them onto the table.

Her eyebrows arched. "You challenge me to a duel? They have been illegal for quite some time, as I'm sure you know," she said, quite satisfied with herself.

"Yes, I do know. And no, not a duel. At least not one with pistols. I would hate for such a lovely creature to die at my hands. Rather a duel of the wits. Skill against skill. The first case I'm given, once I'm released from probation," he added. "We will battle to see who can solve it first."

Amelia gasped. "She's rather gifted, James; you might want to reconsider."

Amelia was a kind soul and she was good for Colin, but her sweetness often blinded her to the truth of a matter. And with this, she saw her dear friend as an actual threat to James's detecting skills. It was laughable, but he restrained himself. Besides, it was unlikely the prim and proper miss would actually accept his bold dare.

"Thank you for the warning, Amelia, but I will take my chances. That is, if Miss Mabson agrees to a little friendly competition." He turned his glance back to the lady in question. "That is, if she's brave enough to prove herself. Or perhaps she's second-guessing her abilities."

"If you think me frightened, sir, rest assured I am not." She made eye contact and didn't look away for quite some time.

This woman meant what she said, which James found amusing.

"I do have a question, though," she continued. "How am I to solve a case when I am not privy to the kinds of investigative details you will have? Not quite a fair challenge."

He shrugged. "I will share all of my information with you. You take the information and do with it what you will. You follow your precious rules and I shall solve the case with my own techniques—and whoever solves it first is the winner."

He could see her fighting an internal battle. She wanted to do it—that much he surmised—but something was holding her back. No doubt that shield of propriety she had hanging around her neck. His mother would love her. And were that not such a terrifying thought, he might have found it amusing.

"What say you, Miss Mabson? It might give you ample opportunity to point out all the errors of my ways. Surely you can't decline such an opportunity." He had her there. He was goading her and she was going to accept—he could feel it in the charged air between them. He should have stopped while he was ahead.

She took a deep breath and nodded. "Very well, Inspector, I accept your challenge."

Chapter 2

The men had retired to the other room, presumably to smoke, although Willow knew that Colin never touched tobacco. But now that she was sitting alone with Amelia, her friend was staring at her with questioning eyes.

"What?" Willow said, unsuccessfully keeping the impatience from her tone.

"Do you still believe him to be the cretin you imagined?" Amelia asked.

James Sterling was the closest thing to a friend that Colin had, and Amelia had been so relieved when they'd resumed communications that Willow hated to be nasty. Admittedly, the man was not exactly how she'd envisioned him. Much to her surprise, he was the very picture of good health. He was obviously athletic and in high form, so her assumptions had been incorrect. But he was as arrogant, if not more so, as she'd imagined.

Amelia's eyebrows arched even further.

"He is not completely as I expected," Willow said, hoping she would not have to elaborate.

"Once you get past the arrogance, he is rather charming and sweet." Amelia raised one finger. "And humorous."

Willow could concede the charming part, if one were susceptible to that sort of overt charm that men who thought too much of themselves seemed to perfect. Were they taught those sorts of skills in school? While she and other ladies were mastering table skills and how to read and speak Greek, were men likewise learning how to manipulate women with false words and glances? In any case, charming he might effectively act, but humorous was a stretch by anyone's definition.

"I can not believe you accepted his wager," Amelia said, not hiding her smile. "I never imagined you would be that bold."

Willow tugged on the hem of her jacket. "I don't consider that bold." Foolish? Yes, but she was not ready to admit that just yet. "I am apparently the only one who is interested in showing this man the error of his ways. This is good fortune for me to see him and his irreverent ways in action, therefore allowing me prime opportunity to bring them to his attention. Once he sees that crimes can be solved within the confines of the specified guidelines, he will cease his wild

ways and become a more respectable employee."
She crossed her arms over her chest. At least that
sounded like a plan.

In reality she'd accepted that challenge because
he'd manipulated her into a corner. He'd seen her
competitive inclination and played her like an exposed chess piece. She shook her head. Ordinarily
she saw moves like this coming before they hit,
but she'd allowed him such liberties.

She'd already asked herself why she was so
fixated on the inspector. Plenty of people broke
rules every day and she never wrote them letters.
Her own dearest friends bucked convention and
ignored propriety all the time, but she still cared
for them. What was it about this particular man?

Her irritation would have made more sense
had she met him before tonight. He was precisely
the type of man that ruffled her feathers, so had
she met him before she had noticed his behavior,
the letters would most certainly have been written. But she hadn't. So why did she bother?

Was it simply because he'd ignored her first
few? Because she'd been so casually dismissed?
She didn't want to admit that that could be part of
it. But she couldn't ignore it. Before she'd mailed
the first letter she'd imagined the kindly inspector
receiving it and being impressed with her wit and
intelligence. She'd imagined he'd write her back,
thanking her for her astute observation. None of

that had happened; instead, her pride had been wounded and she'd allowed this letter-writing thing to get completely out of hand.

"Willow?"

"Sorry." She gave Amelia a nod. "I missed what you said."

"You accepted his challenge for the good of the people, then?" Amelia said.

"Absolutely. What other reason would there be?"

"Oh, I don't know." Amelia waved her hand in the air casually. "A chance to solve a real crime with a real inspector."

Willow's hands seemed to itch with excitement. She couldn't deny the attraction to solving the puzzle, especially in the presence of a professional. His methods might be questionable, but she'd be foolish to deny his skill and experience.

Willow gave Amelia a small shrug—it was all the answer she could muster. Puzzle or not, that was not the point. There were more pressing matters involved, ones that didn't involve her personal interests and curiosities. She had agreed to the wager for more important reasons.

It had very little to do with the excitement and thrill of solving a real crime. And even less to do with the much younger and more virile than anticipated Inspector Sterling.

* * *

"We solemnly swear to unravel mysteries by ferreting out secrets at all costs," they all said in unison.

Willow eyed her three friends. The Ladies' Amateur Sleuth Society was what they called themselves, but they were not a publicly recognized society. As it was, only a handful of people knew of their existence. They were four friends who enjoyed solving mysteries and fancied themselves novice—not to mention unpaid—detectives.

It had all started with Amelia's fascination with Sherlock Holmes stories. She had hooked the rest of them on the serials, and the Society, somehow, had formed out of that.

Willow watched as Meg bit into her cake and Charlotte swayed her leg casually. No, not a real society at all. Were it not for her and Amelia, they would scarcely discuss anything but hair ribbons and Charlotte's latest suitor.

They had recently been involved with some legitimate mysteries, but more so Amelia and Meg. Now Willow had an opportunity to work on an investigation, and try as she might, she was unsuccessful at squelching the flutters of excitement in her belly—even when she reminded herself that solving the crime wasn't her primary motivation. And especially when she remembered that the only reason she was in said position was because James Sterling had orchestrated her reaction so perfectly.

Regardless, she wanted to get this meeting on track and keep Amelia focused so she wouldn't make a big to-do over last night's dinner.

Willow knew she could always get them on track. She need only mention one little name. "Now then," she said. "I believe we all agree that our attempts to entice the Jack of Hearts have, thus far, been futile. We must step up our efforts if we are to snare the thief."

She saw Charlotte perk up instantly. Her leg stopped swaying and she sat straighter in her chair.

"Agreed," Meg said.

"I must interject something first," Amelia said. "It is simply too scrumptious to keep to myself." Her smile was bright and completely mischievous.

Willow sat forward slightly. This would not do well for her. They—in particular, Charlotte—would never allow her to forget. "Amelia, honestly, it wasn't—"

But Amelia did not let her finish. "Willow met Detective Sterling last evening. We had a dinner and invited both, but neither Colin nor I expected quite the show those two put on."

Charlotte laughed heartily.

"You did not tell him you were the one sending

him the letters, did you?" Meg directed her question to Willow.

Willow crossed her arms over her chest. She did not have to defend herself over those letters. They were within her right to send. "It didn't precisely happen in that manner," she muttered.

"In what manner did it happen, then?" Meg asked.

"He knew it was her," Amelia said excitedly. "She said something and he recognized it from a letter." She shook her head. "And then off they went, challenging each other back and forth."

"Oh, I would have paid great money to have seen that," Charlotte said.

"Indeed. It was not a night I will soon forget," Amelia said.

"Nor I," Willow said. This situation might be humiliating had she not been friends with these women for years. It was bothersome, but they jested in kindness. Even so, she did not want to discuss Inspector Sterling.

"Was he as dashing as Amelia said?" Charlotte inquired.

"What has that got to do with anything?" Willow said.

"Oh, then he must be," Meg said.

Willow rolled her eyes. "Honestly. Don't you think of anything other than how dashing men are? There are far more important things in life to fret over." She might not be as interested in men as her friends, but she certainly wasn't blind—although she often pretended not to notice men. She never indulged thoughts and fancies, but she'd be a fool not to take notice of a man such as Inspector Sterling. He was a fine specimen, indeed.

If one prefers men who are overly tall and overly opinionated, she reminded herself. Or men who wear their hair so unfashionably long that it hangs far too much in their face.

"She certainly looks as if she found him rather dull," Charlotte said, not bothering to hide the sarcasm in her voice.

Willow tilted her chin up. "It matters not what Inspector Sterling looks like or whether or not I thought him to be attractive."

"She's right," Amelia said.

That surprised her. She turned to her friend. "Thank you, Amelia."

Amelia flashed her a devilish smile. "What is important is that she and the inspector made a wager."

"How very improper of you." Charlotte sat on the edge of her seat. "Willow, honestly, I didn't know you had it in you."

Willow really could kill Amelia right about now. Her friends stared openly at her. It was too much. She smacked her hands on her lap.

"Oh, stop it. Stop gaping at me."

"Precisely what sort of wager is it?" Meg asked.

Amelia's eyebrows rose, but she said nothing. Apparently she had finished torturing Willow, and was going to allow her to fill in the remaining details.

She sighed and resigned herself to telling Meg and Charlotte the rest, knowing they would not allow her to withhold such information. "After I was exposed for the letter writing," she said, "he tossed down the gauntlet, so to speak. He issued a challenge to see who could first solve a mystery and I accepted."

Charlotte started to make a comment that was no doubt cheeky, but Willow held her hand up. "It is my duty to show this man how to adhere to rules and regulations. Since his superiors have been unable to do so, perhaps he needs practical guidance. I can do that." She nodded once to affirm it.

Meg frowned in confusion. "So you are going to work with him? At the Yard?"

"Not exactly." She hesitated to mention precisely how the wager had come about, about how he'd manipulated her and about how he probably sat, even now, with his inspector friends jesting about the silly woman who believes she's going to work an investigation. But the laugh would be on him. She was already cultivating a plan to ensure that he didn't wiggle out of their wager.

"We are to work a case together," Willow continued. "At the moment, he's on probation, well deserved, if you ask me. Once he's back as a lead detective, I will be privy to all the details of the investigation and we will race, if you will, to see who can solve the case first. Me," she placed her hand on her chest, "by following the rules. Or him, by doing whatever it is that he does." She flit her hand about. "I can assure you all, I fully intend to win." It would be a tall order, she knew, but now that he had made a fool of her, she was determined to turn the tables on him and win, simply to prove her point.

Charlotte chuckled softly. "Of that, I have no doubt, my dear Willow."

Willow took a sip of her tea, and then folded her hands in her lap. "Yes, well, thanks to Amelia you are all quite informed of last night's events. But that is certainly not why we are meeting today," she reminded them. It was too unsettling having them all look at her so eagerly and listen so intently about her life. This was precisely the reason she maintained such an uneventful life—less interest and focus from others. Well, certainly not the only reason, but that was neither here nor there.

Amelia frowned. "We always meet on Wednesdays."

"Yes, I realize that. What I meant was, there are other pertinent things to discuss," Willow said.

"Like our boy, Jack," Charlotte said with a grin. "Naughty, naughty boy that he is."

"Indeed," Willow said. They had long been following the escapades of the now notorious Jack of Hearts, a jewel thief who had a penchant for walking straight up to London's wealthiest people and simply taking their gems. It was a most appealing case for the society, but seeing as their only clues were those left in the papers, the trail to him had led them nowhere.

They had even, on a handful of occasions, ventured out in their finest to try to lure the gentleman thief. To no avail. They had yet to catch the slightest glimpse of him.

"I had an opportunity to attend that opera last night," Charlotte said. "But Frannie convinced me that the Bensen soiree would be a better choice. So of course I missed him again."

The Jack of Hearts had struck the opera house the previous evening, taking no fewer than three private boxes. What always amazed Willow was the willingness of the people to simply hand over their prized possessions without any sort of resistance, as if being robbed by the masked thief was some sort of honor. Were she ever to encounter him, he'd have to literally rip the jewels off her body, as she would certainly not hand them over willingly. There had been no reports thus far of violence on his part, although he was rumored to carry a small pistol.

"How was the Bensen soiree?" Meg asked.

Charlotte shrugged. "Moderately entertaining. Now that Frannie has come out, Mother is hassling both of us to find matches. I think she's beginning to lose hope for me."

"Well, can you blame her?" Willow asked. "You have declined a rather large number of proposals since your own coming-out. I do believe you hold some sort of record."

Charlotte smiled sweetly. "Actually, Jane Portfield has me by at least three."

"Yes, but she never did marry," Willow pointed out.

"She never married because she wanted to continue cavorting with as many gentlemen as she chose," Meg said. "And she certainly doesn't take care to hide her affairs. She's quite bold about them."

"Jane Portfield is nothing like our Charlotte," Amelia said. "She had no desire to be any man's wife. She is content to be a spinster, although I use that word loosely. Charlotte will certainly get married. As will you, Willow."

Willow eyed Amelia and opened her mouth to disagree, then thought better of it. There was no point in arguing with her. Amelia was convinced that all of them would find love as she had. Granted, she'd been right about Meg. Meg had found love at her father's chocolate factory and ended up married to a viscount. And Amelia was probably right about Charlotte. Eventually, the beauty would settle down and find a man who might make her reckless heart happy. But for Willow, having a family was simply not possible. She had enough responsibility already and she could never desert her mother. There was no reason to argue about it, however; she'd never be able to convince her well-meaning friend that not everyone would find her own happy ending.

"So, what are we going to do about the ever elusive Jack of Hearts?" Charlotte asked.

"We must keep trying to catch him," Amelia said. "We simply haven't been at the right places."

"I agree. We can't stop simply because we haven't had any luck thus far," Meg said. "And I have the perfect opportunity." She leaned forward and set her saucer and cup down. "Apparently Gareth has an aunt here in London who is throwing a ball in his honor. And mine," she added with a smile.

"That should be perfect, since we never did get to properly celebrate your wedding," Amelia said.

"Yes, well, Gareth believes his aunt is more

thrilled that Gareth married into my father's fortune rather than finding a long-lost nephew after all this time."

"Perhaps she really is genuine," Amelia offered.

Meg shook her head. "It's doubtful. She still keeps her family's estate, but apparently doesn't have very many funds. She's already hit my father up to actually pay for the ball. Of course, he won't be listed as a host on the invitations."

"How positively vulgar," Willow said.

"Indeed," Amelia agreed.

Meg shrugged. "Gareth tried to talk them out of it, but his words fell on deaf ears. I keep telling him that it will be fun, but I don't think he believes me. In any case, they've now decided to make it a masque ball, and so I'm sure it will be well attended. The perfect place for our masked thief to feel right at home," she said with a smile.

"Or for any other masked man who feels obliged to take people's jewels," Willow said.

"Honestly, Willow, it's not good for you to expect the worst of people," Amelia said.

Willow knew her friend was right, and on most days she could squelch those sorts of feelings, but she wasn't feeling in high spirits today for some reason. Perhaps because her mother had another episode last night when she'd arrived home. She'd missed most of the drama, but she still got to see plenty. She sighed and leveled her gaze on her friend.

"You're right. I shall endeavor to not believe the worst in everyone. But if my jewels are stolen that evening, I shall blame you," she added with a smile.

"Fair enough," Amelia agreed.

"You will all receive your invitations in the post quite soon, I believe. But we'll have time to formulate our plans at the next meeting," Meg said.

The clock chimed and Amelia stood abruptly. "I do hate to rush everyone, but I must go. I have an appointment with the dressmaker and then I'm meeting Colin at his offices."

Willow stood and made her way to the door.

"Don't let your inspector worm his way out of that wager, Willow. You know how men are," Charlotte said.

Willow paused and eyed Charlotte for a moment, then nodded and slipped out the door. Charlotte was rather astute when it came to men, but Willow didn't think her friend had perceived the entire situation.

Still, Charlotte was right: Willow needed to be diligent about the matter and not allow Mr. Sterling to get out of their wager. She'd shaken hands to seal the deal and she wasn't about to allow him to forget such a thing. Perhaps it was time to pay the good inspector a visit.

Chapter 3

James had no sooner arrived at work than he
was called into Randolph's office.

"You beckoned?" James said as he sat far too
casually in one of the chairs opposite Randolph's
desk.

Randolph eyed James with disdain. His supervisor didn't like him. James had known that for
a while now. But Randolph also knew that James
was one of the best inspectors he had, so while
he might punish him, he wasn't likely to dismiss
him.

"You know what your problem is, Sterling?"
Randolph said.

"Please enlighten me."

"You don't need this job or the pay, so you
have this devil-may-care attitude and it gets in
the way of your being an inspector. I should dismiss you. But as it turns out, it's your lucky day."
Randolph gathered some papers and held them

out to James. "A nasty little murder on your side of town."

James tried not to react to the excitement in his stomach. He was so damned tired of working under Finch. He'd worked too hard to run his own investigations and to have his position snatched so carelessly away from him. The last month had been sheer hell. He casually flipped through the papers. The first constable on the scene had written up the report of the murder, but there were very few details to go on. His side of town, indeed.

"You know this git?" Randolph asked.

James scanned the name and it was certainly familiar. "I know of him." He read some more and found the usual lack of detail. "Is the body still there?" James asked.

Randolph practically spit. "That I don't know. Why don't you get yourself over there and see?"

"Why me?" James asked, already knowing the answer.

He shrugged. "They'll talk to you. You're one of them," Randolph said.

"The victim was a photographer, not an aristocrat," he pointed out.

"But he moved in those circles. From what I understand he was Society's most revered photographer and was planning a large exhibit with all the portraits he'd been commissioned to do. 'Portraits of Ladies.'"

"Well, if he was so loved, why would anyone want to kill him?" James asked dryly.

Randolph pointed a finger at him. "That's where you come in."

"It wasn't an actual question."

His supervisor shook his head. "Just get out of here and get to work. I expect a report on this on my desk by the end of the week."

James turned to go.

"Oh, and Sterling—this time, you think you can keep your nose clean?" It was a command, not a request.

James walked out the door, not bothering to answer the question. He'd always gotten his work done on his own terms. First the bothersome Miss Mabson, and now Randolph.

Speaking of Miss Mabson, what exactly had he been thinking last night, making a wager with her? More important, what had a proper lady such as herself been thinking when she'd accepted such an asinine challenge? Who was he kidding? He knew why she'd agreed. He'd baited her, twisted his words in such a manner that he'd made it nearly impossible for her to say no.

Luckily for him, he could pretend that the lapse in judgment had never occurred. She knew he was on probation, so waiting for a lengthy bit of time would ease that little wager into the past and soon it would be forgotten. He certainly did not intend to allow a woman to assist him with an actual investigation.

He looked down at the paper in his hands. It felt damned good to have his own case again. He only needed to gather some things and find a sergeant to assist him, and then he could head to the scene of the crime.

James stepped into the open area that housed the desks of the inspectors and practically ran right into someone. That someone turned and looked up at him. He tried to hide his surprise.

"Miss Mabson, are you looking for someone?" he asked.

"You," she said.

She was tenacious; he'd give her that. "Do you need assistance with something?"

"I stopped by to ensure that you intend to hold to the wager we made last night." Her light and very feminine voice carried through the open room.

He cringed when a number of the men sitting around uttered low whistles and coughs. As if they hadn't ribbed him enough over his probation. The last thing he needed was their pestering him about making wagers with ladies of the ton. More fodder for his bloody nickname. "Bluestocking."

He grabbed her arm and led her out into the hall.

"What are you about, Inspector?" she said curtly, then pulled her arm free of his grasp.

"I thought talking out here might be more the thing. Did it not occur to you that when you walked into an office full of men and mentioned wagers that it might perk some ears?"

Her eyes rounded. "Oh, good heavens. I never even thought. What they must think of me," she said.

"You?" he said. "I work with them. They don't even know who *you* are."

"Well, this is getting us nowhere." Her lips tightened.

"Precisely *why* are you here?" he asked.

"I wanted to make certain you had not forgotten about our little conversation." She said the last part in a whisper. "It occurred to me after you left last night that we never made arrangements for how you would notify me of the case. I thought if I stopped by this morning, I could give you the details you need to get in touch with me."

She was quite serious—although he really ought not be surprised by that revelation. Though he'd never met her before last night, she'd been writing him letters for more than a year and he knew her through her words. He had already surmised a great many things about her.

One of which was that Willow Mabson was nothing if not serious.

Of all the ridiculous things he had gotten himself into, this might top the list.

"Well, as I mentioned last night, I'm on probation and am not working cases alone right now. I'll be certain to contact you with the first one I'm assigned." The lie rolled so cleanly off his tongue, he almost felt proud.

"What are you still doing here, Sterling?" Randolph barked as he walked past. "Get to work on that case before I change my mind and put your back on probation."

It was as if the man came out on cue. James could almost hear Willow's satisfaction at catching him in a lie. He flashed her a smile.

Willow's eyes narrowed. "Off probation, are you? And you weren't planning on telling me that, just as I suspected." She crossed her arms over her chest and eyed him warily.

He was honestly surprised she wasn't tapping her foot. "You would have made a spectacular governess," he said dryly.

"So I have been told before," she said. Her eyebrows arched delicately over her spectacles. She was not going to let him off on this one.

"I wasn't going to tell you about this particular case because it is rather gruesome and I didn't believe a woman such as yourself would—"

"Have a strong enough constitution?" she bit out. "I can assure you, sir, I am quite able to manage any sort of situation. I am not some delicate young flower. I'll have you know I am nine and twenty," she said, as if her age changed the situation.

"This has nothing to do with age. This is a murder." He tapped the file against his leg.

"Well, it's really quite sweet of you to be concerned." She did nothing to hide her sarcasm. "But you can put your confidence in the heartiness of my stomach. I've never once been the slightest bit queasy from the sight of blood."

He wasn't being sweet—he was trying to rid himself of a pest. But no matter what he said, she would not be dissuaded; he could see that clearly enough. He would devise a plan to rid himself of her later.

"Well, let us be off then. I have not been there as of yet."

She opened her mouth to argue, then must have realized he had consented, because she closed it abruptly, nodded, then stepped aside.

He stepped back into the open office and the room fell silent. "If you say one word . . ." James said as he passed Finch.

"She doesn't look like your preferred bit of fluff," his friend said.

James glowered at him. "It's a long story and one I'm not partial to digging into at the moment." He grabbed his coat, and then turned to face Finch. "Make sure none of these gossips run off to Randolph with this."

Finch nodded.

"Bluestocking," one of the others yelled.

He turned slowly.

It was Beck, and he pointed at James' coat with laughter. "Don't forget to toss that on the ground should you happen upon any puddles. You wouldn't want her ladyship's slippers to get wet." The men around him roared with laughter.

James gave them a mock laugh and then stepped into the hall.

Willow did her best to match his stride as they walked around the large granite building, but his legs were far longer than hers and she found it increasingly difficult to keep up. But she wasn't one to complain, so she kept her mouth shut and walked as swiftly as she could manage.

The New Scotland Yard was a majestic-looking building, almost castle-like in its design. With large circular turrets on the corners of the building, and spires and chimneys rising from the top, it was a forceful presence on the Victorian Embankment.

She snuck a glance at the man beside her. He was glowering. Apparently he was none too thrilled at the prospect of working with her. For some indiscernible reason, that pleased her. He should have considered that when he'd proposed the wager, baiting her in such a brazen fashion.

She edged her chin up a notch and faced forward. Stumbling slightly, she regained her footing before she required assistance.

He stopped and leveled his gaze on her.

She braced herself for him to drone on about how her presence was a nuisance, but instead he ensured she had properly regained her balance before setting off again, this time at a much slower pace. Perhaps Amelia was right, and he wasn't a total cretin. No, this only proved he had manners when he chose to use them.

"The carriage house is right over here. We maintain a fleet."

He called for a rig and for a moment she hesitated. Without a chaperone, she should not be alone with him. It seemed foolish to consider that now after entering into a wager with him. Besides, since she was nine and twenty and had no prospects of marriage, precisely what would be ruined? Surely such rules did not count when it came to men in his position. It would be a perfectly acceptable situation had he come to her rescue. She nodded and allowed him to assist her inside.

They sat in silence as the carriage jostled through the streets. Willow had never before been in such close—not to mention private—quarters with a bachelor. She glanced around the inside of the rig, which was modest but considerably better than most hackneys on the street. She looped a finger beneath her high-necked collar and tugged on the stubborn fabric. Her ministrations did nothing to ease the warmth that had begun to spread through her body. She needed some fresh air. The carriage jarred them as it hit a hole in the road, and the inspector's knee jammed into her own. He met her eyes briefly but said nothing of the intimate encounter.

Oh, good gracious, she needed to get ahold of herself and stop acting the green girl. She straightened her back and turned her legs ever so slightly away from his. It seemed quite probable that Mr. Sterling was involved with a woman—although she knew from Amelia that he was not married— but right at this moment it was she, Willow, who was alone with him.

"Precisely what is the nature of this investigation?" she asked, unable to bear the silence a second longer.

"It appears that Malcolm Drummond was murdered."

"The photographer?"

He nodded. "Yes."

"How dreadful. He's rather popular in Society at the moment. The gossips must be twittering this morning."

"I know that my mother will be most distraught at his passing, as she had scheduled a sitting with him in the fall."

Well, that was most curious. "Your mother, sir?"

"Lady Fiona Dandridge," he said dryly.

"As in the Earl of Dandridge?" She couldn't prevent the surprise from seeping into her tone.

"One and the same." He pulled aside the curtain on the window. "We're here," he said as he opened the door.

They climbed the steps to the red brick townhome.

He probably thought this meant she wouldn't ask any more questions about his parents, that she would forget her curiosity. He was sadly mistaken. She simply had to know how the son of an earl had become an inspector. Why had Amelia never mentioned that tidbit? Surely it was noteworthy that he came from a rather prominent family.

Inspector Sterling used the large bronze knocker. Soon after, a short, wiry man answered the door. His old face was all wide eyes over a beak-like nose. Willow barely noticed the man's lips, which were pulled into a tight, worried line. As it was, she could scarcely concentrate on anything save the warm and very masculine hand resting against her elbow.

"Yes?" the man said, his voice frail.

"I'm Inspector Sterling from the Metropolitan Police, and this is . . ." He looked at Willow as if not certain how to introduce her.

She straightened and looked the butler in the eyes. "Wilhelmina Mabson," she provided.

"I'm heading the investigation of the murder of your employer," James continued. "Might we come in to ask questions and look around?"

The butler nodded and moved aside to allow them to step through the entryway. "I am Fenby, Master Drummond's butler and valet."

James pulled out a notebook and pencil. "I understand you found the body," he said without looking up. "Have they come to dispose of the remains?"

So he began the questioning right here in the hall. Murder was a rather crude business.

Fenby made a choking sound. "They have not."

"I'm going to need to see the body," James said. "Might Miss Mabson have somewhere to sit while I examine the other room?"

Willow shot him a look. She opened her mouth to speak, but he grabbed her arm and pulled her away from the butler.

"If you think to argue this point with me," he hissed at her, "consider for a second what you are requesting." He did not allow her to argue. "Under no circumstances will I allow you entrance into that room."

He continued to drone on, but his words were lost on her. His hand still held her arm, preventing her body from moving away from his side. Her heart beat wildly in her chest, but it was not from fear, and that in itself was frightening. He was trying to protect her. Gone was the charming, arrogant man who would flirt and jest with any available woman. In his place was an intense and protective man who shot awareness through her body and made her very glad she was of the fairer sex.

She reminded herself that he would do the same for any woman in this situation, that this wasn't something unique for her benefit. Still she'd be fabricating were she to say his actions had no effect on her.

"You might think yourself prepared to see a deceased body, but believe me, you are far from it," he said.

"Are you quite finished?" she asked. She couldn't handle any more of his close attention.

He nodded.

"Well, then, I was merely going to suggest that I was perfectly capable of waiting in the hall. I need not a place to sit or rest."

He eyed her silently, then nodded. "Very well." He turned back to Fenby. "The lady wishes to remain in the hall."

Willow watched as both men started down the hall, leaving her to her own devices. She took the opportunity to calm her frazzled insides and make some observations.

The wood-paneled hallway smelled of fresh lemon oil and shone from the high, arched ceiling to the cold marble floor. Evidently, photography was more profitable than she had imagined. Then again, it was quite like Society to pay a small fortune in order to participate in something deemed fashionable. And oftentimes all it took was one well-named member doing something different to start the latest frenzy.

It was not long before James and Fenby rounded the corner. James carried his bag as if he was a doctor, but Willow knew there was nothing healing tucked within the folds of the leather case. Instead it would contain evidence from the room and James' notes regarding what he'd seen.

Willow imagined the room covered in blood and she shivered. She might not have gotten ill when Edmond had cut his arm that time, but James was right—she was not prepared to see death.

"Someone should arrive later to remove the body," James said. "Did you ever find the weapon? Or remove anything from the room? Because I saw nothing there that could have caused that damage."

Fenby shuddered. "I touched nothing. I sent for the police as soon as I found him." Then he swallowed visibly. "How was he killed?"

"Knocked over the head," James said.

"Knocked over the head," Fenby repeated. "Then I suppose I might know what the weapon was. At first I thought Master Drummond might have moved it to a new location, but I have been unable to locate it."

"It?" James asked.

"There used to be a rather heavy vase. It was from China, I believe, and was nothing more than a decorative piece. But I noticed just this morning that it was missing."

James nodded, then made another notation. "Did you collect any pieces of the vase anywhere, shards or fragments? Because there were none to be found on the floor."

The butler shook his head. "No. As I said, I thought it had been moved, because there was no sign of it anywhere."

"So it must not have been made of clay," Willow pointed out. "Else it would have shattered. Unless they swept it up. Was there blood on the floor?"

James' eyebrows rose and she thought she detected a slight twitch of a smile. Then he nodded to answer her question. "There was blood on the floor."

"No, the vase was not clay at all," said Fenby. "Bronze, actually."

James eyed Willow briefly but said nothing. She took in his full height. He stood shoulders and head over her and at the moment his dark blond hair hid his eyes as he jotted a note. Hid eyes that she knew were a startling crystal green. Knowing that made her feel slightly uncomfortable, as if she knew a secret he kept. But it was not her fault that she was so observant. It was hard not to notice him. He was such a . . . presence.

"Was anything else missing?" James asked.

"No, I don't believe so."

James nodded. "I trust you are not planning on leaving town."

The old man was gracious enough to look offended. "Of course not. My duties are not finished with the Drummond family. I must facilitate Master Drummond's burial and services. Not to mention finalize the financials with his solicitor."

"So he was doing rather well, then?" James asked. "Financially speaking."

"Oh, yes, sir. All to the help of His Grace," Fenby said.

"And who might that be?" Willow asked.

The butler tugged on his vest. "The Duke of Argyle."

"He was a patron of Mr. Drummond?" James asked.

"Indeed. He gave Master Drummond his very first commission, even passed me to him from his country estate. I much prefer the climate here in London," he explained. "Once His Grace made it known that Master Drummond was whom to go to for portraits, *everyone* came calling. The Duke was even sponsoring the exhibit next month." His voice cracked and he put his hand over his mouth. "Many apologies."

Willow offered him a smile and the elderly butler gave her a weak smile in return.

James' brow creased. "What exhibit?"

"Of his latest works. He had been working for months, photographing ladies, and the His Grace was to sponsor the exhibit at Burlington House," Fenby said.

James made a note. "I don't suppose Mr. Drummond kept a list of the names of the ladies he photographed? And what of the actual photographs? Where are they?"

"Most of the photographs have already been delivered to Burlington House, although I'm not certain. If he kept a list of the women, it would be in his journal. He wrote in that book every day."

A diary. Now finding that would probably prove most helpful. "Do you know where he kept his diary?" Willow asked.

James frowned at her. She ignored him. She had every right to participate in the interrogation. How else was she going to win? Well, technically she had no right. She wasn't an employee of the Metropolitan Police. She was nothing more than a well-bred lady without a cent to her name and nothing better to do with her time. Well, that wasn't precisely true either. She could and should pass the time at her mother's side.

Fenby shook his head. "I don't know where he kept it."

"I believe that will be all for the time being," James said.

Were those all the questions James was going to ask? Well, she had one more.

"And what will happen to you once your work here is done?" Willow asked Fenby.

"It depends on the state of Master Drummond's affairs, whether or not he made provisions for me. Perhaps I shall be retained by His Grace." Then his face soured. "I do not wish to be ungrateful, but I would hate to return to the country."

Willow gave the aging man a smile.

"I will be back tomorrow afternoon," James said as he faced Willow and gestured toward the door. "Miss Mabson."

She supposed that meant they were leaving. She frowned. He had been on his best behavior with Fenby, but when it came to speaking to her, he was nothing but rude. Since there was nothing else she could do here, there was no reason to argue with him, so she turned on her heel and stepped out of the room.

"Is that customarily all the questions you ask?" she inquired.

He sat on the worn carriage upholstery and lurched slightly with the hackney's abrupt movement. "The butler was in no place to answer questions today. I had suspected it might be him, but that old man couldn't pommel a dog, much less a grown man." Why was he answering? He didn't owe her an explanation.

"Are we going back to the Scotland Yard offices?"

"Yes."

He didn't want an assistant. Especially not one who was so opinionated, regardless of her skills at observation. Frankly, if he had to have an assistant, he'd prefer one without breasts. That included some of the portly fellows at the Yard. He let his gaze fall to Willow's chest as she sat across from him in the carriage. The modest neckline of her yellow muslin dress did nothing to hint at any cleavage, but he could tell by the stretch of the fabric that were he to sneak a peek, they would be the most glorious breasts.

He looked up and met her gaze, and both her delicate eyebrows rose above her spectacles. She'd caught him staring. She didn't look annoyed or even scandalized. No, what he saw in the brown depths of her eyes was nothing more than surprise. Now, why would she be surprised that he'd stare at her breasts? It was his experience that no matter how well bred, a man would shift his gaze to the supple mounds of a woman any chance he could.

So why would she be surprised?

And what else would surprise her? Would those perfectly arched eyebrows rise if she knew he'd not only closely examined her breasts (what he could see of them) but also the graceful curve of her neck and fullness of her lips? Would it intrigue her or enrage her to know he'd found himself wondering what it would be like to move his mouth across her sensual red mouth?

It was then that it occurred to him, a possible way to rid himself of her assistance and distracting presence. "Miss Mabson, it has occurred to me that we never set the parameters of our little wager," he said.

"Parameters?" she asked, her voice sounding breathless. "Whatever do you mean?"

He grinned. "Meaning, what do I get when I win?"

"Is it not enough to know you are a winner?" She shrugged. "Or the loser, whatever the case may be?"

He watched her mouth enunciate each syllable. So precise. So perfect.

"Then it is nothing more than a race. But a wager—a wager has consequences. You either win something or you lose something," he said. "It raises the stakes, provides more impetus for success."

"I'm beginning to think, Inspector, that you have given this much thought. What is it you want from me?" Then she smiled. "*If* I lose?"

"A kiss."

Her eyes rounded and her mouth worked itself into a tight line.

"Is that a yes?" he asked.

Those lovely eyebrows of hers fell into a downward point and her eyes narrowed. "No, it most certainly is not a yes. And I find jesting about such a matter completely inappropriate."

"I'm not jesting. And those are the terms of my wager. If you do not comply, then the wager is off." He sat back and rested his arms against his chest.

He could see her mentally stammering—trying to develop an argument, a protest—but the only thing that came was a slight tint of red, settling in her cheeks.

"But what shall I get if *I* win?" she asked.

"Perhaps you would like a kiss as well," he offered.

"I most certainly would not." A few silent moments passed before a slow smile crept onto her face. "I've got it. If I win, then you must write a formal apology for all your reckless antics with a promise to fully adhere to the rules and regulations set forth by the Metropolitan Police, to be published in the *Times*."

Oh, and that reminded him. "I wasn't actually done with my own guidelines," he said. "If I win, I receive the kiss. Willingly, I might add. As well as a promise from you to never send me another letter again."

She opened her mouth to protest, then shut it and frowned.

He almost laughed, but he feared she might actually box his ears if he did. If he wasn't mistaken, she was going to agree to his ridiculous request. So far, she continued to surprise him. Well, if he were to be saddled with an assistant, at least he'd win peace in the end. Not to mention a kiss.

"Are we in agreement?" he asked.

"I suppose I have no choice but to win," she said.

"Let us kiss on the agreement," he suggested.

She stuck her hand out in front of him. "I prefer to shake hands, thank you very much."

He took her gloved hand and shook it gently. No kiss today, but he would taste her lips sooner or later. He knew one thing for certain: Willow would never beat him at his own game.

Chapter 4

Willow had made a deal with the devil, and then she had agreed to kiss him. She had taken serious leave of her senses. His request, though, had taken her aback. Men did not tease her or flirt with her, and they certainly did not request kisses. So, she had been disarmed and completely unprepared to respond to such a ridiculous request.

If she won, however, there would be no kissing, and he would have to publicly apologize. Yes, that was sounding more the thing. Why had she agreed to such conditions? She took a deep breath. She would win, so none of the kissing would come to fruition. She had nothing to worry about. All she need do was keep her eyes focused straight ahead and analyze the facts of the case. This would be no different from any other mystery she'd solved, fictional or real.

Granted, the only mysteries she'd ever solved

were fictional, unless she could include the assistance she'd given Amelia in discovering the whereabouts of her father's missing artifact. So, she did not have an enormous amount of actual experience. It did not mean that she didn't know how to go about investigating.

No, the wager's conditions would not be a problem, because she would ensure she solved the crime first. She could do that. Tomorrow was another day, and they were set to return to the photographer's house to search his studio. Once the body had been removed and the blood cleaned up, they would be able to look for other evidence. She had been unable to accomplish much today, but she had some ideas for gathering additional information.

She was, after all, a member of the only ladies' sleuthing society. Her friends certainly knew of the photographer; perhaps they had some insight into who his clients might have been. Charlotte was generally active enough in Society that she would know if Mr. Drummond had any enemies.

More than likely this was simply a burglary gone awry, but until that was certain, she would sniff about and see what she could uncover on her own.

James eyed Willow as she stood next to him on the stoop. They had knocked and were waiting for Fenby to answer the door. She was enveloped in a brown cloak of wool, and he could see the determination furrow her brow. He knew that look. He'd made that expression himself.

An invisible line passed between them. They might be rather different, but there were some similarities he could not deny. He'd be a fool not to recognize them. Willow had something to prove. Either to him or to herself—perhaps even the world—he wasn't certain which. But he knew what it felt like, and recognizing it unsettled him. A strand of commonness that he could neither touch nor ignore.

A moment later the aging butler cracked the door. "Oh, Inspector. I wasn't expecting you," he said, then opened the door the rest of the way. He nodded at Willow. "Madam."

James cleared his throat. "I've come to further investigate the studio."

Fenby's watery eyes scrutinized them before he moved out of the way and admitted them. "I did as you instructed and locked the door to prevent anyone from disturbing any details."

"Very good," James said.

"I also located the missing vase," Fenby said.

"Whereabouts?"

"The hallway that leads to Master Drummond's studio goes in the other direction, but ends at a wall. He always thought to expand his studio down that way, but it was not to be." Fenby put his hand to his mouth. "The vase is in that darkened corner."

"Did you touch it?" James asked.

Fenby shook his head. "Follow me."

James noted the slight bend in Fenby's back and the cane he now leaned on to walk. It nearly masked a limp. James rattled his head trying to remember if the man had had a cane and limp yesterday, but nothing surfaced.

Fenby led them through the kitchen and down some back steps. He nodded to his right. "The vase is down there."

"We'll collect it on our way back up. I want to gather evidence in the studio right now," James said.

They proceeded to the left end of the hallway, where they came to a large door. Fenby inserted a key, unlocked the door, and then nudged it with the weight of his entire body. The door did not move. James pushed it himself and it creaked open.

"Thank you," Fenby said. "These bones are not as strong as they used to be."

James nodded but said nothing.

They stepped into the room, and had James not been standing so close to her, he would have missed Willow's slight gasp. Rich red and purple silks draped the walls, and plush furniture sat arranged in the middle of the room on an exotic Persian rug. Lining the wall to his left was a large rosewood breakfront. It had a central fitted secretary drawer with side drawers and four base cupboards, and its shelves were hidden behind glazed doors.

Aside from the missing dead body, the room looked exactly the same.

"Mr. Drummond spared no expense," Willow said under her breath.

"No, he always had an eye for things such as these," Fenby replied. Apparently the man might be failing in some of his senses, but hearing wasn't one of them.

James turned to face Fenby. "Thank you. We'll let you know if we need anything." The old man clearly knew when he was being dismissed, but made no immediate move to leave the room. After a long scan around the room, Fenby nodded curtly, then turned and headed for the stairs.

In the center of the room sat an oak tripod topped with a wooden accordion box camera with black hood attached. It was aimed at the settee, clearly ready for the next model.

"My mother is quite fascinated with the advent of photography," James admitted. "I can't really say that I share her wonder."

"The girls and I posed for one at a fair once. I believe Amelia still has the tin reproduction in her room," Willow said. "But they've already made such strides in how these things are done."

James moved to the breakfront. A new Scovill portable box camera sat on the secretary edge; James doubted Drummond had had the opportunity to use it. He bent and began opening the cabinet doors. The shelves were lined with wooden plates, glass screens, pieces of linen, and glass jars filled with liquid chemicals. Everything needed to expose the photographs and print them onto the linen sheets.

"What precisely are we looking for?" Willow asked.

"Anything that might explain why someone would want this man dead. Evidently, the murder wasn't motivated by theft, or this expensive equipment would have been taken and sold. So if something was stolen, then it might be more of personal than monetary value."

Willow's lips parted as if she had something to add, but thought better of it. She was a handsome woman. Not by all standards beautiful, but something about her face intrigued him. He wasn't certain if it was the delicate arch of her eyebrows that framed her unassuming brown eyes, or perhaps the classic bow-and-arrow shape of her lips. The small cleft in her chin certainly demanded some attention, but didn't prevent one from noticing the graceful line of her neck or the creamy texture of her fair skin. He forced himself to turn away from his scrutiny of her features.

Whether or not Willow Mabson was considered classically beautiful had no bearing on their current investigation. And if he were to work with her on this case, he had to find a way to keep his observations of her flawless complexion in the back of his mind lest it cloud his judgment.

He shoved his hand through his hair to push it from his eyes so he could focus on the task at hand. He opened a drawer and rifled through the contents. He found a ledger, bill notes, old copies of some gossip broadsheets, and a small leather pouch full of coins.

"It's not right," he heard her say from behind him.

"What's not right?" he asked as he turned to face her.

"This." She spread her arms out to encompass the room. "It feels wrong to rifle through his belongings. It's his privacy," she added in a whisper.

"He's dead," James offered.

She looked from him to the brocade chaise lounge next to her and then back at him. She shook her head.

He released a puff of breath. Evidently she needed more convincing, and he knew precisely how to spur her into action. "This is what it takes to be a detective. But if you need me to do this part of the investigating, I understand," he said with feigned compassion. "You can simply sit and wait, and then—I don't know—read my notes or something."

She seemed to grow a full inch in height and he suppressed a smile.

"I most certainly will not stand by and just read your notes," she said. "I meant it when I said I could best you in this little competition."

He shrugged. "But if the privacy issue bothers you . . ."

"I'll push aside my concerns for the sake of the investigation," she said sweetly, then turned and immediately began perusing her surroundings. Several ornate frames had to be moved, as well as long cuts of lush fabrics that were strewn about the studio.

It was difficult, but he managed to stifle a chuckle and went back to his own search. He opened the next drawer and found mostly newspapers. He tugged on the next drawer and found it locked. Interesting. He scanned the area for something he could use to open the lock and spied a metal letter opener.

James fiddled with the letter opener and the lock for what seemed like five minutes, but eventually the lock gave way and the drawer loosened. He opened it, fully expecting to find it full of money. The drawer was much more shallow than he'd imagined, and it contained nothing resembling money. All the thin drawer contained was blank parchment. He pulled it all out and fanned through it, but found nothing but page after page of unused paper.

He went back to the deceptively small drawer to further investigate, going so far as to pull the drawer completely out. As he did so, a small, soft leather book fell to the floor.

Before he picked the book up, he turned to see that Willow was busy, bent over a stack of books she was examining. He tried not to notice how nicely rounded her bottom appeared with the bustle out of the way and the dress molded to her curves.

He turned with a groan and grabbed the book. He flipped it open to a random page and saw that it was a diary, no doubt the one Fenby had mentioned yesterday. One more flip, and it opened to a list of names. Certainly this book would be of use. He tucked it into his coat pocket, then bent to examine the hole where the drawer went. Nothing else remained, so he returned the drawer and moved on to another cabinet. The diary would remain his secret for the time being.

James finished searching through all of the cabinets and drawers and found nothing else of importance. Willow had apparently found a stack of letters tied together and was in the process of unbinding them.

"Who are they from?" he asked, walking toward her.

She frowned. "I'm not certain."

"Put them in your bag; we'll take them with us and go through them later. I've gone through everything over there, so if you're finished, we can be on our way. I do have a few more questions I'd like to ask Fenby before we leave, though."

Willow eyed the letters once more before tucking them into her reticule. "There wasn't much else over here besides books, and these chests" —she gestured to her right— "were filled mostly with various fabrics. But buried inside one is where I found the letters."

James nodded. "Perhaps they'll be of use." He would keep the diary from her for the time being, but she might have found something useful herself. "Don't forget your cloak."

Willow gathered her cloak and they shut the door on their way out. They made their way down the long hallway past the staircase and to the empty wall where the hall ended.

"Strange design," Willow said, noting the hall that seemed to lead nowhere.

James nodded, then bent down to retrieve the bronze vase that looked to have been tossed into the dark corner. He slipped a glove on before touching it. "We're still a long way from being able to use fingerprints in our investigation, but Colin said we should try to keep our prints off as much evidence as possible."

"His research is quite fascinating," Willow said.

"Indeed."

"Is it heavy?" she asked as James lifted the vase from the floor.

"It's not light." He moved away from the corner. "It's too dark here to see if there is anything on it. We'll better be able to see upstairs."

She nodded, then headed back for the stairs, all too aware of his presence behind her. If she concentrated hard enough, she could almost feel his breath. It didn't take long to find Fenby; he was waiting in the kitchen for them.

"Did you find what you were looking for?" he asked.

"We'll have to wait to see how the investigation unfolds," James said. "I do have some additional questions for you, however." The bronze vase hung from his hand at his side.

Fenby tilted his white head, then turned and walked away. James gave her a half smile, clearly amused with the butler's behavior. That crooked smile nearly stopped Willow's heart—which was completely ridiculous considering it was quite unlikely that a simple smile could actually stop the beating of someone's heart.

She followed James and Fenby to the front parlor and went and stood by the window. Distance was what she needed. And sunlight. She peeked outside and was met with an overcast sky. So much for the latter. Being in that dank, windowless studio downstairs alone with James had been ... nothing. No matter how she tried to spin it in her mind, there was nothing remotely scandalous about the encounter. He'd been so busy digging in the cabinets and drawers, he hadn't even known she was in there with him.

Lock Meg alone with a man, and she gets kisses stolen and a compromised reputation.

Amelia was nearly killed by a lecherous shop owner.

But no, boring Willow could spend hours alone with a man, and he wouldn't so much as look at her inappropriately. Not that she actually wanted him to.

Oh, this line of thinking was getting her nowhere. And it confused her to boot. She tried to concentrate on the conversation between James and Fenby.

"So there weren't any other investors besides Duke Argyle?" James asked.

Fenby's withered hands fidgeted in his lap. "Not that I ever heard."

"There were no other men that he had meetings with or accepted money from?" James prodded.

"Master Drummond did not discuss his financial affairs with me. I only knew about His Grace's patronage because of the upcoming exhibit."

Willow had to admit, James wasn't handling the investigation as she'd imagined he would. He hadn't yet resorted to violence or bribery or any of the other means she'd heard he used to persuade suspects or witnesses to talk to him. It certainly would be easier to point out these indiscretions if she could actually catch him in the act, but so far he'd been on his best behavior. Being able to chastise him a little would certainly make it easier to ignore how handsome he was and keep her focus on besting him in their little competition.

Instead he'd stuck to traditional modes of questioning and she was left feeling nothing short of guilty for all the letters she'd sent him. Perhaps the information she'd received about his tactics had been inflammatory. Her cousin certainly had a flair for gossip, so it wouldn't be beneath him to embellish some details.

She shook her head. No, James was only behaving because he was clever enough to know she was watching him closely. So, he was making certain to cross all his *t*'s and dot all his *i*'s while in her presence. Sooner or later he'd slip, and she'd be there to notice.

"We'll be in touch," James said to Fenby, then turned to go.

It was annoying how he always decided when it was time to leave and then simply expected her to follow him as if she were some sort of trained dog. It was even more annoying that she *had* to follow him, as he was providing her ride back to her house.

James hated to have to ask for help, especially from his mother, but she would be particularly useful in this case. So he swallowed his pride and stepped into his family's entryway. Craddock, the family butler, nodded when he saw James.

"They're in the drawing room," the butler said, sounding utterly bored.

How was it that the man never seemed to age? It was as if he'd been the very same since James was a child, which obviously couldn't be the case. But he'd always been tall and slender, with lucid blue eyes and a head of thick, bright white hair. Very stately looking, which appealed greatly to his mother.

"You're looking quite fit, Craddock," James said as he handed off his coat.

Craddock gave him a wry smile and draped the coat over his arm. With a slight nod, he said, "And you as well, sir."

After the brief exchange of pleasantries, James made his way to the drawing room, where he would no doubt find his mother worrying over some needlepoint and his father reading one of many papers. He stepped into the room and they sat doing precisely as he'd imagined, as if they were on the set of a play rather than living an actual life.

"James," her mother said excitedly, "what an excellent surprise." She set her sewing aside and patted the cushion next to her. "Come and sit for a while."

His father folded the paper just enough so he could see over the edge. "How kind of you to grace us with your presence. Your mother was just fretting about you only moments ago."

"Harry, don't be so dramatic. I was hardly fretting, merely wondering about your well-being," she said, directing the last sentence to James.

He lowered himself onto the green and gold velvet sofa next to his mother. "My well-being is perfectly fine, Mother, I can assure you."

She smiled brightly. "Yes, dear, but I do like to see you with my own eyes so that I might know that you're eating and sleeping and the like. You know how your activities make me nervous."

"I'm a detective, Mother, that's not exactly an activity. It's an actual paid position."

She pursed her lips. "Your allowance is waiting for you whenever you choose to take it," she said smartly.

His father rattled the paper a little too loudly

for a simple turning of the page, then cleared his throat. It was a gentle nudge in the direction of his wife meant to cool her worried nature.

"I came here to ask for your assistance. With my current investigation," James said.

His mother actually looked affronted. Her hand went to her breast and her eyes widened. "What help could I possibly provide in relation to a crime? You know what is a crime? The fact that you're still a bachelor, and as looks would have it, perfectly content to stay that way. I would like grandchildren while I'm still alive."

"Fiona, don't pester the boy, he'll marry in his own time," James' father said.

James had heard it all before, and it didn't faze him. His mother had a flair for the dramatic; he'd have to be blind and deaf to have not recognized that by now.

"Might I remind you, Mother, that you are already a grandmother." His brother, who had not yet taken his father's place as earl, had already married and secured an heir. A long line of heirs, actually. "Are six grandsons not enough?"

"Well, there is always room for more," his mother said. "I have hopes that you will find a match like Stephen has."

"Yes, well, there's still time," James said, not even attempting to hide the sarcasm from his tone.

"Of course there is, dear. Men can marry and sire children well into their years. It is only we poor women who must marry early, else face life alone on the shelf."

Willow would be considered "on the shelf" already. She had mentioned she was nine and twenty. He pushed his hair back from his eyes. Willow had nothing to do with any of this.

"I appreciate your concerns, Mother, but can we get back to why I'm here?" he prodded. The sooner they could discuss the case, the sooner he could remove himself and perhaps salvage the rest of the evening. At the moment, holing up in his townhome with a bottle of rich port sounded just the thing.

"Yes, of course, dear," she said. "Tell me how it is you think I might be of use and I will do my best."

"I believe you knew the victim."

"Victim of what?" she asked.

"Murder."

"Oh, heavens." Again her hand went to her throat. "I know someone who was murdered?"

"Yes, the photographer Malcolm Drummond."

Her expression fell, clearly disappointed that the deceased hadn't been someone slightly more important, and therefore more notorious. "Why would anyone bother killing him?"

"I don't know yet. But I know you met the man,

and I thought you might provide some other contacts for me."

"Never trusted him," his father said from behind his paper.

"Oh, Harry, you never trust anyone," his mother said. "I met Mr. Drummond on several occasions. We had planned to go to his new exhibit." She shook her head and was quiet for a few moments. "I simply need time to think about it. Try to remember who I might have seen him with at times. You know what might help?"

He knew that look. That twinkle that set in her eyes as soon as she had what she deemed to be a perfect plan. And her perfect plans were nearly always less than perfect for him.

"What is it?" he asked.

"Join us tonight." She looked over at her husband, who met her gaze, shook his head, and went back to his reading. "It's a small party. But seeing people might help my memory, and if you were there, I could point people out to you."

Point annoying girls on the marriage mart out to him, that's what she would do. But it was the only way she'd help him. He knew that about her.

He would have immediate access to them. Plus seeing the news of Malcolm's death spread through Society might actually give him a better idea of who the man's foes and allies were.

"Where is it?" he asked.

He thought he heard his father chuckle, but it was so brief, he couldn't be certain.

"Fieldcrest Hall," she said.

James snorted. "A small party? At Fieldcrest Hall? Mother, do you think me a fool?"

"Of course not, darling. If it's any consolation," she said, "Louise said they invited half as many people this year as last year. And can you blame her, with all the traipsing around in her garden? It took them weeks to put her bushes back together. And the statue garden will never be the same. Insolent, the lot of them."

"Half as many," James repeated. He sincerely doubted that. Lady Fieldcrest prided herself on hosting the first large ball of the Season and had been doing so for years. She still had one daughter to marry off, so no doubt this year's gathering would be larger than ever and packed to the gills with eligible men. He didn't really have the patience to wade through this sort of event right now, but it might be the difference between a break in this investigation and a dead end.

"Here are my conditions," he said, ignoring his mother's glee-filled applause. "I'm going for business purposes only. Which means I will not dance with anyone. Nor will I fetch any pretty miss something refreshing to drink. Is that understood, Mother? I do not want to waste time tonight being paraded around for marriage-minded mothers."

His mother squeezed her lips together then gave him a big smile. "I promise."

Somehow he doubted she actually meant that. But he was stuck now. He would do his best to evade the marriage seekers for the evening and focus on the case.

"Shall we pick you up, dear?" his mother asked sweetly.

"No, I'll take my own rig, thank you."

James poured himself a glass of port and then sat at his desk. He still had a few hours before he needed to leave for the Fieldcrest ball. And Drummond's journal had been weighing down his pocket all afternoon. He practically itched to open it.

Every entry was dated, and Drummond's flourish-filled penmanship was difficult to interpret at first glance. Along with the date, each separate entry started with a name. Always a woman's, sometimes the same as on previous days, but generally different each time. Jane, Anne, Millie, Sophia, Agatha, Eleanor—no surnames, just listed by their first name.

The name would start the page and the text would launch into a monologue on each woman's beauty, poise, grace, her every curve. "Agatha" appeared more often than any other name. Always the same details: her raven-black hair, her crystalline-green eyes, her perfect complexion, her flawless body. The details were worthy of Dickens or Brontë.

Drummond had evidently spent some intimate time with each of them, as he knew of moles and birthmarks and scars and coloring. In addition to their physical beauty, he documented words they'd said, expressions they'd made. But never a mention of one of the women being a lover.

Had Drummond been murdered by a disgruntled lover? Perhaps one had discovered she was one of many, and her anger had driven her to the unthinkable.

Fenby would surely know who these ladies were, could provide him with surnames so he could question each of them. Surely, they knew Mr. Drummond as well as he knew them.

Chapter 5

Willow examined the ballroom, trying to remember precisely why she had decided to attend. It was a lovely place; she could not deny that. The Fieldcrest ball usually was lovely. The room itself was a rather large rectangle with archways outlining doorways on the left, leading to other parts of the house. To the right, the French doors leading to the landscaped yard seemed to mock her with their invitation to freedom.

"I don't know how I allowed you to talk me into coming here tonight," Willow said. She spoke to her brother through her teeth, keeping her gaze on her surroundings. The half balcony lining the room hosted the band, which at the moment was playing a soft collection of Wagner.

"It amuses me how irritating you find these events. I would have imagined you, above all people, would find them entertaining." Edmond gave her a little salute with his glass before downing his champagne.

Willow turned to glare at him. "And what is that supposed to mean?"

"With all the rules in Society, I would think you would be most at home." He grabbed another glass of the bubbling liquid as a footman passed.

"Yes, there are rules. But there are also gossips and mean-spirited people, for which I have no use at all."

Edmond chuckled. "Why are you so surly tonight? It's a lovely evening. There's even a fragrant breeze to refresh us."

She couldn't argue with that. The scent of the potted rose topiaries wafted through the air of the crowded ballroom. She eyed her brother and softened. "I don't mean to be surly. It's a lovely night." She was only irritable because her attempts to uncover any information about the late Malcolm Drummond had failed. She knew no more today than she had when she'd last seen James. It was going to be rather difficult to beat him if she had to rely on him for all of the clues. But she was persistent.

She elbowed her brother in his side. "Shouldn't you be pursuing some young miss tonight? Mama will be so relieved when you find a wife and settle down."

"*You* will be relieved. Mama is . . . well, Mama

is Mama, and she'll be happy for me, but it's not her primary concern. You know that."

He was right. Their mother was far more concerned with her garden than on whether of her children married and started families. But Willow firmly believed that was a product of her illness and not her true feelings on the matter.

Willow toyed with the necklace at her throat. "I do worry about you. All your gambling. Wherever do you find the money for that sort of thing? And the additional funds you give to Papa?"

He gently tweaked her nose. "Willow, you are too nosy for your own good. One of these days that curiosity is going to land you in a heap of trouble that your blessed rules can not work out."

Couples filled the dance floor as the band began a quadrille. Willow immediately spotted Charlotte dancing with the Marquess of Sinclair. They made a striking pair together with their tall statures and attractive features. Willow snuck a look at Edmond and was unsure if he saw the couple before they moved further into the ballroom. She noted that his jaw clenched, and supposed he'd seen everything she had. While she had never received confirmation, she'd always speculated that her brother had fancied Charlotte more than he was willing to admit.

Her eyes traveled back to Charlotte, who now laughed as a new partner twirled her about. Something in her chest pinched. Charlotte, always the beauty. Always the center of some man's attention, more than likely a crowd of gentlemen. Willow tried to hide her wistful sigh. It had been ages since she had been asked to dance. Ages since a man's hands had brushed her own and used his strength to guide her about the sheen of the dance floor.

There had been a time when she'd enjoyed the few moments in which she'd held a man's attention. But then she'd realized she didn't have that sort of luxury with her time, couldn't afford to encourage a relationship of that type. Not when it had become abundantly clear that her mother would require more constant care. This was precisely the reason Willow rarely attended these functions; they made her want things she could not afford to desire.

"Willow?" she heard Edmond ask. "Your mind is elsewhere this evening."

She smiled. "Yes, it is. I apologize. I'm afraid I didn't get much sleep last night and I—" Her eyes fell on the familiar form of Inspector Sterling and her words died in her throat. "Oh, goodness," she said. What was he doing here?

"Oh, goodness, what?" Edmond asked.

"What?" Then she remembered she'd been in the midst of fabricating some story of lost sleep to excuse her flighty behavior. "I merely saw someone, that's all." There wasn't any good way to tell her older brother that she'd unofficially joined the ranks of the Metropolitan Police. "Someone I wasn't expecting." So she couldn't explain her new unladylike relationship with James, but the odds were quite unlikely she'd actually have to. There was no conceivable reason why James would engage her in public. Besides, it looked as if his entire family was with him.

"Who?" Edmond asked.

"James Sterling. A friend of Colin's, an inspector with the police." She'd seen Lord and Lady Dandridge on enough occasions to recognize them, but this evening she could see their resemblance to James. He and his father were nearly the same height, James having an inch or so on the older man. And Lady Dandridge—she had the same dimples Willow had briefly seen displayed in James' smile. "We met at Amelia's earlier this week," she added absently. That was true enough.

"And you do not like him," her brother stated.

It did not matter if she liked him or not. Or found him dashing—that especially did not matter. And it appeared she wasn't the only one who found him so. As he stepped into the crowd, the fans started waving and a chorus of giggles broke out every time he walked past a clump of ladies.

He actually swaggered, no doubt fully aware of the disruption he was causing. Willow tried to turn away, tried not to look at him. She didn't want to be one from the crowd, merely another pair of feminine eyes tracking his every move. But that was just what she was.

With all the beauties in attendance tonight, he'd have his selection of which woman to dance with. Perhaps he would ask Charlotte, if her dance card wasn't already full. Or the hostess's daughter.

If he were to see her, would he nod politely as he walked by? She let her eyes flutter to the ground, trying to stare intently at her feet. Perhaps if he did not see her, she wouldn't have to live through the humiliation of his ignoring her.

"Like him or not," Edmond said, "I believe your new friend is headed this way."

Willow's head snapped up. Edmond was right. James had spotted her and evidently saw fit to speak to her. She mentally calmed the nerves that rattled inside her belly. There was no reason to work herself into a lather. He was being polite; his parents had reared him correctly and since they were present, he was on his best behavior. So they would exchange pleasantries briefly and then he'd be on his way.

Not only had James reached her, but now the entire Sterling clan also stood before her. Willow swallowed what felt like a rather large lump, then painted on what she hoped was a perfectly genuine-looking smile.

James reached for her hand and she watched as he bent his head over it. Such formality. She shut her mouth, which had unwillingly gaped open. A brilliant beginning for behaving properly. She resisted the urge to roll her eyes.

"James, introduce us," Lady Dandridge whispered. His mother was all smiles and ruffles and gems.

He nodded curtly to her but his eyes said something else to Willow. As if he were apologizing. "Miss Wilhelmina Mabson, may I present you to my mother, Lady Dandridge, and my father, Lord Dandridge." Then he introduced his brother and sister-in-law.

She bent in a curtsy and kept her smile in place. "Such a pleasure to meet all of you. This is my brother, Edmond."

"Your family name sounds familiar," the earl said.

"Yes, my father is Viscount Saddler," Willow said. "I'm afraid he has retired from Society in recent years. I expect it won't be long before he passes the title onto Edmond."

"Saddler, yes, I know that name," James' mother said. She looked up at the ceiling as if looking for divine guidance. "Agatha is your mother. I met her on several occasions. Such a . . ." she paused, clearly grasping for an appropriate adjective.

"Energetic?" Willow provided.

Lady Dandridge's face erupted into such an unexpectedly genuine smile, it nearly brought tears to Willow's eyes. "Beautiful. Your mother is truly lovely. How is she?"

It was not the word Lady Dandridge meant to use and Willow could think of a string to give her. *Erratic, impulsive, haunted. Loved* and *protected*—she could not forget those. The list could go on. Edmond placed his hand at her elbow.

"Mother is as lovely as ever. She keeps busy in her garden," Edmond said. "She's quite the accomplished gardener."

Willow was not certain what else could be said. Lady Dandridge was simply being polite. Willow let her gaze fall to the dance floor, where couples passed by in a flurry of black coats and trousers and a multitude of colored silks and satins. She looked down at her own simple dress, which was several years old and while still in prime condition was not the height of fashion. Her ears went warm and she mentally cringed, hoping her cheeks would not redden.

"Would you care to dance?" The question seemed to come from her right and she looked up to find James' gaze on her. The question—had it been directed at her? Had James Sterling just asked her to dance? She felt her eyes widen. He held his hand out and she realized that yes, in fact, the question had been aimed at her. Her stomach leaped in response. *Mercy*. What should she do with that?

She thought she heard Lady Dandridge twitter, but Willow was unable to pull her eyes away from James.

She rarely danced with men at these functions. Mainly because men rarely asked, but also because those who did were generally twice her age and reeked of alcohol or liniment. Her first instinct was to tell him no, she shouldn't dance with him. She shouldn't *want* to dance with him. But she did.

Then she realized that the voices around her had ceased and all eyes were on them. She looked around. The smile on his mother's face was so full of surprise mingled with hope that Willow couldn't bear to let the woman down. So she did the polite thing and nodded and allowed him to lead her out to the floor.

"A waltz," she said numbly.

"You do know how, do you not, Miss Mabson?" he asked.

"Of course. I had a proper presentation at court and a coming-out and everything else required of young ladies." And she did know how, but aside from that first night at Almack's, she had never waltzed again. Here she was, though, in the arms of the most dashing man in the room.

She tried desperately not to notice the feel of his

warm hand at the small of her back. Or the feel of his muscles flexing lightly beneath her hand. Or the rich aroma of sandalwood that was so decidedly masculine, she had to fight not to close her eyes and lean into the scent.

Instead, she focused intently on counting her steps so she wouldn't miss one. One, two, three . . . one, two, three. It wasn't until he chuckled that she realized she must have been mouthing her counts. And had the sound of his laugh not completely captivated her, she would have boxed his ears. But the rich baritone of his voice and the genuine quality of the laugh made it impossible for her to do anything but smile.

And then it was he who missed a step, but he recovered so quickly, she almost didn't notice.

"You have a lovely smile." It didn't sound like a heartfelt compliment, but rather the kind a boy of seven pays when his mother forces him to say something nice to someone.

"Thank you." She probably should have said something equally as kind, it seemed only fair to repay a compliment with a compliment, but when it came to forming one, she was at a loss. His smile was nice as well. More than nice, if she were perfectly honest. The dimples imbedded in his stubbled cheeks gave him a mixed look of dangerous man and boyish charm.

He was precisely the sort of man who would

make Charlotte weak in the knees. Why, then, did Willow's own joints feel so wobbly? She had always been the one unaffected by the charms of men. Had always managed to keep herself collected and calm, and those very skills had enabled her to accept her spinsterhood with ease.

But here she was, drawn to the man who behaved as he desired rather than as he ought. It seemed a cruel trick of irony that the one man she did not want to want was the only man who seemed to stir her interest. Perhaps that's all it was: wanting what one couldn't have. That trick had ensnared poor Eve in the Garden of Eden. It was in a person's nature to behave in such ways, just as it was within her capability to ignore such longings.

His hand tensed, pressing into the small of her back. And try as she might, she could not ignore the sensations radiating up her spine. She was right at eye level with his Adam's apple, more evidence of his masculine nature. The muscles and tendons in his neck tightened ever so slightly and the browned skin beckoned for her to run her fingers over it. She looked at her hand resting against his shoulder and knew if she allowed herself to explore, she'd find more firm muscle just below her fingertips. She swallowed.

It was foolish for her to try to ignore his body so close to hers, or his hands on her body or his breath at her ear. Nor could she ignore the rapid cadence of her heart. She could not have this, she reminded herself. Romance and love, marriage and family—those things were out of her reach. Not that he was offering.

No, James was simply being polite for the sake of his parents. He, no doubt, took pity on the poor spinster for standing off to the side like a discarded wallflower.

So despite the feelings this dance conjured, nothing had changed. She might still harbor desires for that sort of life, but to claim it, she'd have to neglect her mother, and that was a sacrifice she wasn't willing to make. She could control this reaction as well as any other she'd had for the last nine and twenty years. Soon she would forget it had even crossed her mind. At least she hoped so.

"Your mother," James said, interrupting her thoughts. "Her name is Agatha?"

"Yes. Why?" Her words came out more curtly than she'd intended. It was only that her family had spent so much time trying to protect her mother's secret, and Willow knew she became defensive whenever someone mentioned her.

He shook his head. "I simply hadn't realized that our mothers knew each other."

She tried a light laugh, but knew she had not hidden her unease. James was no fool; he would know she was keeping a secret.

The song ended and it took her a moment to realize the dance was over. When she did, she immediately dropped her hands to her sides. She ought to thank him for the dance; it was the polite thing to do. But if he was motivated out of pity for her, she didn't want to appease him with gratitude, so she said nothing.

He led her back over to their waiting parties. His parents still stood there, although her wretched brother was nowhere to be found. Now she would have to search him out so he could drive her home. It was time to end this evening's humiliation. She smiled at James' parents and inclined her head.

"Such a pleasure to meet you both. I do not wish to be rude, but I'm afraid I've come down with a headache and will be leaving."

"James, escort Miss Mabson," his mother said tightly with her hand on her son's arm.

"Oh, no, thank you," Willow said. "That really won't be necessary. My brother is here, I need only find him." No doubt he'd made his way to a card game somewhere in this infernally large home. "I know precisely where to look for him." Then she turned and walked away.

James' mother popped him on the arm with her fan. "You could have offered her an escort home," she said tartly once Willow was out of earshot.

"You heard her, Mother. She already has an escort." Of all the asinine things. He fought the urge to let go a string of curses. Of all the ridiculous things he could have done, he had gone and asked Willow to dance in front of his mother. What had he been thinking? He hadn't been, that was the problem.

He'd seen Willow gazing wistfully at the dance floor and something inside him had tightened. It had not been out of pity, although he was certain Willow thought as much, with her rapid departure. No, pity hadn't led him to ask; he'd wanted to dance with her. It had been some indiscernible urge—an urge to have her in his arms and give her what she seemed to desire. Perhaps he had misread her.

He was so used to acting on impulse that he hadn't paused long enough to consider the repercussions. And those repercussions were about to come flailing out of his mother's mouth.

"She is quite a lovely girl, James, I can't imagine why you wouldn't have wanted to spend more time with her. I realize she's older, but she is still viable."

He nearly winced. "You make her sound like a cut of meat—decided when it has soured enough to toss out. Can we get back to why I came here tonight?"

"And what reason is that? To break your poor mother's heart? Honestly, James, I can't take much more of this. A mother can only suffer so much pain before she simply withers away." She caught a sob behind her handkerchief, then she pulled her husband away.

So he'd chased two women away for the night, both with the same dance.

Chapter 6

James swirled the glass of amber liquid around while he flipped through Drummond's journal. The first mention of Agatha was not far into the leather-bound book. James scanned the photographer's words and felt a stone sink in his stomach. Luscious brown hair, crystalline-green eyes, rounded curves, and a dimple in her chin. Aside from the color of the eyes, Drummond could have been talking about Willow. When he'd first heard her mother's name mentioned at the ball, he'd wondered, but Agatha wasn't that uncommon of a name.

He'd wanted to ask Willow if her mother had known the photographer. The question had been right on his tongue, but every mention of her mother's name seemed to greatly increase her unease. Willow was hiding something, and this just might be it. Perhaps she knew of her mother's connection to Drummond and was trying to protect her.

Tossing the journal on his bed, he poured himself another drink. Regardless of Willow's motives, he needed an opportunity to interrogate her parents. But he needed to do so without her interference. He knew that were Willow to be present during his questioning, nothing would get accomplished.

He might not know Willow very well, but he'd seen enough to acknowledge that she would be fiercely loyal to her family. So, as soon as he could, he'd pay a visit to the viscount and his wife. In the meantime, Willow might be able to assist him in figuring out who the other ladies in the journal might be.

His mother hadn't been the least bit helpful tonight. Once he'd foolishly asked Willow to dance, it was all his mother could think about. He knew she'd immediately begun dreaming about which church and what flowers, and which would be prettier, a spring or fall wedding? He certainly hadn't planned on dancing with her. Or with any woman, for that matter. He'd told his mother as much to keep her pestering at bay. And yet he'd asked Willow and she'd said yes and had spent several moments encased in his arms.

He wanted to pretend those moments hadn't affected him, that the softness of her skin and the clean citrus smell of her hair hadn't caused desire to surge through him. He took a sip of brandy and reveled in the fire that slid down his throat.

Closing his eyes, he could still see how she'd looked as he'd guided her over the dance floor. While her dress wasn't completely unfashionable, it wasn't nearly as revealing as most of the other women's. The creamy pink had looked nice with her skin. The delicate curls of her soft brown hair had laid nicely on her smooth and rounded shoulders. Shoulders he could have spent hours laving kisses and nibbles on.

Bloody hell.

He stepped out onto his balcony and looked to the ground, three stories below. In the dim light it was difficult to see the manicured lawn and pebbled walkway, but he knew from memory that they lay beneath. He tossed the remaining brandy out of his glass and watched the liquid travel into the darkness.

He'd not only wanted to dance with her, but after the feel of her in his arms, the subtle feminine scent surrounding her, and that smile she'd bestowed upon him, he'd wanted nothing more than to pull her close and kiss her senseless.

She amused him. Not in a cruel, jesting sort of way, but in a purely entertaining manner. She was intelligent and her sharp tongue was a testament to that. Despite all of this his attraction to her made no sense. Not because she wasn't deserving of his desire, but because she represented everything he'd stood against for the past twelve years.

Her propriety and aristocratic rules. Her prim and proper ways, all for the sake of Society. He'd learned to ignore it in his own family because there was nothing you could do about the family you had. But to engage in courtship behavior with a woman like Willow—that simply wouldn't do.

He'd not only done that, he'd actually desired kissing her. Which was annoying. He wasn't supposed to want her. Wasn't supposed to desire her kisses, not really. He'd only mentioned that kiss as part of the wager in an attempt to scare her off; instead, it had appealed to her competitive nature. Perhaps he should steal a kiss. While the threat of one might not frighten her, surely the impropriety of an impulsive kiss would insist she walk away from the investigation.

And the further he pushed Willow away from him, the better.

Willow had decided that the dance would not interfere with the investigation. There need be no mention of it. After all, it was only a dance. What they needed to focus on was a plan of action to take with this case. What was next in the investigation?

They'd made no plans to have a meeting, so

Willow had taken it upon herself to seek him out. She had made some inquiries on her own, but hadn't turned up any helpful information. It was important that she be privy to the same information he had. Which meant constant communication.

Her smart heels clicked on the sidewalk as she stepped from the carriage out onto the sidewalk in front of the New Scotland Yard. James' office was on the third floor, while her cousin, who had often passed information to her—quite eagerly, she might add—sat on the first, back in a corner. Clerks weren't highly regarded among the detectives.

There was no need to visit with her cousin today. No need for James to know she had a source within the walls of his sanctuary. That was her little secret. And she hadn't pestered Frederick for details in months. Granted, that could have been because her idle threats of telling his mother about his gaming hell habits had worn thin. Aunt Marietta was so senile these days she hardly knew who her son was much less what he was doing. She knew none of it mattered anyhow. Chances were unlikely anyone would believe him if he told of Willow's curiosity.

She tried her best to walk softly through the halls, but her boots were making such a racket. If she was to be a real detective, she might need to invest in quieter shoes. Rounding the corner, she approached the hall that led to James and the other detectives.

"I mean it, Sterling," a man's voice boomed from an enclosed office. "One more complaint like this and you're gone. For good. I don't care who you are. Your family doesn't have any power here."

Then the office door opened and she came face-to-face with a hefty man about her height with dark, round eyes and sweat beading on his forehead. A small, wiry man with a blackened eye followed him out. The smaller man was looking rather smug.

James appeared next and surprise widened his eyes, but he recovered quickly and scanned the length of her. He had that way about him; the way to make her feel completely aware of herself in a way that she'd never considered. He uttered a low expletive and Willow felt her ears heat with embarrassment.

"Did we have a meeting this morning?" he asked briskly. She was unable to determine whether or not he was surly with her for popping in unannounced or because she'd caught him getting disciplined. It was really rather rude of her and not ladylike in the least, but with a business transaction, those rules did not apply—correct? It was not as if she were calling upon him for tea.

"No, but I felt it important that we discuss the next step in this investigation. Aside from the butler, are we planning on interrogating anyone?" she asked, attempting to shift his attention off the unpleasantness she'd witnessed.

"Just a moment," he said, then he turned and stepped into his office area. He was gone for a couple of moments, but she could hear him rustling some papers. A few snickers filled the air and James cleared his throat, presumably to get the men to cease their badgering.

Finally he emerged with his black leather satchel. "Follow me," he said.

He led her back down to the first floor, then out the front door, all the while not saying a word. Once on the sidewalk, he hailed a hackney, then opened the door for her.

His eyebrows rose when she didn't immediately move toward the open door.

"Precisely where are we going?" she asked.

"To my townhome to discuss the case and to set our plan in motion. Get in, Willow."

It had been on her tongue to tell him she would under no circumstances go alone with him to his townhome. But the sound of her name on his lips seemed to have a soothing effect on her nerves. It rolled so simply off his tongue, she would have sworn no one had ever uttered the syllables but him.

She sat dumbfounded in the carriage and eyed him cautiously as he sat across from her. What was she doing? While the state of her reputation would have no bearing on her spinster status, it still seemed remarkably reckless of her to jaunt about town with a bachelor. A very eligible and handsome bachelor. Desirable as well.

Oh, for pity's sake! She needed to get ahold of herself.

"What?"

She jumped at his question. "What do you mean 'what'?"

"You rolled your eyes and scoffed at something, I wanted to be inside of the joke with you."

I was having silly schoolgirl imaginings about you. Somehow that admission wouldn't just roll off her tongue and she was rather thankful for that.

She nearly scoffed again, but caught herself. "I only just realized that I forgot my spectacles this morning," she said. It was a legitimate excuse and quite brilliant for one thought up off the cuff. "What was that about back there?" she asked.

"What?" he asked, looking up at her.

"Those men. I heard them yelling at you."

"The one yelling, that was my superintendent. The man in charge of me," he said tightly. "The other man is a suspect that I tried to arrest but was unable to do so. He didn't like my interrogation methods, so he came and filed a complaint against me."

"Who is he?"

"Baron Millhouse." His tone was flat.

Willow frowned. "I've heard his name."

James nodded. "You probably have. He has quite the reputation."

Willow tried to pull from her mind what she'd heard. She'd seen his name. Printed somewhere. She closed her eyes. "In the *Times*," she said. "He's been written about in the *Times*."

James leveled his eyes on her. "He buys orphan girls supposedly to save them from the streets and hire them as servants, but instead uses them for his own pleasure. Then, when he tires of them, he beats them and turns them out."

"Loathsome," Willow whispered.

"We can't find any evidence against him. And none of the girls are willing to point any blame in his direction. Not that their doing so would help. He's well protected."

"And you gave him that blackened eye," she said.

James shrugged. "I saw him the other night and he wouldn't cooperate with my questioning."

She sucked in a breath as the realization settled over her. James had used physical violence against a suspect. This was precisely the type of behavior her cousin had reported to her, but never had he detailed the reasoning behind the actions. When she'd received the notes from her cousin, she'd thought James a despicable, self-serving man who bullied and pressured until he achieved his goal. But now, knowing what she knew . . . because surely this wasn't the first incident of this kind. She could hardly fault James for striking a man with such low character. Perhaps she had misjudged the inspector.

She should probably apologize, but her mouth simply wouldn't form the words. There wasn't sufficient proof yet that all of his indiscretions were properly motivated. No, she would withhold her apology until she knew for certain if it was warranted.

It took less than a quarter of an hour to arrive at James' home, and she noted, as she stepped onto the street, that it was just off of King's Road. Evidently he was closer to his family's money than he liked to admit. The black double front door of the three-story redbrick building was flanked with white columns. Bushes in a small grassy area on the left side of the building were neatly trimmed, creating a pristine appearance.

James opened the front door and instantly three servants appeared in the hallway.

"Miss Mabson and I have some business to attend to. We'll be in my office. Tea and cakes when they're available." And with that he led the way down the hall to the last door on the left. It too had double doors leading into it, and upon entrance she could certainly see why he chose this as his office.

It was at the back of the house, so that one entire wall was lined in large windows that, unlike in most houses, weren't suffocating behind heavy draperies. Instead a light fabric outlined them, allowing more than enough sunlight to spill into the room. The butler had followed them in to relieve them of their cloaks, and he quickly disappeared. Without the wool wrapped around her and the servant in the room, Willow was all too aware of their being alone.

There was no reason to fret. He wouldn't take advantage of her. He might have pretended that he wanted a kiss, but she was no fool. She was clever enough to see his veiled attempt for what it truly was—an effort to rid himself of her presence. But it took more than an idle threat to scare her.

The thought of him leaning close and pressing his lips to hers warmed her to her toes and no doubt stained her cheeks. Thankfully, with her coloring, blush was often missed. She sighed in frustration. That line of thinking would get her nowhere.

She cleared her throat on the off chance that her voice would reveal her nerves. "I've considered our options, and I feel it would behoove us to question some other photographers. Certainly he must have had a reputation among them, and perhaps they can give us some additional information regarding his comings and goings and his techniques."

James leaned back in the deep-buttoned chair and the leather groaned beneath the movement. He steepled his hands beneath his chin and eyed her silently for a moment. She realized she was holding in her breath waiting for his response and she blew it out softly. It was puzzling how frazzled she felt around him. As if her insides were showing and she could do nothing to prevent him from gawking at her.

Then he nodded and she felt her shoulders sag. Mentally she chastised herself for such eagerness to achieve his approval. Perhaps it had nothing to do with him. Yes, that was it. She was always eager to please, eager to do things the correct way. This was more about her than him. She settled into the welcoming cushions of the sofa and tried to relax.

"Good idea. We need to question the women involved as well. It takes a long time to sit for a photograph and certainly there was conversation involved," he said.

"Do we know which women sat for him?"

"We can compile a list by viewing the photographs already located at the Burlington House. Fenby might can fill in any holes we might have.

No doubt there are more, those not included in the exhibit, but it is a good place to start. I also tried contacting the Duke of Argyle, but was told he's out of the country for the time being. His solicitor said that he, himself, handled most of the communication between the duke and Mr. Drummond."

"That seems to be the way," she said. "Rich benefactor simply investing in the arts and hoping for a lucrative return."

James had tried repeatedly not to notice how fetching she looked in her plain muslin gown, but he'd failed miserably. The pale lavender fabric might have looked washed out on anyone else, but Willow's complexion positively glowed. It seemed to make her rich chestnut hair even more lustrous, her brown eyes all the more sultry. Good God, he was becoming a damned poet.

Her idea to find other photographers who might have known the victim was really quite good. He hated to admit it, but she just might know some things about investigation. Or perhaps it was beginner's luck. He doubted that, however, as Willow's intelligence had been obvious from their very first encounter.

"So, do we want to plan to go and see the photographs and compile a list of the women to visit?" she suggested.

Just then the butler poked his head in. "I do apologize, Sir, but there is a . . . *rat* at the back door." His white eyebrows rose with the emphasis.

This was simply bad timing. James turned to Willow. "I apologize, if you'll excuse me for a moment." He rose and stepped out of the room. When he reached the back door—the one that led out of the kitchen—sure enough, an informant was standing on the stoop.

"Tumlins," James said. "I didn't think we had a meeting today."

"We don't. I just seen you come home with that lady and thought I'd stop by." His thin mouth curved upward. "I've come for my blunt."

James retrieved the money and handed it to the man. "Be sure you find me some reputable information this time." Then he shut the door in the man's face and turned to find Willow behind him.

She stood with her arms crossed defiantly over her chest and she had a very sour expression. "Is this how you intend to win our wager, Inspector? By bribery?"

He tried not to, but he laughed at her.

"Precisely what is so funny?" Her lip twitched as if his good humor were contagious.

"I am going to win our wager, but not because of bribery." He walked past her and straight back to his office. "Because that was not bribery at all. That man has nothing worthy a bribe."

Her eyes narrowed. "Then why were you giving him money?"

"I don't suppose you'd believe he was a common street urchin and I was being a good Samaritan," he said, hoping she'd at least smile.

"No." No smile, but her features did soften.

"That was Mr. Tumlins. He's in my employ, if you will, and collects information for me. From the street."

Her expression did not change.

"I can assure you, Willow, that it is all perfectly legal. It is often the only way you can get the inside details."

She gave him a small smile and retook her seat.

"You wanted to know about when we could go and visit the other photographers," he said. "What about tomorrow?"

She opened her mouth, then paused. "Tomorrow morning I have another engagement. But tomorrow afternoon should be fine."

"Another engagement?"

"I'm sure you are fully aware of the Ladies' Amateur Sleuth Society. Surely Colin must have said something to you about that. No doubt you've shared a laugh or two about us silly women."

"Amelia's little club. Yes, I've heard about it."

"We've now been instrumental in solving two large cases, both of which had terrible risks involved. As soon as the meeting concludes, I can meet you at your office," she said.

"No, I'll already be out, so I'll pick you up. How about two o'clock?"

She nodded. "You know, I've been thinking the killer must have known Mr. Drummond, and more than on a casual basis."

"What led you to this conclusion?"

Her eyes narrowed slightly and a smile toyed with her lips. "His studio," she said. "Not the easiest room to find, yet the killer found it without alerting the servants." She paused. "He'd been there before."

James watched her eyes light up. She loved this. Perhaps as much as he did. The clues and puzzles, the chase. And she was good; he couldn't deny that. He'd come to the very same conclusion, had even written it in his notes yesterday.

"I noticed the same thing," he said. "Quite clever, Willow."

She smiled in appreciation. Then he leaned back in his chair. A moment passed and neither of them spoke. She shifted. Should she bring up the dance to tell him that it was very kind of him, but he shouldn't feel obligated to ask her again? No, she didn't want to create any delusions in his head that she had spent considerable time thinking about the dance.

Even though she had, in fact, spent quite a bit

of time replaying the moments back in her mind. Where his hands were, what they had felt like against her body. She shivered. No, it was best if it wasn't mentioned.

But why was he being so quiet all of a sudden? Was he avoiding discussing their dance as well? No, that was foolish. Men didn't waste time on such frivolity.

"Willow, I hope my having asked you to dance has not made you feel uncomfortable. If you want to rid yourself of my presence, we can put an end to this silly wager and you can return to your life."

"I should think not," she said. Make her feel uncomfortable. He was so arrogant. "Precisely why did you ask me to dance?"

"I wanted to dance with you," he said.

If he was lying, he was doing an admirable job, because he seemed rather sincere.

"Willow, is it so farfetched to believe a man would want to dance with you?" he asked, his voice gentle and soft.

She wanted to be defensive. To say something caustic and protect herself, but she found herself completely stripped of tart retorts. If she were not careful she would end up trusting this man. Something she simply could not afford.

"I should go," she said. She inclined her head and stood to leave.

He rose to his feet. "Allow me to call for my carriage to take you home. That will be easier than trying to find a hackney."

She nodded and James swore he briefly glimpsed a blush staining her cheek. He'd seen it once before, earlier today, but it was so subtle, he wasn't certain it was there.

After he'd seen she was safely tucked inside his carriage and on her way home, he sighed in relief.

She would have her meeting tomorrow morning with the other ladies. The opportunity he'd been waiting for. A chance to speak with her mother and father without her present. It should be easier to get honest answers without Willow taking offense to every question.

He ignored the nagging voice that told him it was wrong to keep this from her. It was guilt and he refused to answer to such a futile emotion. Were they anyone else's parents, he would have no qualms about questioning them. Why was Willow so different?

But something was different, something that called his actions into question. Something he wasn't yet willing to put a name to.

Chapter 7

Her mother was having another of her episodes. It had only just started when Willow had arrived home the day before, and was in full swing by that evening. Last night her mother had tried to get out onto the balcony to dance beneath the diamond-studded sky. Willow and Edmond had spent more than two hours going over the entire house and making certain that every door and window was locked. Aside from the fact that she could fall off the balcony, it was quite frigid in the evenings, and they couldn't allow her to catch cold.

This morning she wasn't any better.

Willow did her best to smooth her hair down and pin it back. She didn't have time to do anything ornate. She needed to get dressed and get to her mother's side as soon as possible.

There had been a time when Willow and Edmond had followed their mother outside at night to dance under the moonlit sky. It seemed her childhood was full of wistful imaginings such as that. But she was all grown up now and didn't have time for fanciful thoughts. She had to take care of her mother before she injured herself.

Not ten minutes after dressing, Willow descended the stairs to reach her mother's parlor. It was a bright room full of windows that allowed the light to pour in and reflect off the polished furniture. Her mother had always liked shiny things, so this room, decorated mostly in yellow, fit her perfectly.

Her mother stood at one of the windows watching some birds play in a puddle of water.

"Darling," she said gleefully when she saw Willow.

"Good morning, Mother. How are you feeling?" She caught her father's glance from across the room and he gave her a tight smile.

"Well, I feel extraordinary. Come and look at the birds. Wouldn't it be divine to be a bird, darling? To be able to fly about and see the world? I want to see the world." She floated over to her husband's side and sat next to him. "Will you take me on a boat to see the world, Charles?"

He kissed her gently on the forehead. "We might do that, my love."

Her papa, so patient with her mother. It made Willow's heart ache to see them like this. Agatha smiled at her husband, then turned her attention to Willow.

"Have I ever told you the story of Maribel Huggens?" Agatha's face soured at the name. "Such a nasty woman. You can never trust a Huggens." She patted Willow's hand. "Listen to your Mama on this, Wilhelmina. The Huggens women are awful."

Willow had heard the story a thousand times. About how Maribel Huggens had tried to steal Willow's father away from her mother before they were married. Evidently her mother simply couldn't forgive. As far as Willow knew, that was the extent of their contact, but she'd been warned from a young age to not trust any Huggens. It made for awkward interludes with Maribel's daughters whenever she ran across them at balls.

Her mother eyed Willow's skirt. "You need new dresses. Charles, don't you think our beautiful daughter needs new dresses?"

Willow smiled at her mother, then met her father's gaze. Both of them knew the family didn't have funds for anything other than necessities. She certainly got the occasional new dress—they weren't that far into the bottom of their purse—but they were few and far between. And since she hadn't grown since she was eighteen, everything still fit her fine. Even her infernal breasts had been this large at eighteen. Thinking back to her Season, had she worn the sort of gowns that were fashionably low cut, she might possibly have garnered more attention from the gentlemen. But it mattered naught now.

"Yes, we can purchase some new gowns for Willow," her father said. He knew enough that arguing with her in this state wouldn't get any of them anywhere.

Agatha stood and walked back to the window. "Where is your brother? Edmond! Edmond!" She cupped her hand to her mouth as she yelled.

"Agatha, love," said her father gently. "Edmond isn't home right now. But as soon as he arrives I'm certain he'll come visit you."

Willow eyed the clock on the mantel and realized that if she did not send a messenger soon the girls would worry about her. She stepped over to her father and spoke softly.

"I'm going to send a message to Amelia's and let them know that I won't make it this morning. I'll only be gone a second," she said.

"And why aren't you going to see your friends?" he asked.

She glanced over at her mother, who had begun cleaning spots off the window with her skirt.

Her father smiled. "She's fine. I'll stay with her. You go. You deserve this time with your friends, Willow. There will be plenty of time for you to care for your mother. I won't be here forever, but while

I am here . . ." He paused and swallowed visibly. "I love her and spending time with her certainly isn't a chore. You go. I'll keep her occupied."

Willow stood a moment, weighing her options. She certainly didn't want her father to feel as if he wasn't capable of handling things.

"Go," he prodded.

She kissed his cheek. "You're a good papa," she said. "Mother, you should have Papa take you out to your garden. Your roses have looked so beautiful lately."

Agatha smiled broadly. "What a splendid idea. Charles, let us go straight away."

Willow stepped out of the room with one last glance. She hated leaving at a time like this, but her father was right. She would have her time. The rest of her life. Today she could have a few hours with her friends. She couldn't stay long, though, because she needed to rush back and make certain that when James arrived she could send him away immediately. No reason for him to see her mother in the state she was in. That would be positively dreadful.

James retrieved his police badge from his pocket and knocked on the door. Moments later a young gentleman opened the door. James knew from the Fieldcrest ball that this was Willow's brother. The man's eyebrows rose slightly.

"Yes?" he said.

He handed over his badge. "I'm Inspector Sterling. I'm here to speak to the viscount and his wife. Are they available?"

"My sister isn't home," Edmond said matter-of-factly. He allowed James entrance.

But James already knew that Willow was absent. Had planned this very interrogation while she'd be out. He tried to ignore the guilt that was sitting like a cold stone in the pit of his stomach. He should have spoken to her about this, especially knowing how protective she was of her mother.

"I don't require an audience with Miss Mabson this morning." He left out the fact that he would see her later that day. "Only your parents."

Edmond stopped before opening the door. "I'm afraid they aren't taking social callers today."

James nodded. "This isn't a social call. I'm here on official Metropolitan Police business."

"Police business, with my parents? I don't see the connection."

"I appreciate your position, Mr. Mabson, but I really must insist. I'm investigating a murder and I believe your parents were acquainted with the victim. It is really quite imperative that I speak with them. You may remain in the room if you like."

Edmond eyed him for a moment longer, then finally nodded. He led the inspector past the front parlor and further down the hall, stopping at a door. "How much has Willow told you about our mother?"

James frowned. "Not much." He kept his wording evasive. If Edmond knew that Willow had told James precisely nothing of her mother, it might increase Edmond's distrust. "Only that she has some sort of illness and must stay home."

Edmond's features tensed and he inhaled sharply. "My mother suffers from mania, Inspector. It is not widely known among Society, and I know you have ties in that area and we'd implore you to keep your observations to yourself."

James's heart pounded hard and heavy in his chest. So this was Willow's secret. His stomach tightened. Perhaps he should have spoken to Willow first, but it was too late now—he was here.

He nodded reassuringly to Edmond. "I can assure you that everything in my interrogations remains confidential." That wasn't always the truth, but in today's situation, he would make it so. "I only need to ask them a few questions." If she was mad as they said, then she could be quite capable of the crime at hand. A myriad of emotions scattered through his mind over that possibility. Willow would never forgive him. And that thought nearly made him cease his pursuit.

He might be unorthodox with his procedures, but at the end of the day, he was loyal to his duties as an inspector. Surely his position and pursuit of the killer of Mr. Drummond were more important than a woman's forgiveness. But if that were true, why then, did he feel as if he were betraying a dear friend?

Edmond put his hand on the doorknob and twisted it, but did not open the door. "I'm afraid I should warn you that she's having a rough go of it today. I'd appreciate your understanding and would hope you would be sensitive to the situation."

James swallowed. "Of course," he assured Edmond.

Edmond opened the door, but did not admit James entry. "Father," Edmond said as he entered the room. "Inspector Sterling would like to speak to you and Mother about a current investigation." Willow's brother stood in the doorway, completely blocking James' view of the interior. Apparently both Mabson siblings were hell-bent on protecting their family.

He couldn't blame them. He would no doubt do the same. As ridiculous as he found his mother, he would protect her should the need arise.

"Edmond! Come in and visit with your mother. I have missed you so."

"In a little while, Mother, I promise," Edmond said.

He heard a man's voice but could not decipher what was said. Edmond stepped aside and opened the door wider. James walked into the bright room and was greeted by Lord Saddler.

"Inspector," he said.

"Viscount Saddler," James said.

The viscount led his wife over from the window. "This is my wife, Agatha." He leaned closer to the woman's face. "This is Inspector Sterling. He's with the police."

Her pale green eyes widened, and she clapped her hands. "An inspector! Oh, how exciting. Where is dear Willow? She would absolutely love this." She looked around the room searching for her daughter.

James could tell she had once been a beautiful woman, and while the years hadn't necessarily been unkind to her, her eyes had taken on a glassy, faraway look. But he could very much see Willow in her.

"Willow's not here right now, remember?" Lord Saddler said.

She smiled knowingly. "Of course I remember. Edmond, go find Mary and have her fetch some tea and cakes for our visitor." She linked her arm with James' and led him over to the sofa. "Have a seat," she patted the cushion next to her. "Why on earth are you visiting us?" Then her hand flew to her throat. "Oh, gracious, are we in danger? Is someone after us?"

James tried to give her a reassuring smile. "No, nothing like that. I'm investigating a murder and I believe you might have known the victim."

Lord Saddler sat in an adjoining chair and laced his fingers together. "Who is the victim?"

"Malcolm Drummond."

"The photographer," Charles said. "Yes, I read about that in the paper. He was not a very old man, such is the pity."

"Yes, sir. We found a journal in his belongings and he writes of many women." James knew Willow would be extremely angry with him for this visit. She would view it as a betrayal, even though he was doing all he could to make it as pleasant and painless as possible.

"Malcolm is dead?" Agatha said softly. Her eyes filled with tears and she held her hand out to her husband, who reached forward and grabbed on to it. "I had no idea. I wish I had seen him one last time."

She was like a sad child. James' stomach tightened. "So you did know him?" James asked.

"Yes, we knew him," Charles said tightly. "Agatha sat for several photographs. We have them, if you'd like to see them."

James nodded. "He wrote often in his journal about a woman named Agatha and I wondered if it might be you."

"Me? He wrote about me?" she asked with a

smile. "How flattering. What could he have possibly said about me?"

It was unclear from the words in the journal as to whether or not there had been an affair or if the man's feelings were the only ones involved. "He was rather fond of you," was all James said on the matter.

"Do you want some tea and cakes, Inspector?" Agatha asked. "I can send Mary for some."

"No. Thank you, madam."

He only had a few more questions and then he could leave and time his entrance back to meet up with Willow. He would tell her he'd visited with them, as he was certain her mother would mention it. But he wanted to get her alone first so he would have a chance to explain.

The meeting was slow to start because Meg, as usual, was late. Willow tried to suppress her annoyance because she was rather eager to be somewhere other than here.

"Oh, Meg, I received your invitation to the masque ball yesterday and it's so beautiful," Charlotte said.

"No doubt it will lure the Jack of Hearts. He'll find it irresistible and we'll finally catch a glimpse of him," Amelia said.

"I suspect this will be the party of the Season," Charlotte said.

Meg giggled breathlessly before collapsing on a chair. "If the planning doesn't kill us all first. I swear Gareth's aunt is the most persnickety woman I have ever encountered. Not to mention fickle. She's changed the color theme three times already." She waved a hand in front of her face. "Enough about that, though."

Willow scanned the faces of her friends. Regardless of her preoccupation, she loved these meetings. They were good friends, all of them. It seemed ironic, somehow, that she and Charlotte would be the ones left unmarried. She, the plainest woman among them, and Charlotte, arguably the most beautiful woman in all of London.

Her gaze landed on Amelia and the sparkle in her eyes indicated she hid some sort of secret. "Amelia, dear," Willow said. "You look positively bursting at the seams. What secret are you holding in?"

Amelia squealed. "'Lady Shadows,' the first story, is to be printed." She clapped her hands under her chin. "I still can not believe it." She held her arm out to Willow. "Pinch me."

Willow laughed. "I will not pinch you, silly." Instead she leaned in and hugged her friend. "I'm so very proud of you."

"We always knew it would happen," Meg said.

"This is so wonderful, Amelia," Charlotte said. "You must be so thrilled."

"Thank you. I never would have accomplished any of this had each of you not encouraged me and forced me to pursue this."

"Not to mention you found your husband in the process," Meg pointed out.

"Yes, you can't forget that. And went on some amazing adventures," Charlotte said.

"All in the name of research," Amelia said with a smile. "I'll let you know the exact details as soon as I receive them."

After another round of congratulations and a fresh cup of tea, the room quieted down.

"Willow, how fares the investigation with the devilish inspector?" Charlotte asked, breaking their comfortable silence.

She tried to ignore the hard thumping of her heart at the mention of James. With one hand she smoothed her skirts. "We're making slow progress. We've made a list of people to interrogate, but in all honesty, there don't seem to be very many clues. Did any of you have any luck discovering anything of interest?"

Meg shook her head. "I'm afraid no one of my acquaintance knew him."

"I didn't have any luck either," Amelia said.

"All I found out was what we already knew: Malcolm Drummond was well liked," Charlotte said. "I would have loved to sit for a photograph with him. He was really all the rave."

"Indeed," Willow agreed. "Well liked, yet still murdered. Someone harbored him ill will—we simply can't figure out who that might be. I thank you all for trying."

"You'll unravel the mystery sooner or later," Amelia said. "You and James are both quite clever."

"And is the inspector behaving himself? Is he the reprobate you always imagined he would be?" Meg asked with a smile.

"I admit he has been on his best behavior," she said. With the exception of mentioning that he desired to kiss her. A conversational tidbit she had tried desperately to rid her mind of, much to her defeat. It was a nasty ruse, she reminded herself. "I'm certain he won't be able to maintain these good manners."

"Oh, Willow, don't be so negative. Perhaps James isn't as bad as you once thought," Amelia offered.

Amelia was right. James wasn't entirely the man she'd imagined him to be. Yes, he could be brutal with suspects, but did some of them not deserve it? And evidently he paid a man to dig up information, but were it not for those funds, how would that man eat? She had not seen enough yet; he might have some excusable behavior, but perhaps not all of it was so. She simply was not willing to admit complete defeat as of yet. "He's extremely arrogant," Willow said.

Amelia nodded. "But aren't they all? I mean all men? Aren't most of them arrogant to a degree? I know Colin is. He is certain that he is right most of the time. When we all know that that simply isn't the case." She smiled warmly. "But he is quick to apologize when he sees the error of his ways."

"Gareth is certainly arrogant. And stubborn." Meg made a small *oof* sound.

Charlotte chuckled. "He's good for you."

"You just wait," Meg warned.

"Yes, yes, I'll heed your warning. You can all have a good chuckle someday when my parents reach their limit and saddle me with some old lecher," Charlotte said.

"Now, how could that possibly happen?" Willow asked.

"I suspect my insolence in failing to accept any of the proposals I've received thus far is wearing on my poor father's nerves. If either Frannie or myself doesn't marry soon, he's likely to sell one of us to the highest bidder. Maybe I should flee to the Americas. I'm sure many adventures await there."

"Don't be so theatrical, Charlotte," Willow chided. "I seriously doubt your father will sell either you or your sister."

She sighed dramatically. "You're probably right," Charlotte agreed. "So tell us, have you asked the good detective how close the Yard is to identifying the Jack of Hearts? Surely they know more than we do."

Willow felt her ears go hot. She was embarrassed that the thought had never entered her mind. What was so different? There was a time she wouldn't have wasted any time at all before asking such a question. She had simply been distracted. "We haven't discussed the Jack of Hearts. But I'll be sure to probe and see what I discover."

Speaking of which, she should really go. She needed to get home before James arrived.

"I really must go. I apologize for having to leave so soon. But Mother's been having a rough day and I hate to leave poor Papa alone with her for long. He loves her so, but I know he hates to see her like that."

"Do you still believe she's getting worse?" Amelia asked.

Willow sighed. "I'm not certain what to believe. Some days it seems as if she's lost forever, but other days, she's calm and mentally acute. The doctor keeps suggesting we give her laudanum when she has her episodes, but I hate the thought of her living in a fog like that. Papa agrees with the doctor." She shook her head. "She deserves better, though."

"You take excellent care of her," Charlotte said. "But she is not your sole responsibility. Remember that."

"Not now," Willow agreed. "But she will be someday." She smiled at them, then pointed at Charlotte. "I'll be sure to ask about the Jack of Hearts."

Chapter 8

Willow stood in the entryway straining to hear the flurry of voices, but could not make out any words. An unrecognizable baritone voice took up part of the conversation. Funny, she didn't think Edmond sounded that way, even through walls and doors. She followed the sound to her mother's parlor.

Upon opening the door she saw James sitting adjacent to her mother and promptly dropped her umbrella. It crashed to the wood floor, causing everyone in the room to look up at her.

"Inspector?" she said.

He seemed less surprised to see her, but some undeterminable emotion crossed his features. Heat filled the pit of her stomach, turning her breakfast over and threatening nausea. He said nothing to her, but went back to his conversation with her parents.

Willow eyed her mother, then moved closer to

stand at her side. No one outside of the family, except for her closest friends, had seen her in years. It was simply too risky. What had she said to him? What had James witnessed when he'd stepped into this parlor?

"I thought we agreed upon two o'clock." She glanced at the mantel clock, her heart pounding loudly in her ears. "That's still more than an hour away."

"Willow, please," he said softly.

"May I inquire as to what this is about?" Willow asked. She watched her mother worry the fabric of her dress in between her hands. Willow smoothed her mother's black hair in an effort to soothe her.

James met her gaze. He took a deep breath. "This is part of the investigation. I thought it would be best to handle it without you."

Her stomach seemed to fall to the floor. "The investigation? With my parents? It most certainly does concern me then. What made you think it would be best to handle it without me?"

"Willow, this isn't necessary," her father said gently. "The inspector is merely doing his job. No harm has come."

"Papa, I know Inspector Sterling and I'm certain he'll explain himself. You and poor Mama should not be subjected to this," she said.

"All is well, dear, I promise," her mother said.

"The handsome inspector was just telling us about a dreadful murder." Her forehead wrinkled with worry. "I simply can't believe Malcolm is dead."

Willow whipped her head around to face him. She was unable to decipher his expression on his chiseled face. "You mean *that* investigation?" she asked. "Why do you need to speak with my parents about that?"

"Perhaps we could discuss this in private." His voice was tight as he rose from his seat, and she suspected his suggestion wasn't up for negotiation.

She nodded and excused them from the parlor.

Once they reached the hallway, he pushed his hair back from his eyes and sighed heavily. "I was trying to—"

"Do this without me. Yes, I gathered that."

"No, I was trying to handle this without you becoming upset." He paced along the hallway a bit before coming to a halt. "I knew if I mentioned this to you first, you would not allow me to speak directly to your mother. I needed to do this. I needed to do my job. Surely you can agree with that."

She shook her head. Was he trying to protect her? Out of some misguided chivalry? "I'm confused as to how my mother's name got involved. She wasn't on anything we discussed yesterday."

"We still need to see the photographs to make

sure we include all of the women involved in the questioning. But I already have a list to start off with," he explained.

"Where did you get it?"

"From a journal. I found Drummond's journal in his studio, and in it are pages of entries about women. Your mother's name is mentioned more than any other."

Willow balanced herself against the wall behind her. "He mentions my mother by name? And you never said anything to me about your finding the journal?"

James took an even breath. "All the women he writes about, he merely uses their first names."

"Agatha is a common-enough name," she said, folding her arms over her chest.

"Yes, it is. But he described her, Willow. In great detail. And you heard her in there." He pointed over his shoulder. "She knew him."

Her world seemed to stop moving. There were no other sounds than the ticking of the clock on the opposite wall and her breathing. "Are you saying that my mother is a suspect?" She tried to keep calm, but she could feel her heart beating faster and panic flooding her veins. Her parents involved. That was preposterous.

"There's no reason to become alarmed," he assured her.

She nodded absently.

A pulse flickered in James's cheek; it was so small she almost didn't notice. *Oh, God.* Her knees buckled underneath her and his hand reached out and steadied her.

"Don't touch me," she said, quickly recovering and stepping away from him.

"I never said anything about anyone being a suspect. I only wanted to speak to her about her relationship with the photographer," he said.

"So perhaps he took her photograph; that would mean her relationship with him was probably not unlike your own mother's." Her tone graduated up the scale as she spoke. This was not happening. Not to her mother.

"Yes," James said calmly, "but he did not write of my mother repeatedly in his journal."

"Why didn't you tell me you found the journal? You said you would share information with me. To make the wager fair."

He said nothing—only looked at her. Evidently he didn't think his dishonesty meant he owed her any explanation.

"Sir, I don't think you understand the situation," she continued. "My mother is . . ." She grappled for the right word, not wanting to say too much. "Delicate. This sort of thing is precisely the reason we keep her at home. To shield her from the ugliness of the world."

He said nothing for a moment but simply

gazed at her with those green eyes of his. "Your brother explained your mother's condition." His tone was calm. "I understand your concern, but I must run the investigation as I see fit and that means questioning all families who had business with Mr. Drummond." He reached out and put his hand on her arm. "Your mother is a delightful woman; you have nothing to worry about."

She got caught in his glance and tried to determine what it was she saw hidden in their depths. Concern? Pity? She pulled away from him.

"Well, I hope you are satisfied that my parents were not involved with such a dastardly crime and will leave them in peace in the future."

"Willow, I have to go where the clues lead me, and if that is back to your door, then so be it. Surely you can't argue with justice."

She couldn't argue with him about that point, damn him. She wanted desperately to beg him to turn the other way when it came to her family. Surely they weren't involved.

It seemed as if her heart stopped beating. How could this be? She shook her head in disbelief. "I don't understand."

He grabbed her elbow and pulled her further away from the parlor door. "On the day of his death, he was writing about your mother."

That was it. She felt weak, but she steeled herself and kept her feet planted. She might have entered this investigation with a point to prove, but everything was different now. It didn't matter which method they used to uncover the clues. All that mattered now was finding out who the murderer was, to make sure her mother wasn't involved any further.

"If you would please wait here a moment," she said, then turned and entered the parlor again. She had a few words with her father, then stepped back into the hall. It occurred to her that the inspector had no reason to wait for her, but surprisingly enough, he still stood there.

"She wants to take a rest," she said.

He raised his eyebrows.

"Shouldn't we be off?" she asked.

"You still wish to come?"

"Now, more than ever, I need to be a part of this investigation."

He nodded once, turned on his heel, and spoke not a word until they were seated inside his carriage. "I do not think this is a good idea."

She pulled her reticule tighter to her chest and ignored the pounding her heart was making. "I shall be fine, I can assure you. I'm not nearly as delicate as you might believe."

"Then I shall not try to protect your sensibilities," he said.

"I should think not. That's hardly your responsibility." She pulled back the worn velvet curtain to see her surroundings, but her eyes focused on nothing. All of her energy was being spent on keeping her anger at bay. Yelling at him would serve no purpose. He wouldn't react favorably to it—it wouldn't solve anything. "I don't suppose you would show me the journal," she said tightly.

"No," he said.

She nodded. "Where are we going?"

He unfolded a piece of paper and glanced at it before answering. "Back to Drummond's for one last search."

He certainly wasn't giving her much to go on. And after they had been working fairly well together, or so she'd thought. Evidently it had all been a ruse. He had to have found the journal during their last visit to Drummond's home, which meant he had known about it at the dance. An icy chill spread over her skin. That was why he'd asked her mother's name. That was the real reason he'd asked her to dance. Here she'd been caught up in a romantic fantasy—and he'd been manipulating her for the investigation.

She tried to ignore the fact that her feelings were hurt. Ignore that his inability to trust her wounded her pride. Or that he'd used her to further his own needs. She shouldn't be surprised. These were the tactics he used. Instead of physically harming her, he'd coaxed her with his charm. She felt an utter fool. But this was not about her. All she needed to concern herself with now was protecting her mother.

They were headed now back to the photographer's house, as James had found a clue inside Drummond's journal that hinted that something was hidden elsewhere in his house. A box that contained secrets that might prove to be of interest. But James could not focus on the investigation.

Willow hadn't said another word to him, and despite his attempts to ignore it, James was assaulted by guilt. She had been right, he had promised to share information with her and he'd ignored that promise. He was an inspector, however, and it was his duty to perform his job regardless of whose feelings got hurt. Yet, this was different; he couldn't deny that.

There was more though. He was drawn to Willow and although he enjoyed teasing her, he genuinely liked and respected her. But the attraction could get him into trouble.

Willow sat quietly in the carriage, her hands neatly folded in her lap. She was furious with him but was playing the prim and proper lady and stifling her anger. No doubt she was embarrassed and terrified as well. He wanted to say something to make her feel better, something that would take the sadness out of her brown eyes. Wanted to pull her close to him and run his hand down her back. Soothe all her worries.

But the fact that he wanted to do all of those things stopped him from proceeding with any consoling remarks. He was not accustomed to coming to a lady's rescue, and he certainly wasn't going to start now. This was about the investigation and he had to follow the clues—even if they led him to her front door.

She looked so sad, with her perfect mouth drawn into a line and furrows wrinkling her brow. The most disturbing part, though, was that he was aroused. Looking at her—with her need to be comforted, to be soothed—all he wanted to do was pull her onto his lap and spread kisses into her hair, trace his fingers across her body, then push himself into her. Make love to her until they both forgot about Malcolm Drummond and that the poor man had been killed.

He shifted uncomfortably in his seat to alleviate the pressure. He just needed to touch her. Needed to somehow remind himself that he wasn't a heartless beast who would betray people and never look back. Needed to see that smile she'd given him the night they danced. Without thinking everything through he moved to sit on the bench next to her.

She turned sharply, her eyes wide.

Before she'd allow him to touch her, he needed to give her some reassurance.

"Willow." He put his hand on her dress-covered knee. He was terrible at this sort of thing. Terrible at trying to be soft and comforting. And God, she smelled so good, he nearly forgot what he wanted to say. "About your mother—"

She held her hand up and shook her head. "Please don't," she whispered.

"No, listen. You don't have anything to be ashamed of, or concerned with. I know you and your family have worked very hard to keep her out of the Society gossip rags and I respect that. My time with her this morning will not make it to my mother's or any other gossip's ears."

He caught her glance and her eyes glistened with tears. It felt as if she'd reached in and squeezed his heart. He knew she would never allow herself to cry in front of him, to show that much vulnerability. And in that moment, with her pain shining desperately in her eyes, he'd never wanted her more.

He cupped her chin and leaned in. His lips pressed against hers and it was as if the world stopped. She was pliant and soft beneath him, had even leaned in closer to him. He teased at her bottom lip with his teeth and then his tongue until her lips parted and allowed him entrance.

She tensed at first at the foreign assault, but softened as he coaxed and played with his tongue. He kept things slow and gentle, seductively worshiping her mouth. When he heard a sigh escape her lips, deep satisfaction and desire surged through his body and he tightened his grasp on her.

She met his intensity, which surprised him, and he squeezed his eyes, trying to ignore his intense desire to slip his hand beneath her skirt. Not too far. Not with this one. She was different. She needed protection. Even from him. Especially from him.

Her tongue slid against his and he groaned into her mouth. Desire surged through him as her hand clutched his shoulder. He could kiss her forever. Only her. Press her body against his as she met his passion beat for beat. But if he let it go on much longer, kissing wouldn't be the only thing done. He'd already betrayed her enough for one day.

Finally he ended the kiss and briefly glimpsed her glossy eyes before she turned away from him.

"I believe the carriage has stopped," she said. "We must have arrived." And with that, she opened the door and stepped down from the carriage unattended.

He released a heavy breath and followed her up the front steps of the townhome. He'd kissed her with that much passion, and now she displayed no reaction at all. How was that possible? He certainly wasn't hearing the angels sing, but his desire had definitely stirred.

Fenby answered the door and his wearied face could not even manage the slightest of smiles. "Do come in," he said. "Would you care for some tea?"

James looked at Willow, who was focused intently on Fenby. "No tea," she said. "Let us get to the root of our visit today."

She certainly knew how to cut right to it. She turned to James and raised her eyebrows expectantly.

"I need to search Mr. Drummond's private chambers," James said.

Fenby sighed heavily and nodded. "Follow me, then." He hobbled off down the hall and led them up the staircase to the second floor.

They stopped outside a large door and Fenby fumbled with the keys before turning the lock.

It was a moderate-size suite with dark wood paneling and green wallpaper. The four-poster bed was made of carved cherry, and the armoire and secretary matched perfectly.

James caught a glance from her brown eyes, but before he could determine anything about her mood, she looked away. There was no chance that the kiss hadn't affected her the way it had him. He was the experienced one, and that had been a kiss so full of passion, he'd had to fight to control himself. Something he'd never before had to do.

"We'll search the entire area," James said. "It will probably take a while." He dismissed the servant.

Fenby eyed them with caution for several long seconds before stepping out of the room.

"I'll take the dressing closet," Willow said and quickly disappeared into the next room.

James eyed the doorway for a bit longer before conceding defeat. Evidently she was going to pretend that nothing had happened. Pretend that his lips had never pressed against hers. Pretend his breath hadn't meshed with hers.

He nearly groaned as he felt himself begin to harden. This was more than a little annoying. He ignored his trousers and began shifting things around on the secretary, looking for the mysterious box.

The sounds of Willow rifling through the items in the next room was distracting. Perhaps this was why he never liked working with assistants. They made it difficult for him to concentrate. Although he'd worked well with Finch and had never felt out of sorts while partnering on those cases, Willow was different. He simply didn't want to admit it.

No, he argued with himself, it was simply that

she was a woman, and he'd be distracted by any bit of fluff that was in the room—knowing that she stood only a few meters away, with her soft hair, feminine scent, and rounded curves.

It was becoming abundantly clear that it was time he took a mistress. This was getting quite out of hand.

Willow continued to search the dressing closet, examining every detail. Malcolm Drummond had impeccable taste in clothing. Everything was of the finest fabrics and cuts. The cool materials brushed over her hand as she pulled each one out of the way.

They were looking for some sort of box, James had said, but they did not know what size or material or anything. So she simply filtered through the clothes and tried to keep her mind on the task at hand. But that was proving more difficult than she'd have liked, when all her mind wanted to think about was the passionate kiss she'd just experienced.

Why had James kissed her? She'd assumed that when he said he wanted a kiss from her, he had only been trying to make her nervous. Or provoke her. But then he had kissed her most ardently in the carriage. Her cheeks still flamed from the memory.

Were she to close her eyes, she was certain

that she would be able to recapture the sensation of his lips moving across hers. A few moments passed before she realized she'd been moving garments aside but had no longer been examining anything.

She closed her eyes briefly, bracing her hand on the panel behind a burgundy smoking jacket and felt the wall shift. She jerked upright and pulled the jacket and the rest of the clothes out of the way. The paneling was slightly different here from elsewhere in the room. It was barely noticeable but there all the same.

"James, I think I've found something." She spoke loudly, knowing her voice would be muffled.

It didn't take him long to come to her side. "What is it?"

"This panel." She ran her hand across the wood. "Something is different about it."

He looked intently at it before leaning in and knocking gently. Then he continued knocking in different areas around the panel, listening for a difference in sound. "It's hollow," he said.

She smiled, quite pleased with herself. Now he couldn't say that she wasn't useful. She had found a secret compartment.

"How do we open it?" she asked.

He looked around the closet, moving clothes out of the way and kicking shoes away from the area. "There has to be a lever or something that will trip it open," he said.

She bent and scanned the area around the panel and then noticed, off to her right, several inches from the hollow wood, what looked like a door-knob. Peculiar to have a doorknob just attached to a closet wall. So she reached over and twisted it. Nothing. She opted to pull on it and this time she heard the panel slide open.

"How did you find it?" he asked.

She pointed to the knob. "Silly place for a knob, don't you agree?"

"Indeed. Let's see what Drummond was so interested in hiding." James reached into the cubicle and pulled out an engraved and a very old-looking wooden box. Then he reached back into the secret compartment to see if anything remained. "I think this is all. Let's move to the bedchamber."

Her ears flamed and she knew she blushed. His intent was innocent enough, but the words sounded very much like an invitation.

"For more light," he offered.

"Of course," she said.

She followed him into the next room and over to the secretary, where he set down the wooden box. He pulled the lid up and it was full of photographs.

"This was his secret box," James muttered, clearly disappointed.

Willow reached in and grabbed a few to examine more closely.

She felt her eyes go wide and was certain her mouth gaped open. Picture after picture she flipped through showed women in provocative positions. Some were scantily clad; others weren't wearing a stitch of clothing. There were a variety of different-size breasts and women of all statures. She felt James shift next to her.

Her palms began to sweat and her insides fluttered with nerves. Here she was, alone with the man she'd earlier been entangled with in a passionate embrace, and she stood with photographs of nude women in her hands. What should she do? Set them down and step away?

Some of the women were shown lying across the settee they'd seen in Drummond's studio and were touching themselves. Their faces were etched with ecstasy, several of them with their eyes closed. One after another, she couldn't stop filtering through the stack in her hands.

James stirred behind her and brought a new awareness of how close he stood to her. Right next to her while she perused carnal images of other women. Should she drop them? No, that would clue him in on how utterly naughty she felt with the torrid pictures in her hands. Her breathing tightened and she felt warm all over. Pleasant tingles had started somewhere between her legs and her breasts seemed to tighten, peaking her nipples into hard buds that rubbed against the fabric of her corset.

"Perhaps this was how he was making his money," James said absently.

She was certain she'd felt his breath flutter across the bare flesh at her neck. All she'd need to do was close her eyes and lean back into him. He'd catch her, he'd support her. He'd probably kiss her again. Good heavens, she needed to get ahold of herself. She cleared her throat.

"What do you mean?" She forced herself to ask the question, then winced when her voice sounded foreign and cracked. So much for appearing unfazed.

"There is an entire underground market for these types of photographs," he explained. "They sell them to voyeurs and put them in books. Generally you find it more in Whitechapel, not on this side of the river."

Willow couldn't tear her eyes away. She'd set the photographs back in the box, but she could still see a collage of bare breasts as the pictures mingled together. What would prompt a woman to do such a thing? To pose nude for a man who was not her husband?

She supposed that within a marriage there were times when a man saw his wife without any clothes— that seemed unavoidable—but she couldn't even imagine walking across a room nude, let alone posing. Just imagining stripping off her clothes here in front of James had her feeling flushed and embarrassed.

What would he do? Would he want to splay his hands across her body, run his fingers down her backside and cup her breasts? Would his body respond to the sight of her skin? Her flesh felt as hot as if she were standing in front of a flame. She took several steps away from the secretary.

James snapped the box lid closed and cradled it under his arm. "Being a lady with your sensibilities, I know that must have been rather startling for you," he said.

She could not meet his eyes. "No," she managed. She could handle this like a mature adult. Pretend she was a woman of the world for the purposes of this case, despite the fact that she was the furthest thing from it. "It's no bother."

"Willow, you don't need to pretend to be strong. Those images are rather explicit, certainly not taken for ladies such as yourself."

But for gentlemen like him . . .

The unsaid justification hung in the air like a heavy fog. Had the images aroused him?

"I think we've seen enough for one day," he said.

Willow followed him out of the room and

down the stairs. They only briefly spoke to Fenby on their way out to the carriage. Once inside, she wasn't certain where to put her focus. Too many things had happened. The kiss. The sexual images.

It was enough to put a permanent blush on her face. She absently rubbed at her bottom lip, then quickly swiped her hand away. There was no need to give him any indication that the kiss had affected her in any way.

"Why will those" —she cleared her throat— "photographs be useful to the investigation?"

"They provide a potential motive for why he was murdered," James explained.

Willow shook her head. "I'm not certain I follow. You believe one of these women might have killed him? Because he forced them to be in the photographs?" They hadn't looked forced. They'd looked . . . pleasured.

"Not exactly. I was thinking more along the lines of men connected to these women. Husbands, fathers, brothers. Men are fiercely protective of the women in their care. Or at least they should be. Something like this could easily put a man over the edge, were he to discover it."

Fiercely protective? Just the words themselves and the intensity with which he said them sent shivers up her arms.

His logic certainly made sense. She suspected if

she were ever in such a situation, Edmond would surely come to her rescue.

Try as she might, she couldn't ignore the niggling desire that it be James who would protect her instead, should the need arise.

Chapter 9

The carriage pulled to a stop in front of Willow's family home. James put his hand on the door, but didn't release the latch. He met Willow's glance.

"It seems rather foolish of us to pretend we're still working under the pretense of the wager. At least the way the initial conditions stood."

She nodded curtly. "You certainly haven't held up your end of the bargain."

He pushed his hair back away from his eyes and gave her a lazy smile. "Yes, I have not been forthright with you regarding evidence. But I do have my reasons. And I suppose I stole my prize today anyway."

The creamy flesh at her throat blushed a lovely pink shade, and her hand fidgeted with her sleeve.

"I very much enjoyed kissing you today, Willow," he said. "But I recognize that stealing such a kiss was not very gentlemanly of me, and as much as I hate to admit it, I was raised better."

He did hate admitting that. It wasn't that he wanted to be ill-mannered, but he hated that his birth alone dictated a particular type of life or behavior.

She swallowed visibly but still said nothing.

"So here's what I propose. We'll continue working together on this case." He knew now that it would be virtually impossible to rid himself of her. "I will share information and the like, we will visit suspects together, similarly to how we've been working. And whoever uncovers the truth of the murderer first wins."

He saw her take a deep breath. "My primary concern is keeping my mother protected in all of this. The wager would certainly come secondary."

"Of course," he said.

"Do the same conditions still apply?"

She wanted to know if he was going to kiss her again. Damnation, the woman had no idea what a temptress she was, with her perfect lips and silky brown eyes. "I'm not promising I won't kiss you again," he said. "If that's what you're asking."

"It wasn't," she said defensively.

But the pulse at her throat told the truth. She wanted him to kiss her again. Oh, she'd been careful today not to reveal any effect he'd had on her, but he knew it had affected her just as it had him.

He nodded slightly, opened the carriage door, and stepped out. "Until tomorrow," he said. Then he watched her climb the steps to her front door.

The smarter thing to do would have been to tell her the investigation was leading somewhere that a proper lady ought not go. But the truth of the matter was, he wasn't quite ready to not see Miss Willow Mabson on a regular basis. She perplexed him in a way that no other woman had, and he needed time to figure out precisely what it was about her.

Willow stood on the sidewalk alongside Charlotte and Amelia, waiting for Meg to finish giving instructions to her driver. They were on Broad Street, known for its choice, if not expensive, shopping. Willow didn't have much in the way of money with her—just her allowance, which might afford some hair ribbons or a pair of gloves. And she wasn't the most downtrodden among their group. Amelia and Meg both had more money than they knew what to do with, but Charlotte had none.

Meg turned and smiled at them all. "Thank you for meeting me here. I have decided that we must all have new finery for the masque ball, and so today we are going to spend too much money. All of it mine."

Amelia opened her mouth to say something, and Willow was forming her declination when Meg held her hand up to silence them.

"And no one is going to argue with me on this. I've heard it said before that expectant mothers should always get their way." Then she smiled slyly at them.

It took a moment for Willow to comprehend Meg's admission. And Amelia was the first to embrace Meg with congratulations, which Willow knew was difficult for her. Amelia and Colin hadn't had any luck in conceiving in the year and a half they'd been married. Amelia had said that it was difficult to remain hopeful. But here today she showed no signs of discontentment, only joy for her friend.

After they all had dabbed at their eyes and hugged and laughed, they stepped inside Madam Dupont's, one of the finest dress shops in all of London. It had been a staple here for the past thirty years, and Madam Dupont had changed with the times, offering more and more ready-made clothing that people with limited funds could simply purchase and alter themselves. But everyone knew that Madam Dupont preferred creating custom-fit clothing for the wealthiest members of London's population.

Willow got a chance to squeeze Amelia's hand as they maneuvered through the aisles. Her friend looked up in surprise and tears sprang to her eyes, but she quickly swiped them away.

Madam Dupont, with her ample curves, stepped out of the back. "What have we here?" she said in her rich French accent. "Ladies in search of . . ." and she trailed off, fully expecting them to finish her sentence.

"Costumes for a masque ball," Meg supplied. "For each of us. And we want something completely unique and very eye-catching." Then she turned and whispered to them. "We must be alluring, to catch the Jack of Heart's attention."

"Well, let me have a look at each of you. Greta, Ingrid, come with the measuring tapes and let us see what we have for you ladies." Two young and bright-eyed girls popped out from the back room, eager to assist. Madam Dupont stopped first at Meg. "Petite . . . quite the red hair you have. Perhaps something in blue to bring out your eyes." Then she moved on to Charlotte, and as she took in the beauty's full height, she released a low whistle. "A pretty one, you are, and so tall. With your complexion and coloring, definitely a bold, daring color. I believe I have just the fabric. Ingrid, fetch that chartreuse silk that just arrived yesterday."

Ingrid scurried away and Madam Dupont moved on to Amelia. "Nothing wrong with you, my dear, you have lovely hair and lovely skin.

We'll want something subtle, perhaps a soft yellow or gold. That would look quite the thing with your eyes."

Then it was Willow's turn. It seemed as if Madam Dupont stood in front of her for several moments, much longer than with the other girls. She was going to tell her there was no hope. She was too plain for anything fancy. How about a lovely shade of brown?

Madam Dupont's lips pinched and her eyes narrowed. "What is this frock that you are wearing? It will not do." She grabbed Willow firmly at the waist. "Look at this tiny waist and your rounded hips. And if I'm not mistaken," her French accent filled the room, "that is quite the bosom you have hidden beneath all these layers," she said as she pointed at Willow's chest.

Willow shut her eyes. Why did it matter how she looked? It really didn't. It would not make her mother healthy and it certainly would not bring her love. Madam Dupont continued her assessment. Perhaps the floor would open up and she could slide right down. Away from this humiliation.

She opened her mouth to say something—what, she wasn't sure, some excuse for her mediocrity. But Madam Dupont shushed her.

"There is no need to apologize. Some women are uncomfortable with their bodies and do not like to flaunt their figures. But we will change that for you, no?" She moved her finger down to the center of Willow's chest. "A dress with a swooping décolleté. And something lush." Madam Dupont turned and glanced around the room, scanning the bolts of fabrics. "There. Greta, fetch me that red damask."

The petite blonde scurried over to one of the shelves and retrieved a large bolt of the richest, deepest red Willow had ever seen. It shimmered to such a degree, it almost looked to be made of liquid rather than fabric. She longed to reach out and touch it.

"It's too expensive," she whispered to Amelia.

"Nonsense," Amelia said. "You deserve it."

Madam Dupont eyed her again. "I should think we might need a new corset as well."

"Yes," Meg said. "New everything for all of us. I should like to be fitted for some that would allow for my growing belly." She patted her stomach with a smile.

Madam Dupont's face softened into a genuine smile. "Ah, the babies. Yes, we will outfit you for your entire term." She looked at her two assistants. "Let us get to work. There is much to be done." She clapped her hands together twice.

The following several hours passed by in a blur of measuring and fabric swatches. Madam Dupont made Meg and Willow her personal projects for the day. It took her a very long time with Meg, as she had to be measured for all sorts of garments that would work for the duration of her pregnancy. Willow wandered around the store, glancing at fabrics and ribbons and looking at the dresses on the forms.

And then it was her turn. She rolled her eyes against the nerves batting around in her stomach. There was no reason to be this fussy over a simple measuring. Madam Dupont led her to the dressing room and assisted her in unbuttoning her day dress.

A cool breeze drafted across her back and sent gooseflesh in every direction. Then she was being turned and modeled and prodded as Madam Dupont wrote numbers down in a notebook.

"Yes, definitely a new corset. Look at this thing." She tugged on Willow's worn corset as she spoke. "It does absolutely nothing for you and your figure. I should think that a dress with capped sleeves right at the edge of your shoulders, or even falling off, yes, that would be precisely what you would need. Most flattering."

It occurred to Willow that while Madam Dupont was speaking, she was not speaking to her but rather to herself. It would have been more amusing had she not heard things like "bold color," "low bodice," and "bare shoulders." Willow was well aware that she had the sort of body that men wanted to look at. She'd known that for quite some time. The fact that no one else had recognized this fact until now was because she took great care in dressing to disguise it.

It had become so evident when she was nineteen that while she had not inherited her mother's lovely face, Willow had inherited her voluptuous curves. She told herself that she hid her attributes because she needed to remain unmarried so she could care for her mother. But deep down she knew that had never been the reason. Deep down she feared she had more in common with her mother than appearances. Deep down she feared that once she loosened her tight control, her life would unravel, just as her mother's had. That it would happen subtly at first, but then eventually she too would suffer from mania.

The doctors couldn't say what caused it, but Willow knew her mother had always been impetuous and wild. So she had spent her life preventing that for herself. She had followed even the silliest of rules, acted the very picture of propriety, in hopes that all her rule abiding would prevent her mind from splintering. As she had matured, she'd discouraged any early signs of courtship because she knew what it was like for a child to look upon their parent and feel fear and despair. She did not want that for any children of hers, so she had dressed extremely conservatively in hopes that men would not notice her, and it had worked.

Apparently Madam Dupont was about to change that. At least for one night. Willow supposed there wasn't any harm in it now. She was far too old to ensnare a suitor, and besides, it was a masque ball and no one would know who she was. Surely, allowing herself one night of fantasy before fading into the background while her friends continued to marry and start their families would not put her at risk.

Had James and his family been invited to the ball? As soon as the thought crossed her mind, she scolded herself. It certainly didn't matter one way or the other, she supposed, but she couldn't help her curiosity.

"Hold still," Madam Dupont chided. She held another bolt of fabric up to Willow's chest. "No, this one does not work with her color. Bring me another shade."

It seemed as if this went on for hours, although it was probably only a half hour or so. And then, finally, it was all over. They were finished. Willow was unsure how her dress would come out, but she had to admit that the particular shade of scarlet was luxurious. And a lush black velvet had also been selected.

Choosing their masks had been the most fun part of the day. Willow's was a half mask, covering her face to her nose and was the same brilliant red as her dress. It was outlined with gold cording and black plumes sprouted out of the top. Right at the top, in the center, rested a large stone that mimicked the sparkle of a diamond. The dress would not be ready for a week, but the mask she could bring home today.

She smiled thinking about it tucked nicely into the box held at her side. It wasn't the only thing she'd bring home today. No, Meg had insisted they each purchase new undergarments as well as some extras, a few pairs of gloves, and hair ribbons.

Once they reached the sidewalk, Willow was smiling quite broadly. She couldn't remember the last time they'd had such a grand time together. Without thinking she embraced Meg.

"Thank you so much. Your generosity is too kind, but I had the most enjoyable day," she said.

Meg smiled warmly. "As did I. I hope we all did. I can not wait to see us all in our finery the night of the ball. I do wonder if my husband will recognize me."

"With the flame of your hair, I sincerely doubt anyone will mistake you for someone else," Charlotte said.

"I suppose you're right." Just then, Meg's carriage pulled up to the curb. "Can I offer anyone a ride?"

"I believe I'll take you up on that," Charlotte said.

"My carriage is coming as well," Amelia said. "And I already agreed to take Willow home."

They hadn't actually spoken about that, but perhaps Amelia wanted to discuss something, so Willow nodded in agreement. The four friends exchanged good-byes and shortly thereafter, Amelia's carriage arrived and she and Willow climbed inside.

"I hope you don't mind," Amelia said.

"Of course not."

"I'm happy for her." Amelia's eyes glistened with unshed tears. "I honestly am."

Her friend had needed to talk about Meg's baby. "I have no doubt about that." Willow tried to give her a reassuring smile. "You can be sad for yourself and happy for a friend, all at the same time."

Amelia tried to smile. "I fear that we will never have children." She spoke slowly as if selecting each word carefully. "Colin says he doesn't need children, that I am more than he ever thought he'd have in life, but . . ." Her hand flew to her mouth. "I am not so certain I feel the same way." She shook her head as the tears began to fall freely down her cheeks.

Willow wasn't certain what to say. She couldn't say she knew how Amelia was feeling. She certainly did not. She'd never tried to conceive a child and failed. But she did know what it was like to want them so badly that her hands ached to touch them, only to know it was a desire that would never come to fruition. But this was not about her. And Amelia, evidently, needed to talk about this.

"It is not that Colin is not enough for me. His love is perfect." Her hand absently rubbed at her empty womb. "I just want to have children. At least one. I don't remember much of my mother and I always thought that instead of having one, I could be one. But now it seems as if I'll miss out on both."

Willow rubbed her friend's back and realized that she too was crying. "It will be all right," she said reassuringly. Although she was not so certain that was true. She knew all too well that life held no guarantees. And that not everyone found the happy ending the fairy tales might lead one to believe occurred at every turn.

Amelia wiped at her eyes. "I'm sorry to go on about this. It is not fair to you. I know Meg and Gareth will be wonderful parents. And Colin and I might be the best aunt and uncle in London. I have so much to be thankful for. I never thought I would marry, and look what I found?" She smiled. "I am happy . . ."

It felt as if an *although* hung in the air. "No one

doubts for a moment you're happy," Willow said. "And wanting more does not make you greedy. It is within a woman, naturally, to want to have children. There is no shame in the desire."

"Do you want them?" Amelia asked.

With every part of her being, she wanted them. But she, unlike Amelia, would never be in a position to have them. She would never marry and therefore never have relations that could lead to the birth of a child. Her place was at her mother's side. Regardless, she could not lie to her friend.

"Yes, I want them," was all she said.

Chapter 10

Willow was supposed to meet James at his office at approximately two o'clock. Outside, though. He'd had enough of the jesting from all the other men. Being called "Bluestocking" was one thing. Being ribbed about his "lady friend" was another entirely.

They had an appointment at Burlington House, one of London's favored exhibit halls, to examine the photographs of the ladies. James had Drummond's diary in his left hand as he stepped out onto the street. They would compare the photographs with the names in the book and see if more matches could be made.

After meeting Willow's mother, he had some doubts as to whether she was physically capable of the type of murder involved. From the position of Drummond's body, James had to assume he'd been reclining when he was struck on the head. So it wasn't completely unreasonable for a woman to accomplish such a feat, in particular if the victim were sleeping and unaware of the forthcoming blow.

It was unclear whether or not Willow's father was involved. Perhaps he had killed the photographer to protect his wife or as some form of retribution.

Something about that didn't feel quite right. Willow's father had been so patient and loving with his wife, it seemed if a man was capable of such warmth, he couldn't, in turn, be capable of such violence. But James had seen it before: someone who was perfectly civil on the outside but still driven to murder.

"Inspector!"

He looked up and found Willow frowning at him.

"What?" he asked.

"I've only been calling your name for more than a minute." A small smile crept onto her face. "Were you daydreaming? I never figured that for a particularly male pastime."

"No, I was not daydreaming. I was thinking." Thinking about her father being a murderer. Something told him she wouldn't take too kindly to that.

"Shouldn't we be going?" she prodded. "I thought our appointment was at half past the hour."

"Indeed it is." He helped her up into the rig and sat across from her. "You look rather fresh this morning." Something was different. Amiss. "Different, though. What's different?"

She blushed prettily. "You're the detective," she said dismissively.

He chuckled. He let his eyes roam over her, trying to determine precisely what seemed so unusual. She still wore one of her faded muslin dresses with the modest lines and starched sleeves. Her hair, pulled into the usual loose knot at the nape of her neck, looked as it often did. But still, something nagged at him.

"Before we get there I want to ask you about another investigation," she said.

"Now you believe you are privy to details from all of my cases?" he asked.

"Of course not, merely curious. I was wondering about the Jack of Hearts."

His eyebrows rose. "What do you know of him?"

"Only what I've read in the papers." He watched her form each word precisely, sitting straight.

"Your spectacles," he said, finally realizing what was missing. "You are not wearing your spectacles."

She put her hand to her head where her spectacles would rest. "Yes, well, I must have forgotten them today. In any case, there aren't many details of the Jack of Hearts," she continued. "The Ladies' Amateur Sleuth Society has been trying to catch him for months now. We have yet to catch sight of him."

"You've been trying to catch him? You and the other ladies?" He did an admirable job hiding his smile.

"Go ahead and laugh. I'm sure this is all rather amusing to you." Instead of her usual severe tone, James thought he detected a bit of embarrassment.

"Willow, in all honesty, I have not been involved with that investigation. The inspectors who have been working that case are under a different superintendent within the Criminal Investigation Division."

"So you don't know anything?"

"You sound disappointed," he said.

"No, I only hoped you might be able to shed some light on him. He is rather elusive."

"Yes, he is. They will catch him, however. It's only a matter of time. If people would fight him off or call for the authorities instead of treating it like a spectacle, then we probably would have caught him by now." He shook his head. "Foolish people."

"Yes, I've been saying the same thing." She met his gaze and gave him a shy smile.

The ride didn't take long and before he knew

it he was escorting her down from the carriage. She smelled lovely and clean. Not unusual, but he'd gotten a nice whiff as she'd swept past him. He wanted to bury his face in the soft skin of her neck and really allow the scent to assail his senses.

He wasn't supposed to want her, let alone touch her. She was a lady. There were rules about that sort of thing. And despite the fact that he wasn't one to follow rules, he knew these rules, if broken, came with stiff consequences. Like a special license and a quick marriage.

He desired Willow; he couldn't deny that. He could even go so far to admit that he wanted her more than he had wanted any other woman. Something in her called out to him and he answered. He needed to touch her, but more than that, needed to comfort her and chase away those shadows that hid behind her eyes. But doing so would surely ensure their marriage, and he simply wasn't ready to marry. Certainly not her. If for no other reason than his mother would approve. She would practically weep with joy.

The great double wooden doors opened to reveal a large hallway with galleries on both sides. A man stood just inside and he nodded as the doors closed behind them, causing an echo to travel through the marbled space.

"I am Finneas Burton, the curator here. If you will follow me," the man said.

He led them to the back of the hall and out two more double doors into a spacious courtyard. Pebbles popped beneath their shoes as they continued to follow the curator. Then finally they entered the original Burlington House with all its splendor. A few twists and turns later, and they were in a back room.

"We've been storing the portraits in here, waiting to hear from His Grace on how to proceed." Burton rubbed his hands together excitedly but never smiled. "We only just heard this morning that he wishes to proceed with the exhibit."

The room was small and contained two bookshelves and one large table in the center with a sheet hung loosely over it, dragging on the floor.

"Let me just remove this." Burton clapped his hands and a bevy of crisply uniformed maids appeared to gather the sheet and fold it nicely. He eyed Willow and James, and then looked at the table holding all of the portraits, then back at them. "Do be careful. These are quite delicate and obviously irreplaceable."

James nodded, then waited for the man to shut the door behind him before stepping up to the table. He handed Willow a sheet of paper and a pencil. "For our list of names," he said.

"Did you bring the journal?" she asked.

He retrieved it from his pocket. "Yes."

"May I see it?"

"No. You make the list, I'll look in the book."

Her features tightened. She wanted to argue with him, he could see it in her eyes. "Why not?" she asked, her voice awfully calm.

"Willow, there's no reason for us to get into this today. You know there is mention of your mother in this book, and that affects the investigation. I simply can not allow you to look at it. As it is, I could lose my position with the Yard by having you work this investigation with me."

"So, she is still a suspect?" she asked.

He released a heavy breath. "I will not discuss this with you. Now can we look at these portraits and formulate our list? If we do not start questioning these women soon, I'll be reassigned and this case will remain unsolved."

"Very well." She stood at the table's edge, careful not to stand too close to him, and looked at the portraits.

He recognized a few of the women and said their names so she could write them down. One was a fairly good friend of his mother's. Of course, that was the purpose of this exhibit, "Portraits of Ladies"—to display ladies of wealth and privilege. They had wanted to be among the first, he assumed, to be photographed and have their image shown in a gallery, for all of their friends to look upon with envy.

"Do you know this one?" He pointed to an older woman who sat ridge still on the edge of a wooden high-backed chair. The photograph perfectly captured her lined face and the fervor in her eyes.

"I believe that is Lady Geraldine Rappaport," she said.

She was still angry with him. He could hear it in her tone and feel it in her stiff movements. But it could not be helped. And it bothered him that he would even allow such a feeling to interfere with his work. Since when did he care if a suspect's family member was angry with him? It was an occurrence that happened with every investigation. Why should this one be any different?

He didn't even want to begin to decipher that puzzle. He would not allow himself to develop tender feelings for Willow. It was simply an impossibility.

He looked back at the portrait. "She looks surly," he said. "And there is no mention of a Geraldine in the journal."

"She *is* surly." Willow stepped around to the other side of the table. "This is Lady Mona Thatcher," she said, pointing to a fair-haired woman. "She was raised poor, in the country, but met Lord Thatcher at a fair, and now she is one of the wealthiest women in London. Not to mention happily married." She met his gaze and her smile faded. "Those details aren't important."

She was embarrassed for some reason. As if he'd caught her thinking about something she ought not think about. Happy marriages?

He flipped the journal open and looked at the pages he had marked. Jane, Anne, Millie, Sophia, Agatha, Eleanor. Were any of them here?

"Do we have any Eleanors on the list?" he asked.

"No."

"Do you see any here?"

She circled the table and looked at each portrait carefully. "No, I don't see anyone here with that name. There is an Esme, but not an Eleanor."

"Do you recognize all of these women?"

"Yes. I do not know all of them, haven't spoken to a good many of them, but I do know their names. I've always had a gift with names and faces. I remember people and their names from seeing them only once." She gave a halfhearted shrug. "It's an odd skill."

"Seems it would be rather useful. Or at least amusing, if you want to trip people up when you know they won't remember you."

"I could never do that," she said.

He smiled. "I would do it."

"You enjoy teasing people, though," she said. Her tone wasn't accusatory; she was simply stating a fact.

"I do. If you knew my family, you would understand."

She placed one hand on the edge of the table. "Explain it to me," she said.

"My mother is the pinnacle of propriety, and she did everything she could to raise me and my brother that way. She succeeded with my brother. He's so straight, he's practically made of wood. I, on the other hand, was not so pliable. Doing things a certain way because someone has deemed it the right way never appealed to me. I wanted a better reason. I suppose I'm more like my father, although no one seems to remember his rebellious side. Now he's simply old and accommodating of my mother and her proper ways."

"They don't sound that bad, James. In fact, they sound perfectly normal to me."

"Yes, but you're one of them."

Her brow furrowed. "You say that so disdainfully, as if being polite and following rules is repulsive. I can assure you, there are quite many of us out there. I know you can be on your best behavior, because you've done so, for the most part, for the duration of this case."

"I can behave." He shrugged. "I simply don't see the point. The world continues to turn without my following every guideline Society has created. I solve as many cases, if not more, than the other inspectors." He leaned against the wall and crossed his ankles. "In short, nothing terrible ever comes from my not following the rules."

"They are not really different from law, yet you enforce that," she pointed out.

"Laws created by our government are very much different from so-called rules, created by a group of pompous men, that people must adhere to in order to be considered civilized. You do realize there is an entire population in this city who are not privy to Society's guidelines."

She said nothing, merely eyed him suspiciously.

He pushed off the wall and swaggered toward her. "For instance," he said. "Who decided that I can not introduce myself to someone without being properly introduced by a mutual acquaintance?"

She stepped away from the table. "It is the polite way," she said softly.

"But say we had not already met before I saw you at the Fieldcrest ball." He closed the distance between them. "I would not have been able to invite you to dance until someone introduced us."

She swallowed visibly.

"What of the rules we're breaking right now?"

He traced a finger over the tiny ruffle at her neckline. "Do those not count?"

Her eyes widened.

"No chaperone, and you are very much unmarried, Willow, as am I, yet still we are here together." He leaned close and whispered, "Alone. Tell me, Willow, what do I have to gain by trying things your way?"

She stiffened and took several steps away from him. Then she pointed her pencil at him, looking very much like a strict governess. Oh, the games they could play with that vision. He had been rather naughty as a boy, often in need of punishment. With a brief closing of his eyes he was able to picture Willow standing before him in nothing but her spectacles, her rounded body taut with desire and her expression stern. She looked so damned alluring.

"I don't have to prove anything to you," she said, jarring his image. "Entire societies are built on rules and laws and guidelines, yet you seem to believe that *you* are above them. That somehow you're untouchable. It makes no sense to me at all. But then I'm simply one of the sheep, blindly following rules, simply because they're there to be obeyed, right?"

He'd evidently touched a nerve.

"I have all of the names written down," she said, then stepped over to the door.

They were finished and he'd made an ass of himself. Nothing unusual about that.

She wasn't angry with him. She was angry because she actually *was* a sheep. She'd never once stopped to consider whether or not rules had any worth or foundation; she simply adhered to them because that was what she was supposed to do. She was a sheep.

A foolish sheep.

He sat across from her and said nothing. The carriage rolled along steadily, heading for her house, where he was to drop her off. She had wanted to ask him today if he were planning to attend Meg's masque ball, but the moment had passed. Now the air sat saturated with awkwardness.

It mattered not anyway if he were planning to attend. She was going to celebrate with her friends and try to catch a thief. It was rather disgraceful that the thought of him seeing her in her beautiful gown excited her. She'd run a scenario over and over in her mind about what it would be like when he first realized it was she. His eyes would roam down the length of her, then settle on the bodice that was entirely too low cut. And he'd shamefully admire her voluptuous bosom.

"You can't possibly be thinking about following rules with a blush like that on your cheeks," he said. The deep rumble of his voice washed over her skin like warm water.

He was smiling at her. That seductive smile with those dimples of his. Her heart seemed as if it had chugged to a stop. Good heavens, but he was so dashing. How was it possible that a girl such as herself could warrant such a smile from such a man?

He was a wolf, teasing and taunting women. She knew that. It had nothing to do with her. Still, part of her wanted to hope that it did. If only a little bit. Just a fragment of him wanting to smile just at her.

She put her hand up to her cheek. "I'm just warm," she managed to say.

His brow shot up. "In this weather? It's damned chilly out."

"Perhaps I'm coming down with something." She was a terrible liar. They both knew that. No doubt he could see right through her.

The carriage rolled to a stop and she leaned forward to open the door, but he caught her wrist.

"I shouldn't do this . . ." His words trailed off and he pulled her to him. She fell onto his lap and he brought his lips down on hers in a hungry kiss. Her eyes fluttered closed and she tried to remind herself that this was a very bad idea, but she, the she on the inside, wasn't listening. Instead she was just kissing and very much enjoying being kissed.

He released her abruptly. "Believe it or not," he said. "That's a rule I've been desperately trying to keep as I know I shouldn't toy with you. But damnation, woman, you make it hard for me to keep my hands off of you." And with that he opened the door.

James closed his eyes for a brief pause, then he stepped into his parents' dining room. He should have known his mother's casual invitation would have been for more than a simple dinner with her and his father. Oh, no. The entire family was there. Stephen and his wife, although none of their children were to be seen. Which was for the best, considering there were six, all boys, which meant nothing but rowdiness.

"James," his mother said. She glanced at the large clock in the corner by the sidebar. "I thought perhaps you weren't coming. I'm afraid we started without you."

James made his way over to the empty seat inconveniently sandwiched between his mother and brother. The glaringly empty seat across from him was for his wife. He was convinced his mother had developed this seating arrangement for that precise purpose. Her primary method of attack had always been guilt. He supposed it was the way of mothers.

"I apologize, Mother." He placed his napkin in his lap and leaned back to allow his plate to be served. "I'm afraid my investigations are often more pressing than my meals."

"Nonsense," his mother said.

He filled his mouth full of juicy beef before he could say another word.

"Stephen was only just telling us about some of the debutantes who've been introduced this Season. Ellen, did you say it was your cousin, dear?" she asked her daughter-in-law.

"Yes. Felicia is my mother's brother's youngest daughter. She's such a lovely girl," Ellen said.

"James, I'm certain we can secure you an introduction," Stephen said.

"I'm certain you can," James mimicked. "But I'll meet my own ladies, thank you." Why had he come tonight? He knew the conversation would end up in this direction. It had only been a matter of time, and judging by the clock and the fact that he'd only been in the room all of fifteen minutes, his mother had pulled a record tonight. He tossed an annoyed glance at his father, who, he could have sworn, hid a smile behind his wineglass.

His father had long ago given up on interfering with his wife and her will. So, he sacrificed his poor children to her whim and then sat back and enjoyed it. If for no other reason, James should marry so he could do the same to his own seed.

"How is the brood?" James asked.

Ellen practically beamed. "Delightful, and as rambunctious as ever." She smiled at her husband. "I keep asking Stephen if he was as mischievous as they, but he won't admit it. Tell me, James, was your brother a scamp when he was a boy?"

Before James could even form a reply, his brother piped in. "I told you, love, James was the rotten one. I was perfect from the beginning. Right, Mother?"

"You were both awful," his father said, finally breaking his silence. "Terrible, loud, disobedient, all of it." He pointed at Ellen. "Don't let him fool you. We Sterling men are all scamps."

"Perhaps," Stephen agreed. "But it was James' fault we went through so many governesses. I was so relieved when I went off to Eton. Just to be rid of the pest and all of his nefarious plans."

"Come now, brother, I wasn't that calculating. There were never plans, I merely seized upon opportunities as they arose." James took a bite of warm bread.

"I suspect Governess Wilkens never worked with children again," Stephen said. "At least not boys."

"Wilkens? Which one was she?"

"The one with the, uh . . ." Stephen let his words trail off, but he motioned to his chest.

James snapped his fingers. "Right. The one with the very large breasts."

"James!" his mother exclaimed.

"Well, they were. I always wondered how she managed to keep her balance. And as a grown man today, I can say I have never seen a bosom that rivaled hers. In size, that is."

"Nor I," his father said quietly, which garnered a laugh from both of his sons and an "Oh, dear" from his wife.

"This is not the sort of talk gentlemen have in front of ladies," she chided. "I shouldn't have to remind you of such things." Then she began to mutter as she often did when her patience was tried. All James could catch was the occasional "grown men" and "so improper."

His mother really would love Willow. She would be utterly convinced that Willow could put James on the straight and narrow, be a good and proper influence in his wayward life. But it was he who wanted to be the influence. Persuade Willow into his arms, where he could kiss her and touch her until the desire subsided.

"We received word today that your Uncle Felix is ill," his mother said. "I am still trying to decide if I should journey all the way out to that infernal bit of country to see how he fares."

"He doesn't deserve it," James said.

"Honestly, James, he is your uncle," his mother chided.

James downed his wine, then motioned for a refill. There was no reason to have that conversation with her. Evidently he was the only one who thought what Felix had done unforgivable; the rest of them seemed content to pretend that the little incident had never happened.

"If you wish to make the trip," Stephen said, "I would be more than happy to accompany you."

"Thank you, dear." She gave James a wounded look, then turned to face her daughter-in-law. "Ellen, have you received your invitation to Henrietta March's masque ball? I believe it is honoring Viscount Mandeville and his new bride."

"Yes, he married Meg Piddington a few months ago, I believe. Her father owns the confectionary," Ellen commented.

"Oh, those delicious chocolates," his mother said.

"Have you tried their latest? The milked chocolate? It's positively divine."

"No, I don't believe I have. Harry, we must get some of the new chocolates."

His father nodded but never stopped eating his dinner.

"We did receive our invitation and I immediately sent out a notice that we will attend. It looks to be the biggest party of the Season," Ellen said.

Meg Piddington, why did James know that name? Oh, that was right; she was one of the lady sleuths, one of Willow's friends. A ball to celebrate one of her friends. Surely Willow would be in attendance. A chance to dance with her again.

"Will your cousin be in attendance?" his mother asked.

Ellen smiled knowingly. "I believe she will be."

"You must attend, James," his mother pled. "At least pretend you are attempting to secure yourself a wife before I pass into the grave. At least the appearance of it might give me some peace."

He doubted that. "If you must know, Mother, I was already planning to attend." Now he needed to get home and dig through all of his mail that had stacked up during the last few weeks. Surely he had been sent an invitation. If not, then he would simply attend with his family.

Lady Fiona's eyebrows rose and she dabbed lightly at the corners of her mouth with her napkin. "Indeed. Well, that is splendid. Splendid, indeed."

With his mother finally pleased and his belly full, James excused himself before the men left to smoke. It mattered not that none of the men in his family, himself included, had ever smoked; they still retired after dinner to his father's study for a "smoke." But he had no desire, tonight, to chat about politics or the latest inventions.

By the time James arrived home, he found himself whistling as he mounted his front steps. He frowned. Precisely what the hell was he so damned cheerful about?

Chapter 11

The next evening James paced his office for hours, long after the other detectives had gone home for the day, running the scenario over and over in his head. The scenario where Willow's mother went to see Drummond, perhaps to end an affair, or merely an obsession, and things had gotten out of hand. But none of it lined up.

You could shoot a man during a confrontation, but he hadn't been shot. He'd been hit over the head with something heavy and so hard that it had cracked his skull. Which, more than likely, meant that the killer had snuck up behind him and hit him before he'd even known someone was in the room. And James had a nagging suspicion about the murder weapon that might eliminate any of the women involved, including Willow's mother.

But he needed to test his theory, so he'd sent a carriage and a note to pick up Willow. There was certainly a chance she might not agree. After all, it was a quarter of nine and well past dark. It was risky, but he hadn't wanted her in the offices again with all the other men. The way they leered at her unnerved him.

He peeked out the window in time to see the carriage he'd hired pull to a stop. It only took him a moment to race down the stairs to the back door. He opened it in time to see Willow ducking out of the carriage. Her eyes were wide and she met his glance with concern.

"Is everything all right? Your note sounded so urgent," she said.

The tenderness in her voice caught him right in the chest. For a moment no words would come, he could only stare into her deep brown eyes. Then he shook his head in an attempt to shake some sense into himself.

"Everything is well. I didn't mean to alarm you." He took her arm and led her forward. "Let's go inside before someone sees you."

Once inside, she turned to face him. "I'm not accustomed to scurrying about at night. Might you enlighten me as to why you called me down here?"

"Follow me." Then he led her up the stairs and past the office door and down the hall to another door. "This is where we keep the evidence," he said as he fingered through his keys, trying to find the appropriate one. "Here we go." Then a click of the lock and he opened the door.

Scotland Yard had been wired for electricity once they moved to their new location, so he turned the switch on and the surge crackled and popped as the light flickered on.

"All of this is evidence for existing investigations," she said, her voice lined with wonder. She was looking at everything as fast as she could, as if to memorize it should he whisk her away.

"We haven't always been diligent about keeping and protecting evidence. But as investigative techniques improve, so must our procedures. So now we hold on to items such as bullets or bloodied clothing because we've learned how to use these items to help identify either the method of a crime or the perpetrator."

She gave him an excited smile. "It's wonderful."

She was wonderful. Intoxicating. He could have stood in that moment, simply watching her amazement and been perfectly content.

"Over here." He forced himself to walk around a row of shelving until they hit the correct one. "This is what I want to show you. Well, in actuality, I need your assistance with something."

He had laid out the evidence on one of the black-topped tables, and he stood back to allow her to examine the items: the bronze vase, still streaked with Drummond's blood, the man's shirt and trousers, the contents of his pockets, and a few other miscellaneous items.

Her eyes narrowed in confusion. "How would you like me to assist you?"

"I want you to pick that vase up and hold it over your head." He grabbed the vase and held it out to her.

"You could not get one of the other inspectors to assist you with this?" she asked, clearly confused.

"No. I need you to do this."

Her hands did not move. "This is about my mother." Then her stance went rigid and her chin tilted up a notch. "I will not help you convict my mother of this crime. I can not even believe you would have the audacity to call me down here and assume that I would help with such a thing. Have you paid no attention to me at all to believe that I would not put my mother's well-being, not to mention my belief in her innocence, above all things?" Her hands moved to her hips. "Precisely what kind of fool—"

He put one finger to her lips. "Willow," he interrupted her. "Might I explain?"

She clenched her jaw, but nodded slightly.

"It occurred to me that this vase was rather large and I was trying to imagine a woman, especially one of your mother's stature, holding it above her head and then bringing it down on someone with enough force to kill him." He shook his head. "The image doesn't fit. I brought you down here tonight because you have a similar form as your mother and I thought this little experiment might prove her innocence."

She eyed him a moment more with some unidentifiable emotion crossing her features. Then she reached out and placed her hands on the vase.

He didn't release his hands immediately. "Do you have a firm grasp?" he asked.

She nodded, so he released the vase. She managed to keep her stance as it was, but her arms sagged beneath the weight. "It's quite heavy," she said.

"Can you lift it above your head?"

She managed to raise it above her head.

"Now swing it down upon my open hands as hard as you can," he said.

She frowned. "I will hurt you."

"I don't believe so." He nodded. "Go ahead."

She did as he instructed, heaving the vase downward until it smacked into his hands. The impact stung and pain shot up to his elbows, but there was no great damage. He took the vase from her and set it back on the table.

"Precisely as I expected. There is no possible way that your mother could have killed Malcolm Drummond. She simply wasn't strong enough. In fact, I'd wager that none of the women he wrote about or photographed would have the necessary strength to have made that blow."

He could tell she was trying to suppress her relief, but her shoulders sagged in confirmation. "I have been telling you that all along."

He reached over and gently squeezed both of her arms, kneading the flesh ever so softly. "Are your arms sore?"

"I am stronger than I look."

Always so defiant and hell-bent on proving herself to those around her. "I never doubt your strength, Willow. You are the strongest woman I've ever known."

"How are your hands?"

He wiggled his fingers. "I'll survive." He took a step forward and she, in turn, took a step backward and stopped at the edge of the table. There was only breath between them—no light, no space. "You don't always have to be so strong, though."

For several moments they locked eyes and James' breath caught as her brown eyes pulled him in. With one abrupt movement, he lifted her off the ground and set her on the table. It moved under her weight and made a scraping noise against the flooring. She tried to move away, but he settled himself between her legs, trapping her in front of him.

He traced one finger down the side of her face, then lightly stroked her jaw. "What is it about you that I find so appealing? I haven't been able to figure it out. You" —he moved his finger farther down so it rested on her collarbone— "are a mystery to me. You are all starched and proper, yet I've seen hints of the woman you hide inside." His finger trailed down her throat.

She swallowed. "I'm not hiding anything."

"Yes, you are, and I simply can not decipher why. Why you would want to hide such a passionate and beautiful creature?"

Her pulse flickered beneath his touch and her breath came in short gasps.

"You must know I enjoy a clever mystery. I'm stubborn, Willow, and I won't give up until I unlock all the secrets."

She licked her lips, then chewed at her bottom lip as she fought to keep her eyes open.

"What kinds of secrets will I discover if I keep investigating you?" he asked.

"I don't have any secrets," she said in barely a whisper. "I am afraid I'm rather dull."

He leaned in and feathered kisses along her cheek and ear. "You, my love, are far from dull."

An almost imperceptible moan escaped her lips, and he felt her lean in to his touch.

It was enough of an invitation to him to take what he really wanted, so he tilted her chin back and devoured her mouth. He didn't ease her into the kiss, but allowed his passion to pour through as his tongue delved deeply into her. Her hands clenched his shoulders, her nails biting into his flesh despite the fabric between them and his skin. She met him with as much fervor as he delivered.

She wanted him.

That thought sent blood rushing to his groin. Never had he wanted a woman to want him as badly as he did tonight. But the thought of her wanting his touch, craving his mouth, the way he had wanted and craved her, nearly sent him over the edge.

Their tongues molded to each other and stroked and grazed, and the kiss went on for what seemed like blissful minutes. Her passion was heady. Her legs flexed at his sides and while she did not wrap them around him, he had the distinct feeling she'd thought about it. That her body had wanted to envelop him, but still a modicum of her restraint remained. Nevertheless, her knees were tight at his hips.

He pushed himself closer to her core, wanting to press his hardness against the ache he knew she hid between her legs. But if he went too far, too fast, he would frighten her. So as much as the blood pounded in his ears and his guttural instincts screamed for him to take her, he forced himself to slow down.

With one hand he clutched at her hip, pulling her gently toward him. All the while he kept his mouth on hers, seducing and loving her lips and tongue. Then both hands were on her hips, inching closer to the roundness of her bottom, which he could feel quite perfectly through her dress as she wore no bustle this evening.

God he wanted her. And she wanted him. He let his mouth trail off of hers to kiss down the thin column of her throat. Her skin was pure like honey, so soft and supple, he longed to trace his tongue over every milky inch of her.

He let his right hand move to her breast and he squeezed her flesh gently. She released a deep moan, which fueled his exploration. Bolder and bolder he became, until his attentions beaded her nipple and he could feel it through the thin fabric of her dress. He flicked at it and she nearly came off the table.

Her eyes flew open and abruptly pushed at his chest. "Enough," she said breathlessly. She shook her head. "We can not do this. It isn't proper." She squirmed, trying to inch herself off the table, so he assisted her down.

He forced himself to step away from her. More than anything he'd wanted to continue touching her, to continue to feel her passion wrap around him. But she was right. It wasn't proper. Not with her. And he'd nearly lost control, which simply didn't happen. At least not in this type of situation.

She smoothed her skirt and then her hair. "I appreciate your experiment this evening. It gives me great relief to know that my mother is no longer a suspect."

No, her mother wasn't a suspect, but her family remained in question. He had to be honest with her. She needed to know. She would hate him regardless, but perhaps if he told her himself. "Someone who was close to one of those women has to be the one who killed him."

She blinked up at him, not comprehending.

"Willow, your mother is no longer a suspect. But your father still is."

Her face went pale as she absorbed his words. "You are a bastard," she said, then walked away.

He caught up with her. She was right; he was a bastard. It was one thing to do his job and follow the investigation, but it was quite another to sully her with his advances. More than likely, she wouldn't be so angry with him had he not kissed her first.

"Willow, wait."

"I have nothing to say to you," she said, her voice thick with anger. She clipped quickly down the stairs and headed for the front door.

"I know you're angry." He wanted her to stop and pound on his chest or yell at him. But she did none of those. She simply stepped out the door and immediately into the awaiting carriage.

He let out a heavy breath. He was an excellent investigator; he knew how to find the hidden clues, how to persuade a victim to talk and how to induce a confession out of a perpetrator. He did not, however, know what to do when a woman was angry with him.

It was not as if he'd never before made anyone angry. Ever since he was a child, he'd infuriated his mother. But she pouted and occasionally raised her voice, although not often. But Willow, however, had been clearly angry, yet had not yelled or struck him across the face, which he very much deserved.

This was uncharted territory for him. He couldn't apologize. It was not his fault her father was a suspect. He could apologize for the kiss, but he'd done that before and then gone back on his word and kissed her again. It seemed that when it came to Willow, he was unable to control his words or his actions.

James put the last of the evidence up, then swore loudly. He shouldn't have told her, should never have said anything about her father. Then what? Hope for the best that he wouldn't have to arrest the man?

His attraction for Willow was beginning to interfere with the investigation. He simply could not allow that to happen. Especially when her family might very well be involved.

If he wasn't careful, he was going to wind up married. The moment James committed himself to a marriage, not only would he be saddled with a wife, but his mother would begin her incessant nagging for grandchildren and would badger him to quit his dangerous position with the Yard. He could hear her right now.

Despite the fact that a small part of him wanted to protect Willow from wherever this investigation led them, he could not do so. His first priority was the Yard and solving the cases assigned to him. If that meant arresting Willow's father, then he would have to follow that through, even if it meant she would never forgive him.

Besides, this attraction to her was more than likely exaggerated by the close proximity in which they were forced to work. Once the investigation was over, his fascination with her would wane and he could return to his regular carefree self.

It seemed as if every emotion was waging a war inside her, fighting for dominance. Willow pulled the tiny curtain back on the carriage window and glared at the moon hanging brightly in the sky. The full, rounded orb seemed to be mocking her with its beauty, daring her to find some romance in the air.

There had been kissing and there had been touching, but there could be no romance. Not with James. Not when he was hell-bent on destroying her family. Her heart beat a sporadic tattoo, and try as she might to ignore the sensations, she could still feel his hands on her.

She should have had more strength. Should have been able to push away from him. She should be ashamed of herself. Acting the harlot while he did his best to dig up evidence on her poor father. Her father, who had already been through enough in his lifetime. And now he was to be a murder suspect. She shuddered.

Yes, she should be ashamed, but no matter how must she tried to muster the feeling, that one simply would not come. She was angry, so angry she wanted to hit something, preferably someone.

She was hurt, of that she was certain. More than anything, she felt betrayed. Yes, by James, but more so by herself. How could she feel such intense desire for a man who made himself an enemy to her family? Allowing him to touch her betrayed her family and her loyalty to them. How could she, even now, knowing what she knew, still close her eyes and feel desire coursing through her body?

She was the worst sort of woman.

Had he been distracting her with his caresses in an attempt to soften his accusations? Her hand strayed to her breast and she closed her eyes against the moonlight. With a tug of her dress, to ensure it was properly in place, she forced James out of her mind. She had worked too hard her entire life to practice restraint and control and be a true lady, and then he'd come into her life and it had all fallen apart.

Well, it would happen no more. She might be a tarnished lady, but no one need know that. Most of her virtue was intact and that is how it would remain. The investigation and proving her father's innocence would take precedence over all things. She would not stand by and allow her family to be persecuted.

They had endured enough.

Chapter 12

Willow was quite certain she might lose her dinner at any moment. She pressed her hand against her fluttering stomach to try to calm the racket within. It was not as if she'd never been to a ball before, but for some reason this one had her nerves tied in knots.

It had been two days since she'd seen or heard from James. She knew he was probably working on the investigation without her, but she hadn't been able to bring herself to contact him. She hadn't given up; she simply had needed a bit of time to regain her strength and resolve. But tonight's affair was not reinforcing either, as she felt rather weak and terrified at the moment.

Thankfully, she would not have to go it alone. Because it was to be a rather late affair, she was attending with Amelia and Colin. So, they'd agreed that she would arrive at their house early and she and Amelia would dress themselves together. But now as she sat at the dressing table while one of the maids worked magic with her hair, she felt nothing akin to excitement, merely dread.

"Willow, you look so pale," Amelia said as she stepped into the mirror's reflection.

"I think my corset is too tight," Willow offered.

"Do you want me to loosen it?" the maid asked, her hands stilling over Willow's head.

Willow shifted in her seat and found she still had ample room to breathe. So that wasn't it. "No, I shall be fine."

Amelia disappeared briefly, then returned with a glass of red liquid. "Here, drink this. I think it might help."

Willow took the wine and sipped it cautiously. Ordinarily she wasn't one to imbibe, but tonight seemed like the perfect situation. She knew what caused her unease—the thing that had her nerves so frazzled. Once the package from Madam Dupont had arrived at her house, she'd nearly fallen over.

Her gown for this evening was not only the most luxurious and beautiful confection she'd ever seen (let alone owned), it was utterly sinful in design. As the maid put the last of the pins in her hair, it became clear that the time had come for her to slip it on.

She stood and allowed the young maid to completely take over. The cool silk sent a shock of chills across her arms as the dress slid into place. Willow raised her arms to allow the fastenings at her side to be closed. Then she stood in front of the mirror looking very much a woman, and not one she readily recognized.

The gown, while mostly red with a delicate embroidered design, had black velvet right at her bosom, with red lace lining the bodice. Below her breasts, three sloping strands of black pearls came to a point at the center where a lovely broach tied it all together.

From there the dress fell in at her small waist then draped to the floor. The skirt was not wide, as fashion had seemed to demand earlier in the year, but was subtle and accented her narrow waist and wider hips.

There was no denying her body in this gown, no way for her to hide her curves or pretend men would not stare. She was rather thankful to have a mask for the evening. Perhaps it would make the ordeal less embarrassing. Red silk gloves slid onto her arms all the way to her elbows, and then the maid looped the fan around her wrist; a rather large fan configured of black ostrich feathers. Suitable for a weapon should she have need of one.

"Oh, Willow," Amelia said from behind her.

Willow turned abruptly, embarrassed to have been caught gawking at herself in the mirror. "I—"

"You've never looked more beautiful." Amelia's eyes actually filled with tears. "You will be the envy of every woman in the room tonight. That dress is stunning and no one else could wear it quite the same way."

"Yours is equally lovely," Willow said, pointing at Amelia's purple confection.

"Don't be a ninny." She waved a hand in front of her face and stepped toward her friend. "This is your night." Willow felt a chill at her neck as Amelia slid a necklace into place. "That should be perfect."

Willow put her hand to her throat. Pearls. She looked in the mirror and found a strand of black pearls sitting right above her collarbone. "Where did you find them?"

"They're perfect, aren't they? Here." She placed two pearl-drop earrings in Willow's gloved hand. "Put these on too."

"Amelia, it's all too much."

"Now, tonight we will have none of that. Willow, you have spent the better part of your life caring for those around you. You can take one evening for yourself and have a glimpse of what your life might be like if you'd allow yourself a different course."

"There is no choice, Amelia, I have responsibilities."

"There is always a choice. Now, let us put our slippers on and head downstairs. If we don't pry Colin away from the library soon, I fear he might stay in there all night and we will be left without an escort."

The carriage ride to March Estates took less than a half hour, although their rig did have to line up and roll slowly to the front walk behind all the other waiting parties. Tonight's ball evidently was a success.

Masque balls usually were. Everyone enjoyed the opportunity to step into someone else's shoes for the evening. Indulge in a bit of imagination. Perhaps she might try to loosen her restraints, provided she was capable of such a thing. Willow had to admit, if she could look beneath her nerves, that even she was caught up in the excitement of the evening.

There were other things she had to admit, only to herself as she dared not so much as whisper them to anyone else. Already, she felt very much the traitor for feeling them. But she had to admit that she very much wanted James to be in attendance. Wanted him to see her in this dress. Wanted to see and feel the desire brewing behind his sea-green eyes.

She felt the stab of betrayal, knowing she ought

to forget about the girlhood fantasies James put in her head. Fantasies of love and family and children. He knew nothing about the meaning of family if he could touch her so reverently one moment, then admit her father was a suspect in the next. It seemed the worst bit of irony that he would be the one to make those desires surge up within her.

It was not an option now to walk away from the investigation. Her family's innocence was at stake. She would endure her foolish desires for James but ensure she kept both eyes open in order to uncover the true perpetrator of this crime.

She wondered, too, if her brother would attend. For weeks she'd been meaning to ask him, but she had scarcely seen him.

In a flurry of movement, she was escorted out of the carriage and up the wide steps into the foyer. She could barely hear the voice announcing them, and then she was whisked into the ballroom.

With her mask securely in place, it was odd to view the room through the eye slits, as if all her surroundings were neatly tamed. Willow and Amelia and Colin stopped to greet their hosts, first Gareth's aunt, then Meg's father, and then the happy couple themselves.

Meg's eyes grew round. "Willow? Is that you?"

"Of course it's me," she said, trying to pretend as if she always wore such revealing dresses.

"You look wonderful," Meg said. "Charlotte isn't here yet. I suppose she'll make her grand entrance fashionably late, as usual. I fear we'll be greeting people all evening. Enjoy, and have some champagne."

Willow followed Amelia into the crowded ballroom and snatched a champagne glass from a passing footman's tray. She smiled as the bubbly liquid tickled her upper lip. Perhaps Amelia was right. She could afford one night to indulge the life she might have had.

The ball was well under way by the time James arrived. He spotted Colin above the crowd and moved in his direction. As the crowd thinned out, he could see the people standing with Colin: Amelia, with her hand on her husband's arm, the Barnetts, and . . . he froze. He knew that woman. The magnificent creature in the red dress had to be Willow. He could tell by her mannerisms, the way she held her glass, and the slight tilt of her head.

He let his eyes take her in and immediately his body responded. He had had his suspicions about the figure she hid beneath her usually modest gowns, but this was not what his mind had conjured. He had been wrong. She was more exquisite than his imagination could have created. Encased in the formfitting dress, her virtues were outlined and showcased for all to see. The tiny waist and slightly flared hips, a perfectly lush décolleté, and those creamy, rounded shoulders.

His first instinct was to pull her into his arms and touch her everywhere. His second was to pull her out of the ballroom so no other man could ogle her. He had no right to do either. He might be reckless, but he was no fool.

But he would dance with her. She would be in his arms, if only for a little while. He closed the distance between them, never taking his eyes off of her. Once he reached her side, though, he took the time to greet Colin and Amelia. He needed the distraction of trivial conversation to prevent him from devouring Willow. But then he turned his attention to her.

"Dance with me," he said.

Before she could answer, Amelia grabbed the champagne glass out of Willow's hand. "Go ahead," Amelia said.

Willow eyed her friend, then held her hand out for James. Even beneath the red satin gloves he could feel the heat of her skin. He swept her into his arms as the music began. They danced in silence for several long moments.

"How did you know it was me?" she asked.

"I know you. I know how you move, your mannerisms." He suspected he'd know her without that. Somehow his body would sense her presence.

"I see." The pulse at her throat flickered.

"I don't know whether to cover you or parade you around the room," he said.

"I beg your pardon?" He couldn't see her frown because of her mask, but he could tell from the tone of her voice.

"Every man in the room is looking at you. I don't know whether to feel pride that you're in my arms and not theirs or angry that they're all ravishing you with their eyes."

She swallowed. "No one is looking at me."

"I am."

"And?" she dared to ask.

"I can't take my eyes off of you. I want nothing more than to throw you over my shoulder, haul you upstairs to the nearest bedroom and kiss every inch of your glorious body."

She stumbled but he caught her before she fell. Blush covered the parts of her cheeks the mask left uncovered.

"Walk with me outside," he said.

She met his gaze. "I don't know, James."

"People do this sort of thing all the time," he said.

"But I do not."

"What if I promise not to ravish you?" He smiled in an attempt to reassure her.

The song ended and they just stood on the dance floor as couples moved in and out around them.

"I promise," he said again. "Your virtue will remain intact."

"Well, it is rather warm in here," she conceded.

"Yes, and the breeze is perfect. And this hall has a garden that is really worth seeing."

"I can not simply walk outside with you. Allow me to go first, and we can meet on the balcony," she said.

He nodded and she strode off in the direction of the French doors.

He had made her a promise, which meant he would have to keep his hands off of her. It would be challenging because he wanted to touch her so badly. Perhaps he could get by with one little kiss.

Willow reveled in the cool breeze that brushed her bare neck and shoulders as she stepped out onto the balcony. It wasn't crowded, which served her well, since she really ought to take care that her reputation remain spotless. She made her way to the stairs that led from the balcony into the garden area and stood against a large potted fern.

What was she doing? Tempting the fates, not

to mention betraying her family. She was behaving recklessly, which she was not accustomed to doing. Something she never even had the secret desire for. Yet, she was engaging in it with full mental capacities. Well, she supposed she might be a tad impaired from the glass of wine and two glasses of champagne, but for the most part she simply felt slightly less nervous.

She should turn around. Walk away from this interlude and go back home, where she belonged. But Amelia's words kept ringing in her ears. Could Willow not have one night away from her responsibilities? One night to allow a handsome man to steal a kiss beneath the moonlit sky? It was a regular occurrence for many of the women inside that ballroom—why should she be excluded?

The fact that James suspected her family of murder certainly complicated things. But when it came down to it, James was the one she wanted. His touch the one she craved. His kiss the one she waited for.

Besides, she was going to prove her father's innocence, then James would have to apologize for his shortsightedness. Tomorrow she would pay for her behavior. Tomorrow she'd be plagued with guilt. But tonight—tonight was hers. And tonight she wanted James.

He appeared in the doorway, looking very

much the handsome rogue. It wasn't a costume, though, it was all him. Dressed head to toe in nothing but black, even the half mask, he looked dashing. Her heart flipped. He hadn't bothered to grease his hair back, so his blond locks hung daringly across his forehead.

He was dangerous. This interlude was dangerous. But no matter how much she reminded herself of that very important detail, she made no move to return to the ballroom. Instead she stood waiting for him to come to her.

And come to her, he did. In determined and focused strides, he moved to her side and held his arm out to her. She glanced around and no one outside was paying them any mind, so she linked her hand in his arm and allowed him to escort her down the staircase. Away from the majority of the lights and the sound.

They were alone as they strode toward the garden. Tiny pebbles crunched beneath her slippers as they followed the marked trail. Jasmine and freshly turned earth filled the night breeze. She inhaled deeply.

Neither one of them spoke for several minutes. They simply walked arm in arm in silence. She wasn't certain why, perhaps she didn't want to speak and remind herself of how very foolish this was. Perhaps he said nothing because he had nothing to say. Because once he got her out here, he realized there was nothing between them.

She stopped walking and turned to face him. He looked glorious standing against the backdrop of jasmine bathed in moonlight. It took her a moment to remember what she had been about to say.

"Why did you bring me out here?" she asked.

"To discuss something. The man we are set to visit tomorrow—I don't believe you should come with me," he said.

Anger surged through her. "Why not?"

"It will not be safe. Neither in location nor situation. Willow, I can't allow you to go."

Here she was looking the way she did and he wanted to discuss the investigation? And to prevent her from aiding him? "Can't allow me?" She poked a finger in his chest. "You said we would work this investigation together. Now, if this particular man is dangerous or whatnot, then it sounds as if you need to do whatever possible to prevent any harm from coming to me. But my staying home is not an option." Then she stood back from him. "You owe me this."

"I lied," he said.

She frowned. "It isn't dangerous?"

"No, goose, about why I brought you out here. It wasn't to discuss that. I brought you out here so I could do this." He wrapped his hand around the back of her neck and pulled her close to him.

She felt every second tick by as she waited for him to lower his mouth to hers. When he finally did, time stood still. Her anger melted beneath his kiss.

His hand at her neck was firm and warm. But his lips betrayed his control. In his kiss, he made no attempt to hide his desire or urgency for her. The realization of that flooded her body. She could try to pretend it wasn't true, pretend that it was merely a convenience. But she'd be a fool to do so. He wanted her. Her. Not any other woman at the ball, but her.

Their tongues intertwined and desire shot through her, hardening her nipples and dampening the space between her thighs. She wanted him too. Wanted him to touch her. To kiss her.

He ended the kiss and gently touched his lips to the top of her head. Then without another word, he laced his fingers with hers and led her farther into the garden. The simple gesture of holding her hand threatened to stop her heart. Kissing was one thing—tied up in desire and carnal needs. But holding hands, that was intimacy. Warmth spread through her and she should have run from him, run from the danger in which she'd just placed her heart.

The greenery around them loomed larger and the lights from the hall began to fade away, leaving them in nothing but the glow from the moon.

They stepped into an alcove hidden within the shrubbery and found a bench.

"I promised you your virtue would remain intact, and I meant it," he said. "But I need to touch you."

They locked gazes for what seemed like hours and she was caught by the raw intensity in his eyes. Something there beckoned to her and she found she had no words to refuse him. She tried to think of something to say, but her mouth wouldn't move. So she did the only thing she could think of —she pulled his mouth down on hers.

Desire coiled through her so quickly, she felt dizzy. She grabbed onto his shoulders and used his strength to steady herself. His mouth left hers and trailed down her chin to the column of her neck, where he licked and nibbled until she thought she would go mad.

Lower and lower his mouth moved until his hot breath lingered over the rise of her breast. She squirmed in a vain attempt to relieve the pressure that mounted within her. The moisture between her thighs was increasing and she knew this night would end in nothing but frustration. Yet she couldn't bring herself to put a stop to it.

In one swift movement, he reached into her bodice and edged the fabric beneath her breast, exposing her aroused flesh to the cool night air.

She didn't have to endure the cold for long, because his mouth covered her bare nipple, sending waves of pleasure shooting through her.

He alternately suckled and nipped at the tender bud and she arched against him. She hadn't realized his other hand had been making attempts to dive beneath her skirts until she felt the warmth of his fingers on her thigh. He knew she needed something, knew she was filled with intense urgency.

His fingers slipped through the slit in her drawers and touched her at her most intimate core. She nearly came off the bench at the pleasure of it. He teased around her opening, toying with her flesh and sliding through her moisture. And then finally he gave her what she needed. With one finger, he slid inside her, all the while sucking fervently on her breast.

A burst of pleasure shot through her in ripples. She clenched her toes inside her kid-leather slippers. When the sensations had quieted, he brought her close to his chest and smoothed his hand down her back. She felt his heart thumping wildly beneath her head.

He moved her dress back into place and helped her to her feet. "You are the worst sort of temptress, Willow."

She looked up at him. "But I'm not—"

"Not a temptress?" He released a strained

chuckle. "The worst sort because you don't realize you're doing it. You don't realize that by simply being yourself you tempt me beyond belief. I know a fire burns inside of you. I can see it in your eyes and hear it when you speak. So controlled, so careful to keep those inclinations reined in. I see it, Willow. I know you believe you aren't meant to marry, aren't meant to be in the arms of a man. But you're wrong."

She opened her mouth to say something, but found no words. How did he know that? She'd never said anything to him about marriage. For all he knew she'd chosen spinsterhood. She had. She'd chosen it before *it* had chosen her. But no one knew that. She'd never told anyone.

Clearing her throat, she finally found her voice. "I should go back in. People will be looking for me."

"Willow." He cupped her cheek. Then he shook his head and said nothing more. He said nothing else as he gently led her out of the garden. More people had filtered out onto the balcony, probably to enjoy the cool evening air.

"Perhaps I should walk in alone," she suggested.

He nodded.

She looked at him for a moment more, waiting to say something, waiting for him to say something, but neither of them spoke. He'd seen so much, noticed so many things about her she thought no one had seen. She felt bare and exposed.

Meant to be in the arms of a man, he'd said. In order to do that she would have to marry, they both knew that. And he hadn't offered to be *that* man.

Chapter 13

As Willow climbed the stairs to the balcony, she noted the crowd was rather thick and everyone was talking excitedly. She tried to tune in to their words as she passed by, but without pausing to join a discussion it was difficult to latch on to one conversation, and she simply felt too vulnerable to talk to anyone at the moment. She was terrified someone could tell what she'd been through by the expression on her face or the tremble in her voice.

Stepping into the ballroom, she discovered that the music had ceased playing and that people were standing in sequestered pockets. What had happened? It took a moment, but she was able to locate Amelia and made her way over to her. Meg and Charlotte had joined their party, and her three friends were exchanging glances and whispers.

"What did I miss?" Willow asked as she eased up next to Charlotte.

"You missed everything," Charlotte said with a big smile. "He was here."

Willow frowned. "Who?"

Amelia grabbed her arm. "The Jack of Hearts."

Willow glanced around the room and then back at her friends. "Are you quite certain?"

She felt the heat of her shame on her cheeks. While she had been out in the garden pretending to be someone she simply could not be, the elusive thief they'd been after for more than a year had finally made an appearance. And she'd missed it. She peeled off her mask; there was no use in trying to hide who she was.

"Of course we're certain," Charlotte said. "He took the rings off my very fingers," she said with a sigh, as if he'd kissed her hands rather than taken her jewelry.

"Where is James?" Colin asked.

Willow's stomach flipped. Could everyone tell? Tell that she'd been alone with him? That he'd touched her and kissed her most inappropriately? "I'm not certain," she said, which was the truth.

Colin frowned and scanned above the ladies heads. "Stay here together and I'll return shortly." He placed a sweet kiss on Amelia's cheek, then strode across the ballroom.

"Did he say anything?" Willow asked Charlotte.

"He ran his hand down my cheek," Charlotte

said, then closed her eyes and cupped her face.

"Honestly, Charlotte, you act as if he was a gallant gentleman. He is a thief." Willow knew she was more frustrated with herself than anything and she shouldn't take it out on her friend, but sometimes her impertinence was very frustrating.

"He was not the least bit disrespectful," Charlotte huffed.

"She's right," Meg defended. "He was very kind."

Willow rolled her eyes at Meg's use of the word *kind*, but swallowed her irritation. "Tell me how it all happened," Willow said.

"We had moved to the billiards room for a game of whist because Meg was feeling weary and wanted to sit for a while," Amelia explained. "There were at least ten of us in there. All ladies. He came in, locked the door behind him and explained who he was and came up to each of us and asked us to put all of our gems into his black bag. It was all rather efficient."

"And then?" Willow said.

"Then he stopped in front of Charlotte and personally took her rings off, touched her cheek, then left out the same door he came in," Meg said.

"And no one tried to stop him or screamed for help?" Willow asked.

"It all happened rather quickly," Amelia said.

"And he did have a pistol," Meg added.

"See," Willow said. "I've been telling you all along that he's a dangerous cad."

"Well, he didn't *use* the pistol," Charlotte said, actually sounding affronted.

"But he had it out?" Willow asked.

"Yes." Charlotte crossed her arms over her chest. "But he never pointed it at anyone. Merely showed it to us, then carried on with this business."

"Oh, well, as long as he didn't aim it at anyone, then he's a perfect gentleman," Willow said, doing nothing to hide her sarcasm. She shook her head. "I simply can not believe that after all of this time, not one of you had the sense to call for help."

"You weren't there," Meg said softly.

She was right. Willow hadn't been there. No, she'd been in the garden in a passionate embrace, finding pleasure for the first time. Her cheeks steamed. "I'm sorry. I suppose I'm only envious that I wasn't here to see him for myself." But she suspected her shame had more to do with her frustration. That and the fact that without even asking herself she knew if she had to make the choice between time alone with James and a glimpse of the Jack of Hearts, she probably wouldn't have made a different decision.

"Where were you, anyway?" Charlotte asked.

"I was walking in the garden. I found it rather

stuffy in here earlier and needed some air." She offered a smile in an attempt to cover her lie. "Perhaps it's this new corset," she whispered.

"You look so lovely," Charlotte said.

"Thank you."

It was then that James and Colin walked up to them.

James eyed Willow, then looked at Meg. "There's no sign of him. Is there anything you ladies can tell me about him? Did he have specific mannerisms or an accent? Anything identifiable at all?"

"He sounded educated," Amelia said.

James nodded. "We've been under the impression, for quite some time now, that he's a member of the aristocracy. Or at least someone who fits nicely within Society. Are any of you hurt? Did he touch anyone?" James asked.

Meg and Amelia both looked at Charlotte. But the tall beauty simply shook her head.

Willow should say something. Admit to James that the thief had touched Charlotte. But it wouldn't help to identify him, and telling James would only embarrass Charlotte. So Willow bit her tongue and said nothing.

"He was rather polite," Meg said.

"Yes, we hear that a lot in regards to him. Very polite, always the gentleman. I wouldn't be surprised if the people were keeping his identity a secret simply because his presence guarantees a good story for all who survive," James said. "It makes catching him all the more difficult."

How quickly he could move from being the passionate man in the garden to the focused detective. Willow tried to ignore the disappointment. She should not be vexed if he seemed to recover more quickly than she.

"James, what has happened?" His mother appeared from behind them, worrying her handkerchief.

"Nothing, Mother." He shook his head. "Nothing to worry about. It was the Jack of Hearts again. Would you like me to take you home?"

She frowned. "Of course not. I'm not a ninny." Her features softened and she smiled at Willow. "So lovely to see you again, Miss Mabson. I trust you are doing well."

"Yes, my lady. Thank you for asking. Might I introduce you to my friends?" Willow introduced everyone around them. It was a bit satisfying to know that James' mother seemed to think rather highly of her. Unless the woman was a complete fraud, which didn't seem to fit.

"If you don't wish me to see you home, Mother, I'm going to leave," James said.

Willow met his gaze briefly before looking away. Did this have something to do with her?

"Whatever for?" his mother asked.

"There has been a crime here tonight and I am an inspector. It is my duty to go into the office and put it on file." Then he turned to Meg. "A sergeant will stop by and get the details from you tomorrow, including everyone who was in the room with you. Could you provide a list of names?"

"Certainly," Meg agreed.

He nodded. "Ladies." He kissed his mother's cheek. Then he took Willow's hand and brought it to his lips. The warm breath was there only briefly, but long enough to scatter chills over her flesh. "Miss Mabson," he said, then he turned and strode away.

Willow eased her front door open and closed it as softly as she could. She slipped her shoes off and tiptoed across the floor, trying not to wake the entire house. She wasn't accustomed to coming home so late—or early, depending how one looked at it—but there was no reason to announce her arrival to her sleeping family.

She was halfway up the staircase leading to the bedrooms on the upper floor when she heard a chuckle behind her.

"Look who's sneaking around."

She turned to find her brother leaning against the banister.

"Edmond," she whispered.

"Come and have a drink with me," he said. He

meandered across the hall and into their father's study.

She thought longingly of her bed, but knew her mind was too active to relent to sleep, so she followed Edmond.

He was pouring himself a brandy when she closed the door behind her.

"Do you want one?" he asked.

She fell into one of the chairs and the leather groaned on contact. "No, I've had enough imbibing for one evening, thank you very much."

"My sister has taken up the life of the worldly woman," he said, sitting back against the sofa.

She had become worldlier tonight, but of course he hadn't meant it that way. He was jesting with her, as he always did about her board-straight way of living.

"I was quite serious, Edmond," she said. "I did imbibe tonight. Two glasses of champagne and a glass of wine. Perhaps I should have some brandy."

He leaned on one elbow and eyed her. "You're quite serious."

"I am."

"Well, good for you. Did you have a nice time?"

She hoped the stain on her cheeks wouldn't reveal too much. She'd hate for Edmond to feel as if he must defend her virtue. Or what was left of it. "It was a lovely evening."

"Meg's masque ball, right?"

"Yes. Did you come?"

"Only briefly. You know how I feel about the dances and all the eager girls and mommas. It's enough to send a single man to bed early."

"Not you," she said.

"No, I don't suppose so. But I prefer much more civilized activities to flirting with women I have no intention of marrying."

"Gambling." It was not a question.

"Not gambling. Cards. There is a difference. A game of odds rather than chance. There is skill involved, and I'll have you know I'm rather good at it."

"Of that, dear brother, I have no doubt. But I—"

"Worry," he interrupted. "Yes, I realize. You spend much of your time worrying about me and the rest of the family. 'Tis a wonder you haven't had some sort of apoplexy."

Her smile faded. Is that what her brother thought? That it was only a matter of time before she began to show symptoms like her mother? "Edmond, that's not funny."

"That's not what I meant. Besides, Mother's episodes can hardly be considered apoplexy. You are nothing like her." His words seemed to echo.

Nothing like her. Willow's heart seemed to wilt in her chest. *Nothing.*

"You don't normally dress like that," he said, eyebrows raised.

"Meg insisted," she said swiftly, "and since it was her night, I didn't want to be difficult."

"But, Willow, you're always difficult. It's what you do. And I wasn't suggesting you dress any differently. I admit it's probably best I didn't see you at the ball tonight, else I would have had to defend your honor. I'm certain every roaming male eye was on you." He sat up and frowned. "Why didn't I see you tonight?"

She chewed at her bottom lip, then shrugged casually. "I don't know. It was a rather large crowd. Perhaps you were there before I arrived. And I did go for a walk in the garden for a bit when I got too warm in the ballroom."

"That must have been it," he said.

"Were you there when the Jack of Hearts made an appearance?"

"No, I must have missed that too. Evidently I missed everything tonight. Except winning a bit of blunt from some poor old fools."

"I'm sure you noticed the lovely Charlotte. You wouldn't have missed her."

He met her gaze and held it for a moment as if deciding whether or not to respond. "She looked stunning as usual."

"Why do you never ask her to dance?" she asked.

He leaned forward. "We've danced on occasion. You know me, I was never much for dancing."

She had suspected that her brother fancied Charlotte, but perhaps that had passed as they'd all grown up.

He drained his brandy glass and stood for another.

"You will have to dance with ladies once you decide to marry. You certainly can not woo and court without dancing."

He released a humorless laugh. "In good time, my sister. I am still young and father is not going anywhere anytime soon."

"What are you waiting for? To win a great fortune? Perhaps love?" Were it she who had the freedom to love and marry, she would do so as soon as she was able. Edmond, however, spent more time at his club than he did in ballrooms.

He sipped his brandy, then set the glass down. "I'm not waiting on anything in particular. I do have more in my life, though, than considering the fact that I'm an eligible bachelor." Then he shrugged. "Love would be nice, but some people never find it."

She considered his words but said nothing. How did you know you were in love? The question was on the tip of her tongue, but after Edmond answered her question, he'd have questions of his own, like why she wanted to know. She couldn't tell him that.

Besides, it mattered not. She didn't love James; she'd know it if she did. Surely that was the sort of emotion that came with a modicum of certainty—not the myriad of questions that had plagued her since first meeting him.

Theirs was a mixed-up relationship built on competition and desire. That wasn't love.

Edmond stood. "You should be off to bed." He placed his empty glass on the decanter tray. "I believe I shall retire as well."

They walked silently up the stairs and along the hall toward their individual rooms. Willow reached her room and opened the door, then paused.

"Do take care of yourself. I look forward to the days when you have a wife to care for you."

He leaned in and kissed her forehead. "All is well, Willow. I promise. Off you go to bed."

Willow rang for her maid to assist her out of the tight corset. In the meantime she unfastened the dress and began removing the pins from her hair. Tonight she had tried to pretend she was carefree, that she could be reckless and passionate. But she wasn't any of those things.

She was Willow. Cold, dull, and proper Willow. Edmond was right; she was nothing like their mother. She had been so afraid she would lose control and become like their mother, who seemed to be a slave to her feelings, when in reality there was no chance Willow would end up that way. She lacked the sparkle and fervor for life that her mother had. She lacked her mother's charm and engaging personality.

No wonder her father loved his wife so much. Her mother had been like a shooting star, bright and beautiful and so full of energy. How could he not love her?

Willow, on the other hand, was rigid and judgmental and utterly alone. Neither James nor any other man would ever love her. She simply wasn't enough.

So, it should be a huge relief that she did not love James. Perhaps she'd feel relieved later.

The following morning James waited in the Mabson foyer for Willow. It didn't take long for her to step into the hallway, looking very different from the woman who'd been in his arms the night before. Today she was Willow, in her practical and modest dress of pale yellow muslin. There wasn't even a hint of the passionate woman he'd brought to pleasure. He knew her secret. Knew of the passionate woman hiding just beneath the surface. The thought shot desire through him.

It was going to be a long afternoon.

"I apologize for keeping you waiting," she said. "I was in with my mother."

"Do you need to stay with her? Because I can go and do this alone," he suggested.

"No. She's napping now, and more than likely will be for a few hours." She fastened her cloak. "You still don't want me to go with you for this, do you?"

"No, I do not."

"But you came here regardless."

"You were right, I owe you," he said.

"Shall we?"

If it were possible, Willow seemed even more reserved this morning than he had ever seen her. No doubt she was ashamed of their embrace. Perhaps he should say something, ease her nerves a bit.

He nodded and led the way to the carriage. He did owe her. For all of the confusion he'd served her. Not to mention himself. He knew how to live with desire. He knew what to do with those feelings. But the other things that seemed to emerge whenever he was with Willow put him at a loss.

He wanted to make her smile, make her laugh, slay her dragons, so to speak. He wanted to smooth back her hair and hold her hand and tell her the ridiculous stories his mother told him. These were the things he didn't know what to do with. So he ignored them as best he could.

Once they were seated inside, he pulled out his notes.

"According to my sources the man we're going to see is somewhat of a broker for the types of portraits Drummond was taking," James said.

"So Drummond and any other photographer taking those sorts of pictures would go to this man and he would find buyers for them?"

"Exactly."

"How charming," she said dryly.

"Yes, well, some people will go to any means to make some blunt." He eyed her for a while as she peered out the tiny window. "Willow, I'm fully expecting this man to be unsavory by every facet of the definition, which means we must be extremely careful with you there. Stay close to my side."

Her large brown eyes blinked up at him and he felt a catch near his heart.

"I don't want you to be frightened," he clarified. "Simply cautious."

"I'm always cautious," she said. But then her expression changed and she turned again to the window. He suspected she used to be always cautious. Until he came into her life and started stealing kisses and touching her when he had no right to do either. Taking advantage of the tight control she held over herself. He'd seen a weakness in her fortress and he'd pushed on it.

Neither spoke for the remainder of the trip to their destination. It was in Whitechapel and James glanced at his note to ensure he'd located the right place. He certainly didn't want Willow to be on the street any longer than necessary.

"This is it," James said as he located the appropriate sign, then knocked on the carriage ceiling. Mulligan's Pub. What had he been thinking? He should have left Willow at home. He turned to her as they rolled to a stop. "Perhaps you should stay inside. This is the worst sort of neighborhood, Willow."

"Whitechapel," she said. "Where the Jack the Ripper murders took place." Her jaw was set and she showed no sign of fear. "Well, I can't say I'd like to purchase a flat in the area, but I don't suppose any harm can come to me at this hour. And I shall stay close." She swallowed, then met his gaze. "I'd rather be next to you than alone in here."

Perhaps she was right. At least if she was next to him, he could guard her closely. He gave instructions to the driver to wait for them, then he assisted Willow down from the carriage.

"You might want to pick up your skirts as we step out onto the street. I don't think this is rainwater out here."

Willow made a face and adhered to his suggestion. They quickly made their way into Mulligan's

Pub, and a bell above them announced their entrance. The room was small and dark and over-filled with mismatched tables and simple wooden chairs. It smelled of old ale and tobacco and already two tables were occupied with dirty men: one chewing on a partially smoked cigar and the other with his head on the table. It wasn't even noon and these men were well into their cups.

"Be right there," a raspy voice called from the back room.

"No need to wait," James said and led Willow around the bar and through the doorway to the back.

A short and round man with thinning hair and two days' worth of beard turned and started at them. He snarled. "I told you I'd be right there. You can't be back here." His right eye didn't seem to focus on anything and it drooped heavily. With his good eye, he scanned Willow up and down. "Especially with your lady friend."

"Are you Mulligan?" James ignored his protests.

"I might be. Who's asking?" he managed before hunching over as a terrible cough ravaged him.

"Inspector James Sterling. I'm here to ask you some questions about Malcolm Drummond."

Mulligan's left eye narrowed. "If you see that bastard, you tell him that he owes me portraits. Already paid for. I've been waiting for nearly three weeks." The pub owner let his good eye roam over the length of Willow, then he licked his dry, peeling lips.

"I don't think you'll be seeing those portraits," James said.

"And why the hell not?" Mulligan demanded.

"Mr. Drummond was murdered."

Mulligan's face contorted in confusion.

"Did you not read about it in the papers?" James asked.

"I ain't got time for the papers. Can't believe that louse got himself offed before I got those pictures and they're already paid for." He released a string of curses that surprised even James. Mulligan stomped his right foot like a portly, spoiled child. "What the hell do I tell my customers?"

James ignored his question. "I need to see your outfit. Where you handle the business of selling those portraits."

"It ain't illegal or nothing," he said.

"I'm not here for you, Mulligan, I only need you as a resource."

Mulligan coughed wildly again. "Follow me."

He led them through a dingy curtain and up a short staircase. The room was dark and it took a moment for Mulligan to light a few lamps, spreading a hazy glow across the room. The walls were covered with lurid images of women in various positions. James instinctively pulled Willow close.

"Just keep your eyes down," he whispered to her.

She nodded tightly, but kept her eyes pinned to the floor.

Mulligan spread his arms out. "This be it." He leered at James. "You looking to buy?"

"No. What I need is some information. Namely a list of whom you sell your . . ." he paused, grasping for the right word, ". . . merchandise to."

"I don't keep no list. It's all confidential, you see," Mulligan said. He chuckled. "You got money, I'll give you a picture. It's as easy as that."

"What can you tell me of Drummond?"

Mulligan shrugged. "Fancied himself a gent, that one did. But he was no better than any of the rest of us in the business. He thought just because he took respectable portraits, that made him mannerly."

"Did he provide you with many portraits?" James asked.

"He was my top supplier. People liked seeing the ladies bared to the skin." He nodded to Willow. "Is she one of 'em?"

James took a menacing step toward Mulligan. "Don't look at her. Understand me? While I'm here asking questions, you look only at me."

Mulligan snarled but nodded in agreement.

"So how did you know they were ladies?"

"Drummond said so." He shrugged. "You can

tell, though. By the way they look with their clean hair and bright smiles. His ladies brought in a fine price."

"What kind of person bought them?"

"Gents like you." He gave a mocked bow. "The rich and noble."

"Ever have anyone get angry at what they saw? Perhaps recognize someone in the pictures?"

"No." Mulligan scratched at his greasy hair. "And you said Drummond's dead?"

"Murdered. But I don't suppose you know anything about that," James said.

Mulligan just eyed him blankly until James' words hit him. Then he stomped his foot again. "No. I don't even know where to find the man. He always came to me."

"Can you give me the names of the other suppliers?" James turned to glance at Willow, who stood beside him with her eyes focused on her shoes. He was the worst sort of gentleman and she was the wrong lady to bring to a place such as this.

"I can give you their names. At least the ones they've given me," Mulligan said. Then he winced. "I don't know how to spell any of them."

James retrieved his notebook and pencil. "I'll worry about the spelling. I want their names and how you reach them."

Willow watched a small beetle scurry across the floor. It was difficult to find anything appealing to look at in this small, dusty room. She'd seen them when they'd walked in—walls lined with provocative images. One after another, pose after pose, women showed off their bodies and flaunted their sexuality.

She'd never known any woman who enjoyed that much freedom. Not even her mother. Yet this man, Mulligan, claimed he'd sold some pictures of gentle-bred women. Had there been some from the box she and James had found? She hadn't recognized any, but she hadn't exactly been looking at their faces.

Part of her twinged with envy, not because of their raucous behavior, as she certainly had no desire to entertain such an activity, but rather their freedom. She was not even comfortable being nude while alone. She envied their ability to let themselves go, to embrace their desires.

What would happen if she did the same?

Which desires would she embrace?

James' strong hand held tightly to her lower back, warming, protecting. She looked up and focused in on an image of a plump woman with large breasts and dark, curled hair. She stood completely nude in front of a mirror, so that two images of her body shone in the portrait. There was no shame in her face, no fear, just a slight hint of a smile, as if she knew she was doing something naughty and simply didn't care.

Willow knew she'd never be such a creature, but she'd never imagined she'd be as wanton as she had been the other night in James' arms, either. The thought of his caresses and her sweet release sent pleasure rumbling through her body. Even if she wanted to, she wasn't certain she could prevent James from touching her again.

Chapter 14

He felt the need to protect her, James real-ized. That did not bode well for him. Men typically only wanted to protect those they cared about. Which meant he had developed feelings for Willow. Feelings that, more than likely, went beyond mere desire.

It could simply be a matter of feeling guilty that he'd put her in such dangerous situations, and therefore felt responsible for her well-being. But something in him argued against that point.

This urge to protect her, coupled with the in-tense desire to touch her, made him nervous. She was not a woman he could trifle with. Her heart would get broken, and he wouldn't want to be re-sponsible for that. She deserved a man who could love her and provide her with a happy and re-spectable home. Neither of which he could do.

He couldn't be the upstanding and proper man she needed. No, he was the brute who took her to pubs in Whitechapel and subjected her to illicit images of women. Willow needed a man who would protect her from the likes of him.

He eyed her sitting silently across from him in the carriage. He wanted to say something, to ensure she was all right, but he wasn't sure what to say. That he felt like a cad for taking her to such a place? Or perhaps that he was trying desperately not to touch her because he did respect her, despite appearances?

He sighed.

"James." She leaned forward and placed her hand on his knee. "I insisted on going with you to that meeting. It is my fault, not yours."

She was being brave, he admired her for that, but it did not expunge his guilt. "I should have *insisted* otherwise. That was no place for a lady. Your reputation could be ruined if anyone saw you anywhere near that place."

"My reputation could be ruined by being alone with you. Which I have been on several occasions."

"Are you not concerned?" he asked.

She frowned. "It's not that I'm not concerned. I certainly do not want to tarnish my family's good name, or bring about any gossip—we have been victim to that enough. But I'm nearly thirty years old, James, and have been shelved, for lack of a better term. I consider what I'm doing with you work, and I should think that people would understand if you were to explain it to them."

Yes, but if people had seen the way he looked at her. Seen the desire he bore her, they would know it was a charade. "It's a risk," he said.

"Yes," she nodded. "It is a risk. But proving my father's innocence is far more important to me than my reputation. I sincerely doubt anyone is talking about me in any case. Besides, my existence thus far in Society has been so boring that no one would believe that I was having an illicit affair." Her face went pale and she leaned back in her seat. "I certainly didn't mean to imply . . ."

"I have taken liberties with you, Willow, liberties I had no right to take. But it doesn't prevent me from wanting to take them again. Right now, I want nothing more than to pull you across my lap and kiss you senseless."

There was no time for her to react to his words as the carriage pulled to a stop in front of Amelia's house, where he was letting Willow out for her Ladies' Amateur Sleuth Society meeting.

"Would you like me to walk you up?" he asked.

"No, I can manage." Her voice shook ever so slightly.

"I'll be in touch."

She nodded, but said nothing else as she climbed from the carriage.

What sort of game was he playing? Toying with her like that. She was the perfect woman for him. Someone who met him intellectually, who was not afraid to stand up to him. Someone he desired. But then there was that other bit, the fact that she was someone whom his mother approved of.

He'd spent his entire life fighting what that stood for and he couldn't very well walk away from that now. Not for a pair of brown eyes that seemed to reach in and squeeze his very heart. He knew that solving this case wouldn't right the wrong of so long ago. None of the cases he'd solved in the last seven years had. But that mattered naught. He simply had to try.

Poor Willow was caught in his life's battle between what was right and what seemed right. He owed it to her to cease his flirtatious behavior and treat her like the lady she was. He had a job to do and his attraction for her was muddling everything up. Her father might very well be the culprit. If James wasn't careful he might lose his heart and the murderer. And then where would that leave him?

Willow took several deep breaths trying to rid her mind of the things James had said. He wanted to kiss her senseless. So he still desired her. Not that any of that mattered. He desired her carnally, not for anything substantial.

But that's what she wanted too, wasn't it? She couldn't have more, so there was no reason to be disappointed if he didn't drop to one knee and declare his undying love. She made another pass over her dress and hair to ensure she was still intact before opening the parlor door.

"Willow," Amelia said.

The room was empty except for she and Amelia. "I see the other two have not arrived just yet."

"You are a bit early," Amelia pointed out.

Willow glanced at the mantel clock. "So I am. I hope I am not intruding."

"No, of course not. You are always welcome. Any time. Colin has a new case that is taking up much of his time and I have been trying to work on my newest Lady Shadows story, but the writing is simply not flowing today."

"Perhaps tomorrow will be kinder to your writing."

"Come and sit. Tea will arrive shortly."

Willow took a seat and straightened her spectacles. "How are you doing?"

"I'd say fair," Amelia said, trying to offer a smile.

"Did you tell Colin?"

"About Meg being with child?" She sighed. "Yes, I did. We had another long discussion about the entire ordeal. He said we'll find a way to have children." She looked down at her dress. "Silly man thinks he can fix anything."

"Perhaps he can," Willow suggested, not knowing what else to say.

"Willow, I don't want Meg to know." Amelia looked up, her eyes brimming with tears. "I don't want to ruin this for her. I hate that I feel jealous sometimes. That's terrible of me. But if she knew about our troubles, knew how I felt, it would take away some of her joy, and I refuse to do that."

Willow felt a catch in her throat. "Amelia, it isn't terrible. It's natural. There is nothing wrong with wanting children. You aren't wishing she wasn't having a baby."

"Of course not," Amelia said emphatically.

"Right. You simply want one of your own."

"Or five or six," Amelia said with a smile.

"That would be quite the brood," Willow said, but she understood. A houseful sounded good to her as well. She knew it would be full of disorder, loud and disruptive, but it would be wonderful too.

Amelia swiped angrily at her tears. "Enough of this," she said with a forced smile.

"They won't be here for a bit longer," Willow said, "if you want to continue."

"No, honestly, I can't talk about any more of this today. It has the tendency to drain everything out of me and" —she shook her head— "I don't want that today. So enough about me. Tell me how you are fairing with your wager."

Willow had been waiting for an opportunity to share with Amelia everything that had happened. She'd longed for a sympathetic ear. She certainly couldn't discuss it with her family, as there was no reason to alert them of her father being a suspect until absolutely necessary.

"It has taken a bit of a turn," she explained.

"Are you losing, then?" Amelia asked.

"No, that's not it. In fact the wager itself seems rather unimportant now." She leaned forward. "Amelia, you must promise to keep this a secret. It could be devastating if word got out."

Amelia sat up straight and nodded decidedly. "Of course."

"My father appears to be a suspect."

Her friend frowned. "For murder?" She waved a hand casually. "Well, that is preposterous."

"I believe so too."

"You sound hesitant."

"I know my father isn't a murderer. The clues simply aren't leading us to any clear suspects. And as much as I hate to admit it, James is a good detective."

"That doesn't mean anything. It's very early in the investigation. You will, no doubt, find other suspects."

"I believe so. But it's been more challenging than I expected."

"How are *you* doing with all of this?"

Willow shrugged. "I'm frightened," she said, her voice barely above a whisper.

Amelia stood and approached her. "Of course you are."

Before the discussion could continue Meg and Charlotte appeared in the doorway. Amelia gave Willow a wistful smile. It was probably for the best that they not say more, Willow supposed.

"We actually met at the doorstep," Charlotte said.

"And it was a good thing too, as she had to assist me inside," Meg said. "I have been positively green today."

"Oh, dear," Amelia said. "You could have stayed home since you are not feeling well."

"No, it's been passing every day. Eventually. It tends to pop up at the most inconvenient times, though," Meg said.

"Let me go check on the tea," Amelia said.

"I have had no fewer than two gentlemen inquire about the mysterious buxom beauty who attended the masque ball," Charlotte said as she settled onto the settee.

"About whom?" Willow asked. Evidently she'd missed more than just the Jack of Hearts at the ball.

"You, silly," Charlotte said. "Not to worry, though. I haven't revealed your secret."

Buxom beauty? Her? That was enough to make her laugh, and on another day it might have. "I wasn't exactly trying to have a secret. Everyone was wearing a mask that night."

"Yes, but you hide your . . ." Charlotte paused ". . . attributes in your regular clothes, and you certainly revealed a secret that night."

Willow waved a hand in front of her face. "Did people simply believe I did not have breasts?"

Amelia stepped in at that precise moment and her mouth dropped. "Oh, I do believe I missed something good. What are we discussing?"

"Evidently Willow's breasts," Meg said.

"No, we are not," Willow said. "We were talking about the ball the other night, and evidently my dress caused quite a stir. Well, now you know why I dress so modestly."

"I do believe if I had your figure," Charlotte said, "I would scarcely wear clothes at all."

"Because you don't garner enough attention as it is?" Willow said rhetorically.

"Perhaps we should address the meeting topics now," Amelia said.

"Splendid idea," Willow said. She'd had enough discussion of her body. She had every right to hide her attributes, as Charlotte put it. There was no reason to flaunt herself in front of everyone. It would only garner stares and she had no use for that.

"Did James uncover anything about the Jack of Hearts?" Amelia asked.

"Another inspector is leading that investigation, but no, another trail that simply ended," Willow said. "He does agree with me, however, that the reason he's never been caught is because no one will fight with him or call for authorities. They simply stand there and hand over their belongings as if he has every right to request them." She glared at them pointedly.

"He did have a pistol," Amelia pointed out.

"You can never be certain that a man will not use a weapon if he carries it with him," Meg said.

"You're right, of course," Willow said. "I was not there and I'm sure it was a frightening experience for all of you."

"Where is our list that we've been keeping on him?" Charlotte asked. "Surely we have new tidbits to add since we've all seen him now. Well, most of us."

Willow shot her a look. "Yes, I missed out on all the fun whilst walking in the garden," Willow said.

"At the precise moment Inspector Sterling was walking in the garden," Charlotte said softly.

"What?" Amelia said, sitting on the edge of her chair.

Willow felt her cheeks go warm.

"Were you in the garden with James?" Amelia asked.

She eyed each of her friends, who sat anxiously

awaiting her answer. Charlotte smiled smugly. How had she known? Willow could not lie to them. For one, because they were her friends and lying would be wrong. Secondly, because she was a dreadful liar and they'd see right through her.

"We were discussing the investigation. We found these letters in Drummond's studio, and we expected them to lead us to someone, but they were a dead end." Perhaps if she gave them details they would believe she'd only been out there talking. "It seems the letters were from many years ago, when he lived in Paris." She shook her head. "It was bad timing on both our parts, and we should have saved our business for the following day," Willow admitted.

"You were in the garden with James?" Amelia repeated. "Alone?" Her friend completely ignored all the other details, focusing only on that one aspect.

"Oh, for pity's sake, Amelia, you traveled overnight with Colin," Willow said.

"Where I lost my virtue," Amelia said with a chuckle.

"Well, I can assure you that I did not lose my virtue. I am still as virtuous as ever." Why did that suddenly annoy her? Her virtue had always been a point of pride, but today it felt more like a nuisance. She shouldn't be so annoyed; she wasn't nearly as virtuous as she used to be.

All three of the other girls chuckled.

"Laugh all you like." Willow retrieved her notes on the Jack of Hearts. "Now, do we want to dally all afternoon, or shall we get some work done?"

"She's right," Charlotte said. "She's the same old Willow."

"Very amusing," Willow said.

"He has brown eyes," Charlotte said.

Amelia looked up from her tea. "What?"

"The Jack of Hearts," Charlotte continued. "His eyes are brown." Everyone just stared at her. "You said you wanted to get started."

Amelia nodded. "Yes."

Willow jotted the note down. "That will certainly narrow the field some, but brown eyes are fairly common. Everyone in my family has brown eyes except for my mother."

"True," Charlotte said. "But I would recognize them again, if I saw them. They were such a rich brown."

"Well, if we see Charlotte gazing into all the gentlemen's eyes for the rest of the Season, we'll know why," Meg said.

They chuckled and Charlotte crossed her arms over her chest in a huff.

"What we need to figure out is why this time worked," Willow said. "Was it simply a feature of it being a masque ball, so he could easily blend in with everyone?"

"He's had such an easy go of stealing before, though," Amelia said. "Perhaps it was just a matter of being in the right spot at the right time. We've only barely missed him in the past."

"But he always knows precisely when to act," Willow said.

"Yes, he seems to know plenty about us, but we know very little about him," Amelia said.

"Except his brown eyes," Charlotte said.

"Yes, Charlotte, except his eyes," Willow said.

"And his voice," Meg said. "He is most definitely educated and well-bred. Of course servants can mimic their employers, but I don't think that's the case here. I believe he is most certainly a gentleman."

"Which adds to the intrigue," Amelia said.

"And excitement," Charlotte pointed out.

"Well, we all know a fair number of the gentlemen in this town," Willow said. "If not personally, then by name. Surely we could cross off a considerable number based on coloring and body stature. How was the Jack of Heart's form?"

Charlotte sighed with great drama. "Athletic and strong. All in all, he was positively dashing."

Everyone ignored Charlotte's laudation.

"Let us compose a list, then, of all of the gentlemen we can think of," Willow suggested.

"We can use our invitation list as a reference," Meg said.

Amelia clapped. "Brilliant idea."

"Meg, can you bring that with you to our next meeting?" Willow asked.

Meg nodded and her red curls bobbed with her head.

"In the meantime we can each work on a list separately and then we'll put them together when we next see one another," Willow said. They could catch him. The thought was exhilarating. She wanted to tell James. Share with him their clever detecting skills.

But she could not continue to nurture a friendly relationship with him. Could she? So far, it had led to inappropriate embraces and her father as a suspect. Because, had they not conversed that night at the Fieldcrest ball, had his mother not said her mother's name aloud, then he would never have known who Agatha was.

Like the other women in the journal, her mother's name would have faded into ambiguity and James would never have questioned her parents.

Upon arriving home, Willow found Edmond sitting in a chair next to their mother, reading some of her favorite poetry. Willow's heart caught at the sight of them. Her brother, who gambled too much and stayed out way too late, yet was so gentle with their mother.

It wasn't fair to him. She should be sitting there

reading. She should be taking care of their mother as she slipped further and further away. Edmond needed freedom from this, needed to marry and start a family.

Her own body ached to know the love of a man and the heaviness of a child within, but none of that mattered. She had a duty to her family. If she tried to do both, if she found love and married and became a mother, how could she balance it all?

Would not her children or her husband or perhaps even her mother suffer? She could not divide her attentions in such a way. When it came to her mother, she needed to be able to give her her full attention.

As it was, this investigation was taking her away from home more than she'd ever been away. And her brother and father were having to take her place. Were the investigation not so important for the good of their family, she would cease her dalliances with James and get back home where she belonged.

Perhaps she could help him speed things along. She needed to secure her father's innocence and then she needed to hang up her detecting hat and stay by her mother's side.

Chapter 15

Willow placed the spectacles on her nose and reached for her bag. On her way out of her bedroom, she caught her reflection in the mirror and stopped to observe. Yes, that was more the thing. She felt herself. She looked herself.

Today was the most important part of their investigation so far. They were finally going to question the ladies from the exhibit photographs. James had felt certain that these women would hold the key to Drummond's secrets.

Some of the women might even be mentioned in that journal of his. It would be nice to have other suspects aside from her poor father. James had not yet returned to finish questioning him on his whereabouts the night of the murder. Willow suspected it had little to do with her assurance that her father had been home in bed, and more to do with not having the opportunity to do so without her by his side.

Willow simply couldn't have him questioning her father without her being present—not because she was concerned her father would say something wrong, but simply so that she could reassure him that all would be well, and to ensure that James was on his best behavior.

With a last pat to her hair, she headed out her bedroom door and down the stairs. James was picking her up today as they had many houses to travel to. Thankfully she did not know any of the women personally, although she knew most by name. She was certain they wouldn't know her. James could simply tell them she was his clerk and there to take the notes or something.

She didn't have to wait long before he knocked on their front door. She caught her father on the way to answer it.

"It's for me." She kissed him on the cheek. "I promise this will not continue much longer, Papa. I am only doing this for the good of our family. I hope you understand."

"No one is concerned," he assured her.

"But I have been gone so frequently these last few weeks."

He nodded.

"I worry about Mother's care."

"Willow, my dear, no one in this family holds you responsible for your mother's care save you.

Go and live your life, we will all be here when you return," he said.

The doorbell rang again. She kissed him again, then slipped out the front door and closed it behind her, not even allowing James entrance into the house.

"Eager?" he asked.

"We have much to do today," she said.

He nodded and led the way to the carriage.

"We are not making as many visits today as we'd planned," he said as the carriage lurched forward.

"Why is that?"

"I'm questioning my original theory on the motive of the murder. And these visits seem redundant when we are going to see these women at the exhibit and can question them there."

She was unable to decipher if this change of events was positive for her father. "Where are we going?"

"To the Duke of Argyle. He's finally returned to town. He was the primary fund patron of Mr. Drummond. Presumably he knew the man to some degree."

Before she could ask any more questions, the carriage stopped in front of a sprawling brownstone estate complete with ivy climbing up to the second story windows.

Willow stood silently at James' side as he

showed his badge to the butler and waited for entrance. The butler led them to the music room and turned to go. It was a huge room, but it held very few windows, and those that were there were lined with heavy dark green draperies. The electric lighting gave off a yellow glow, providing the only light, as the fireplace sat like a cold, empty box at the end of the room. A large black piano sat in one corner and next to it was a harp.

Within moments a slightly plump but very attractive woman swept into the room. "I'm afraid my husband is not home this morning. How may I be of service, Inspector?"

"This is Miss Willow Mabson, she's assisting me today," he said. "Might we ask you a few questions regarding Malcolm Drummond?"

The duchess looked at the door behind them, her hand paused at the side of her face. "Please sit," she said with a tight nod. "Would you care for some tea?" The tea service was set up on an ornate table right in the center of the sitting area.

James absently stirred his tea, which Willow now knew he liked with sugar but not cream. He seemed different today, distant perhaps. He'd deliberately sat away from her in the parlor and had only made eye contact when absolutely necessary.

"Now then," the duchess said, "what's this

about Mr. Drummond?" Her hands worried the fabric of her skirt.

"He's been murdered," James said.

She swallowed her sip of tea, then set her cup aside. "I didn't realize," she said, her face and tone completely devoid of emotion.

"So you didn't see anything about it in the papers?" James asked.

She smiled sweetly and Willow guessed the woman was only a year or two older than she, while, Willow knew, the Duke of Argyle was a much older man. "I don't read the papers very often, Inspector. My husband tends to tell me what he thinks I need to know or what I might find of interest. The rest, I'm afraid, remains a mystery to me," she said with an airy laugh and a wave of her gloved hand.

James nodded and smiled politely. "Then forgive me for being the bearer of bad news, Your Grace."

"Please call me Camille." She shook her head. "It is a shame." Camille took another sip of her tea. "Murdered, you said? How dreadful. I suppose my husband did not *deem* this information appropriate for me."

Willow wrote down everything: every moment, tone of voice, anything that might add to the woman's answers. The duchess was young and pretty and evidently was very well kept by her wealthy and powerful husband. She seemed perfectly content to sit idly by and allow him to dictate her life. Something Willow could not abide.

She felt a twinge of sympathy for the woman. The duchess might have immeasurable wealth and a man to warm her bed, but she did not seem to have a mind of her own. 'Twas a pity.

"How well did you know Mr. Drummond?" James asked.

"I can't say that I knew him all that well. But I did sit for portraits on more than one occasion. For my husband, you understand."

The Duke of Argyle was, after all, the photographer's most lucrative supporter. Willow allowed her eyes to wander around the room and they landed on James. He was thoughtful with his questions, probing without being disrespectful. Willow knew from the broadsheets that many felt the plainclothes detectives were an infringement on their rights, unassuming men who milled about among them gathering up their secrets. Evidently James knew how to handle the aristocracy being civil and polite but not too friendly; yet, he had been a completely different man when they'd visited with Mulligan.

There he had been strong and almost overbearing, standing at his full height and speaking loudly, in short, curt sentences. Here, he had one leg crossed over the other with his hands folded in his lap. He spoke softly in long, languid questions and with a subtle smile on his face.

He was charming, Willow had to admit that.

"Mr. Drummond and your husband must have known each other fairly well," James said. "Your husband was the sponsor of Drummond's upcoming showing, is that not correct?"

"Yes, my husband is a friend to many artists of varying styles. He has a soft spot for those who struggle to bring beauty into our world." She smoothed her coral silk skirt and smiled prettily.

"So, there are others whom your husband financially supports?" James asked.

"Not at the moment, but there have been others. In the past. Let me think." She counted silently on her fingers. "There was a poet once. A handful of painters. I'm certain there were more before we married, but those are the ones whom I have known."

"And how was your husband's relationship with those men?"

Camille blinked her wide eyes. "My husband is a difficult man," she said cautiously, "but a prudent businessman. He invests in these artists because he generally feels they can earn him some income." She smiled. "He's practical that way."

"So, in other words," James said, "your husband was not a friend to these men—he merely paid them and hoped for a healthy return."

"You could say that. I understand this is a practice among many."

"Indeed it is, Your Grace," James said.

Willow continued to jot down all of his questions and Camille's answers. She couldn't help but wander back to what James had said in the carriage about there being a different motive for Drummond's murder. Up until this point, they'd been running on the assumption that it was a disgruntled husband or lover of one of the women mentioned in the photographer's journal—as James suspected these women had had relationships of sorts with Drummond.

But her mother wouldn't have had an affair with the man. Perhaps she had known him at some point before she'd married Willow's father, but she hadn't left the house very often in the last ten years. That was just one more reason why she knew her father was innocent. Perhaps James' new feeling regarding why Drummond had been killed would point them in the direction of the real murderer.

"I'm so sorry my husband was not here to answer these questions himself," Willow heard the duchess say. "I'm certain he would have been more helpful than I have been. I can give him a message if you would like," she offered, "as I most certainly can not speak for him."

James stood. "Thank you, but I believe we'll

see him at the exhibit this Friday. I trust you will be in attendance as well?"

"Indeed," she said.

"Very well, we will see you both there."

Willow nodded to the duchess, then followed James out into the hallway and then out the front door.

Once they were settled back in the carriage, Willow handed James the notebook. "I'm not sure how helpful any of this will be."

He glanced down, then nodded. "Thank you."

"Will you explain more about what you said on the way here?"

"About the motivation? Not now, but soon. I want to do a bit more digging to see if I'm onto something, and then I'll let you know," he said.

She frowned. "That doesn't enable me to participate in the investigation, James."

"I know. But you've already seen and heard too much that a lady like you should never have to endure. I will not present any more of that environment to you. Allow me this concession and I will fill you in on all the details. You have my word."

She knew he wouldn't offer his word lightly. He might go about things differently than she would, but once he gave his word, he was a man of honor. She nodded. "I don't like it," she said.

"I know you don't. You will have to trust me in

this, Willow, because I can not give you any more than that."

She met his eyes and knew she did. She completely trusted him. And that was terrifying.

Willow found her father as he was leaving his bedchamber, closing the door behind him. He gave her a weary smile. "I finally got her back to sleep. She's been so restless these last few days."

"How about some tea?" Willow suggested.

He inclined his head and followed her down the stairs to her mother's parlor. After she'd rung for tea, she sat and eyed her father. He looked old and tired. Not sleepy tired, but weary tired, tired from the inside out. She reached over and patted his knee.

"I know she's difficult, Papa."

"She is your mother. And I love her."

"Of course you love her." She had been wanting to ask her father and hadn't had the opportunity of speaking with him without her mother present. Willow poured him a cup of tea and then waited until he'd taken a few sips before she proceeded. "How well did you and Mother know Malcolm Drummond?"

He stopped in mid-sip and set the teacup down. "It was several years ago—you and Edmond were quite young. Malcolm had only been in town a short while, and photography, as we know it today, was still in its infancy. Your mother and I met him at a weekend house party. She agreed to sit for a photograph as a gift to me."

He reached for his teacup and set it in his lap. "You have to understand that this was the beginning of your mother's episodes and her behavior was new to me. I wasn't certain what to make of her outbursts. I thought perhaps she was unhappy in our marriage." Draining his cup, he leaned back in his chair.

Willow's nerves had tightened and apprehension filled her. She had been expecting her father to tell her they knew him briefly, he took some photographs and that was it. That what appeared in Drummond's journal was a fabrication by a lonely, lovesick man. But that did not look to be the case.

"This isn't anything I should discuss with you," he said.

"But Papa, any information you have might be helpful to the investigation." She didn't want to tell him that James still considered him a suspect. "I am nine and twenty and more than old enough to hear whatever it is you have to say."

He stood abruptly and moved to the mantel, facing away from her. "One photograph turned into three and I admit I suspected that she might be having an affair with the man." He released a harsh laugh. "That was not the truth, however; she loved me and I should have trusted her. Should have protected her."

"Protected her from what?" Willow prodded.

"From that bastard. She went over there one day and was having one of her episodes. I'm not certain how it all happened, but he convinced her to pose for him again. This time in nothing more than her flesh."

The words raked over Willow like hot coal and it seemed as if the world had stopped turning. No longer could she hear the clock ticking in the corner. The crackle from the fireplace seemed to have disappeared and even her breathing was silent. Her mother had been one of those women.

Her father turned around with anger brewing in his eyes. The hardened features startled Willow, as she'd never seen her father so much as swat at a fly. "I wanted to kill him," he said. "With my bare hands I wanted to suck the life from him for doing what he did to my beautiful wife. She didn't know what he was going to do with those photographs. But he" —his face tightened even more— "he knew exactly what he was doing."

Willow had nothing to say. No words of comfort came to mind, because all she could hear were her father's words. *I wanted to kill him*. She didn't even hear him approach until he was seated once again across from her.

"I'm sorry, child," he said. "You should never have had to know about that."

"That was what the big argument was," she said.

"Sorry?"

"You and Mother had that big fight, and after that she stopped going out, stopped going to balls and the theatre."

He nodded. "Yes, that was when it all changed. After that she got much worse. Perhaps if I hadn't yelled at her the way I did."

She wanted to tell him no, that that couldn't be the reason her mother's illness had progressed. But again she found no words. She needed to be alone.

"Excuse me, Papa," she said, and left the room.

Climbing the stairs to her room, her mind wandered. Betrayal, fear, confusion—she felt them all. Was James right? Could her father have been the one who killed that man?

She shook her head fiercely. No! Her father was incapable of such an act. It was wrong to question what she knew in her heart to be true.

Willow wanted to scream. Wanted to open her mouth and yell as loudly as she could, but she couldn't do that; it was improper and would not solve anything. Reaching the second landing, she turned to the right to head to her bedchamber and stopped. Perhaps she could take a walk, get some fresh air and clear her head.

Turning around, she headed back down the stairs and out the French doors in the back of the house leading into her mother's small but lovely garden. It was already dark out and the cool night air hit her bare forearms and hands. She walked down the first row, the moonlight and her memory her only guide.

"Willow dear, is that you?"

Willow turned to find her mother standing behind her.

"What are you doing out here? Papa said you were asleep. Are you chilled?" Willow tucked her mother under her right arm.

"I was asleep, but I woke up and needed some fresh air." Her mother chuckled. "You always were a bit mothering, even as a small child. It used to make Edmond batty."

Tonight it seemed that her mother was rather lucid. Willow loved these moments. She linked their arms and they strolled amidst the fragrant bushes.

"I have the very best family there is," her mother said. "It would be my greatest joy for you and Edmond to find the same."

"I encourage Edmond all the time," Willow said.

"But what of you, my dear?"

"I am happy here. With you." She smiled at her mother.

"You take very good care of me, and I know I am rather trying at times." She shook her head. "But there is more to life than caring for your parents. You need love and a life of your own."

It all sounded nice and Willow did want those things, but it seemed unlikely she would ever find them. "Papa loves you so very much," she said.

"Yes, he does. You will find that too, I know you will. But if you're not out there making yourself available to the single gentlemen, then they will not know how wonderful you are." Her mother cupped Willow's face and kissed her cheek gently. "I wanted you so badly, did you know that?" Her eyes glistened with tears. "After your brother was born, I knew I was becoming more and more ill and I had had such a difficult birth with him. But I knew I was destined to have a little girl. I knew you would come to me."

Emotion welled up inside of Willow and threatened to spill over. She had never heard such words from her mother. Willow couldn't tell her mother that she'd spent the better part of her adult life acting the content spinster. It would break her heart to know her daughter had done everything she could to remain unmarried.

"Willow, dear, is everything all right?" her mother asked.

No, everything wasn't all right, but she couldn't burden her mother with that. "Everything is fine," Willow said.

Her mother smiled, but there was a sadness to her eyes. "Promise me something." She grabbed both of Willow's hands.

"Anything," Willow agreed.

"Promise me you'll find love and make your own life. Promise me that you won't sacrifice yourself for my sake. I couldn't bear that." She shook Willow's hands as she spoke.

She could certainly promise to try to find love, but Willow knew that was unlikely. "I shall only marry for love, Mama."

Her mother squeezed her hands. "You're a good girl, Willow, you know that, don't you?"

"Let's get you inside before you catch a chill. The wind is beginning to pick up."

"Very well."

Willow walked her mother inside and stopped beside the staircase.

"I won't forget that promise, my dear," her mother said.

"Nor will I. Good night, Mother."

Her mother climbed the stairs and disappeared inside her bedchamber.

It had been an empty promise, Willow knew that. She'd never find love. Not now. Perhaps there had been a time when she was younger, when love might have been an option for her. But now it was too late.

It was wrong, she knew it, but for once she wished life had delivered her something different. Everyone had their problems, she knew that, but she had seen so many other women her age whose lives seemed less complex.

Her parents would not live forever, so once her duty to them was completed, where would that leave her? Alone. Completely and totally alone.

She could probably find a man who would take her for a wife, an older gentleman looking for companionship during his last years. But a marriage without love, that would be no worse than a lifetime on her own.

Oh, she wouldn't be completely alone. She had her friends. And surely Edmond and his family would care for her. She'd be the cranky old aunt to his children, and they'd put bugs in her shoes and hide her spectacles. But was it enough? Is it what she would want were she able to choose?

No. The answer was simple and immediate. No matter how much she'd tried to deny herself, how often she'd swallowed those desires in an attempt to completely dissolve them, they still remained.

She wanted more.

She wanted James. That was undeniable.

And if she were to choose, she would want James to love her.

He'd been so civil with her today, too civil. As if they were no more than acquaintances who saw each other occasionally at the theatre. Yet, they were more than that, weren't they? Hadn't they developed a bit of a friendship? Some trust for each other? There was the desire that neither of them could deny.

Could she give in to it? He'd already brought her the most intense pleasure she'd ever known. Would he do it again?

Instead of having that life she'd promised her mother, she could have the memory of what might have been. What might have come to be were she a different person. Were she the kind of woman a man could desperately love.

What would happen if she allowed herself this indulgence? Would she still be able to retain control over the rest of her life? Questions poured through her mind like sifting sand.

Perhaps if she did give in to her wants, it would strengthen her resolve. Give her even more control over everything else. If she allowed all of her weaknesses to fall away in those moments she allowed him to touch her body, then afterward, she could put on her restraints just as she put on her dress.

Chapter 16

Willow had come to a decision. She sat huddled in the center of the carriage seat, wrapped in her brown wool cloak. It was a risky decision, she knew that, but she also knew that if she did not allow herself this one thing, she'd never be the same. She felt safe with James, safe to let go, safe to feel.

Nerves threatened to sour her stomach, but she was resolved to do this. Or at least try. It was the perfect opportunity for her to indulge her need to experience freedom without losing control of her life. One night of passion with him, one night where she allowed herself to be free, to simply feel and see how life might have been had she been a woman more like her mother. One night couldn't cause too much damage.

No one would know. She did not love him, she reminded herself, so her heart would not get broken. And she knew he did not love her, so his heart was not in danger either. It would be pure bliss, a safe environment for her to abandon her restraints and experience life's ultimate pleasure.

But would he say yes? That was her only concern. She knew he wanted her. Had felt the evidence of his desire pressed against her. She felt it in the way that he kissed her, the way he traced his fingers across her skin. As if she were the most delicate woman he'd ever met.

Perhaps, though, his want for her was fleeting. It would come to an end eventually, she knew that. There was nothing about her to inspire any kind of desire that would endure for more than a whisper of time. She hoped his need had not yet waned.

Tonight she would go to him. There would be no forced seduction. Things would simply progress. Being alone at his house would prevent any interruptions.

For one night she would know what it was like to let go of herself and experience all the pleasures life had to offer. For one night she'd allow at least her body to be loved.

James looked up at the sound of the bell. He glanced at the clock on the mantel: nearly ten o'clock. Who would come calling at that hour? He could hear a light rain pattering against the window as he moved his chair away from his desk.

He peered out the window to the side of the door and could only see a cloaked figure; it was too dark to determine any other details. With one movement he swung the door open and was startled to find Willow's large brown eyes looking back at him.

He pulled her inside. "Whatever are you doing out so late? And in this weather?"

"I couldn't sleep." Her voice shook. "I had some thoughts about the investigation and I knew you'd be up working too. I simply thought it might be more productive were we to work together," she said.

He wasn't so certain he believed her, but she had come to see him for some reason. It wasn't like her to lie, though.

"Come in by the fire before you catch your death." Perfect. He was beginning to sound like his mother. He pulled the cloak off her shoulders, draped it across a leather chair, and went to work stoking the fire. "Have a seat on the sofa. Do you want some tea? Or a chocolate?"

"Something warm to drink would be nice," she said with a smile.

James stepped into the hallway and made his way into the kitchen, where he found Marjorie. He asked that she prepare a plate of cakes and chocolate and bring it immediately to his study. Then he went back to Willow.

"You couldn't sleep." He repeated her earlier words.

"Correct."

She seemed agitated or distracted. He waited until Marjorie had brought their tea tray before he spoke again.

"You have thoughts about the investigation?" he asked.

She sipped her tea and nodded absently. "I've been thinking about something Mulligan said," she began. "About the images of ladies going for a higher price than those of common girls."

James nodded, curious to where she was going with this. Willow was clever and more than likely was coming to the same conclusion he'd already made. "Go on," he encouraged her.

"Yes, well, I remembered that statement and then the box of photographs we found at Drummond's house. It seems highly likely that among those images are some wealthy aristocratic ladies."

And there she had done it. "I believe you might be right."

"Really?" she asked, seeming surprised.

"I had already come to this conclusion, and am in the process of wading through those images trying to locate anyone I recognize."

It was a good conclusion for her to make, but surely this discussion could have waited until the morrow. Yet, she had risked being seen as she snuck into his townhome unescorted.

"I could help," she offered.

"I don't think that's a good idea."

She eyed him warily, then nodded. "Do you have anything a bit stronger?" she asked, holding up her teacup.

"Willow, is everything all right?"

Her mouth tightened and she nodded.

He complied with her wish and brought her a glass of brandy. "Careful, it's strong." Then he sat on the sofa next to her. She smelled so good, an intoxicating mixture of lemon and soap. He watched her bring the glass to her lips and take a swallow. Her tongue slid out to catch a wayward drop and his abdomen tightened.

"Kiss me," she whispered.

He wasn't even certain he'd actually heard it or if his mind had fabricated it because he so desperately wanted to kiss her. But she'd leaned toward him and closed her eyes and seemed to be asking him to do this as if it would be some great gift to her.

When the truth was it was a gift to him. Every moment he spent in her warmth was undeserved.

He leaned in and cradled her face with his hands. She released a soft whimper and he gently placed his mouth across hers. Slowly he placed tender kisses on her lips, reveling in the feel of their velvety softness.

Her arms wrapped around his neck and she pulled him tightly to her, deepening their kiss. The urgency in her response fueled his desire. She wanted him.

He kissed her hungrily, not holding back any of the passion he felt. Her fingers dug into his back and she arched against him. His hand moved up and pressed against her breast; he felt the nipple bead beneath his fingers. Blood surged through him and his erection pushed tautly against his trousers.

He laid her back against the sofa and positioned himself atop her. Having her pressed against the length of his body was nearly his undoing. But what of her virtue? He paused, not moving, not saying anything. It was one thing to dally with an experienced woman, but this was Willow.

Then he leaned back to see her face. "Are you certain? There are some things that can not be undone," he said.

She nodded. "Touch me," she whispered. Her eyes pled with him.

It was those eyes that proved to be his undoing. She didn't have to ask him more than once. He continued kissing her as he fondled her breasts, slipping his hand beneath her dress and inside her shift to touch the warmth of her skin.

So smooth. So hot.

Willow couldn't get enough of his mouth on her mouth, his hands on her skin. She wanted more. Wanted to be even closer. His skin on hers. She started tugging at his shirt, attempting to pull it free from his body.

Eventually he pulled his mouth from hers and leaned up enough to release the buttons so he could slip from the confines of the shirt. His athleticism was more than apparent in the muscled sheet of his chest.

Dark blond hair curled across the wide expanse and then tapered to a thin line that traversed his rippled abdomen, only to disappear beneath his trousers. He was a fine specimen, to be certain.

She reached out, ran her hand down the length of his torso, and watched as the muscles tensed beneath her touch, which only fueled her desire to touch him more. She allowed her fingertips to linger at the waistband of his trousers, then looked up to meet his eyes.

She didn't want to ask for this, she'd already asked for too much. But she did want him to take. Take her body and make it his own. She leaned up and captured his mouth with hers, all the while continuing to run her hands across his abdomen.

He reached behind her and began unclasping her buttons, trying to free her from her dress. She allowed her mouth free roam over his warm skin, loving the contrasting feel of the crisp hair and sinewy plains. It was an exploration unlike any she'd ever known.

She felt her dress give way; then warm hands were gliding across her shoulders.

"Stand up," he said.

She did as he said, stepped out of the dress and it pooled at her feet. He then unfastened and unlaced each layer of her clothing until she stood before him in nothing more than her pantaloons and stockings.

He ran his hand down the center of her torso, gently brushing each breast as he did. Her already hardened nipples puckered even more and she desperately wanted to cover herself. But she had asked for this. She had come here tonight for him to touch her and love her.

"You are so beautiful," he said. "Take your hair down."

She reached up and began unpinning her hair. Curls fell one by one and brushed against her shoulders and neck, shooting chills across her sensitive flesh. When she was done, she bent and placed the pins inside one of her slippers, then stood again to face him.

He took one step and was pressed against her, kissing her fervently. His tongue slid against hers and desire coiled through her body so rapidly she nearly fell to her knees. She knew her hands were everywhere, trying to touch him all over, but she could not help it.

She closed her eyes to listen, not wanting to miss one single sound around them. He made a low groan as he pressed his erection against her and she heard herself moan in return. Their breath mingled in hot pants. She inhaled deeply to absorb their scents; he smelled of sandalwood and brandy.

One by one, she involved her senses to commit to memory every detail about this night. The way his hand felt as it grazed her nipple. The sweet taste of him and the brandy against her tongue. His hard arousal pulsating against the thin fabric of her pantaloons.

He gave her one last passionate kiss, then began to kiss his way down her face, onto her neck, across her collarbone to both breasts, onward to her belly, until he presented himself before her on his knees. With one swift movement he brought her pantaloons to her ankles, then slowly rolled down each stocking.

She heard him suck in his breath and for a moment he knelt before her, hands on her legs, eyes closed, simply breathing. Perhaps he too wanted to memorize their experience. Surely he knew tonight would be their only chance.

He stood and went and locked the door, then

stoked the fire until a warm, golden blaze filled the room. He turned the lights down so that only the flames lit their surroundings. The plush red carpet was warm around her toes and she wiggled them to dig in further.

She had said nothing for a long while, had found she did not want to ruin the moment with the sound of her own voice. She wanted to tell him how beautiful he was, how there never had been a man in more magnificent shape than he. But her mouth would not move. So, she hoped that her deep admiration would shine through her eyes and she let them gaze at him freely.

He came back to her, took her by the hand, and led her to the center of the room so that they were closer to the hearth. Warmth radiated to her body. She pulled him to her and kissed him while allowing her hand to trail down his chest to the fastenings of his trousers.

She must have been working too slowly for him, because he swiped her hand away and finished it himself. He removed the rest of his clothes, then pressed his body against hers so that they were skin to skin. He caught her eyes and held them, the green of his swimming with desire.

Her heart beat as rapidly as if she'd run a thousand kilometers. With one hand he grabbed her bottom and pressed her hard against him.

"I want you," he said.

She swallowed. "I want you," she managed in a hushed whisper.

He brought her down on the floor next to him and continued his exploration of her body. His hands and mouth were everywhere and sensations were firing so rapidly she was certain her body would combust. She writhed and moved against his touch, fighting for release.

He inserted one finger inside her and she bucked off the rug. Slowly he moved his finger, in and out and around, finding new sensations with every movement. With another finger, perhaps his thumb, he found that sensitive nub. The two at once created a contrast of pleasure that pulsated through her, building and building until she wanted to cry out.

She bit down on his shoulder and he moaned in response. His hand kept up its delicious torture until she was certain she could take no more, then her body froze as her climax shook through her. Her eyes closed and she let out a cry, and then it subsided.

Then he positioned himself above her and she could feel this tip of him pressing against her.

She slid her legs up until they wrapped around him.

"Willow," he said in a raspy voice as he pushed into her.

Sharp pain rocketed through her and she clenched around him.

"I'm sorry," he whispered, then feathered kisses across her face. "I'm sorry."

She wiggled beneath him, trying to adjust herself to his invasion. Then he began to move, slow and shallow at first, teasing her with sensations between pain and pleasure. Deeper and faster he went and her desire began to mount quickly.

Her legs tightened around him and she pulled his face down for a kiss. She forgot about the remaining uncomfortable twinges and focused on him. His lips, soft and passionate moving across hers. His body pressed against her. Him making love to her.

Pressure was mounting within her and she felt something similar to before. That night in the garden. Only this was deeper, farther away, yet more intense. Then she heard his guttural moans as he spilled himself inside her.

He kissed her neck. "I've wanted you for so long."

She could not form a retort, so she pressed her lips to his forehead.

"I'm sorry that was uncomfortable. That is the way for women with their first time."

"I know," she said.

Then he gave her one of those lazy smiles of his. "It will be better the next time." James smoothed her hair as she snuggled against his chest. "You came here tonight for this, didn't you?"

She met his eyes. "I did."

"Why didn't you say something?"

"I didn't want you to say no."

"Willow, I can never say no to you."

James tried to concentrate on his work but couldn't stop replaying last night with Willow in his arms. He'd tried to keep from touching her. And he'd been successful yesterday while they worked, but last night, when she'd come to his house—when she'd asked him to touch her—he could not deny her. Could not deny himself that which he'd wanted for so long.

She had been a wanton and he had loved every minute of it. But with the light of the day came the realization that he could not leave things the way they were. He refused to be the bastard who would strip a woman of her virginity, then leave her to clean up the aftermath.

He set a file aside and ignored Finch's questioning glance. He might loathe Society's rules, but a woman's reputation was at stake. A woman he admired. A woman whose virtue he'd stolen. So, retribution was up to him. He was the only one who could make this right.

First he would need to secure a special license, then a visit to her father. He had no title to offer her, but he had a good family name and wealth.

"Sterling!" Randolph hollered. "Get yourself out here, you have a visitor."

James stood and could see through the windowed area near his office, where Randolph stood beckoning.

"Another lady friend, Bluestocking?" Beck asked as he strolled by.

Duchess Argyle stood next to Randolph, fidgeting with the fan that dangled from her gloved wrist. Her purple hat was wide enough to shade her shoulders, and was completed with a large purple plume.

He made his way out into the hallway and closed the office door behind him.

"Duchess," he said. "What a surprise."

Randolph grunted something, then walked off.

"Is there somewhere we can speak privately?" she asked, glancing around them.

He nodded and led the way to the evidence room, as it was usually empty. The very room where he had placed Willow up on a table and kissed her. Soon she would be his.

Once they were secured in the evidence room, he turned to face her. "Is there something wrong, Your Grace?"

She chewed on her lip and continued fidgeting with her fan. "The other day, when you came to visit my husband and you asked those questions, well ..." she looked down at her shoes, "... I wasn't completely honest with you."

"And?" James prodded.

"I knew Malcolm Drummond a bit better than I led on. He was actually very dear to me." She looked up and her blue eyes were lined with tears.

"You loved him?"

She nodded. "We were lovers."

"For how long?" James asked.

"Nearly five months."

"You were still together when he died?"

She squeezed her eyes shut. "Yes," she whispered. Then her eyes popped open. Two tears fell from the right eye. "My husband does not know, Inspector, and you can not tell him. He is rather particular about how I spend my time. I believe he loves me in his own way, and I am..." she paused as if grasping for the right word, "... fond of him. I should not like to hurt him."

James nodded. "Why did you wish to tell me this?"

"I do not like being dishonest, and keeping the affair from my husband has been necessary but difficult. This was my chance to finally tell someone." She winced. "Selfish, I realize, to use you to make this confession."

"And that is all?" James asked, feeling confused. She bit down on her lip and shook her head.

Her eyes filled with tears. "No, that is not all. I also just wanted you to know that Malcolm was loved. We were very happy together. He called me 'Millie,'" she said, and then her voice cracked and she took a moment to compose herself. "I wanted you to know that despite some of his indiscretions he was a good and wonderful man. And I just thought that perhaps this would ... I don't know, I feel so helpless, and I just wanted to do something to assist in the catching of his killer."

She did love him; that much was evident. "Do you have any idea who might have wanted Malcolm dead?" James asked.

"No, I don't. I know that on occasion he dealt with unsavory people, selling special photographs. Aside from that everyone he knew is genteel and would never harm anyone. Could it not have been a burglar?" she suggested.

James shook his head. "As far as we could tell, no. The butler has also verified that nothing was missing. I appreciate your candor."

"I ask one favor, if you will, Inspector. If you do find that this must come out, please allow me some time to tell my husband first. He will not take my infidelity in stride."

He nodded.

Willow finished her row of stitches, then looked up to check on her mother. The older woman sat in her chair by the window looking out at her garden. It was raining today so they hadn't allowed her outside.

"Mama, are you all right?" Willow asked.

She turned and faced her daughter. "Yes. I simply wish I could be out there. My roses desperately need pruning, and did you see the buddleia bush? It's positively out of control. Butterflies would as soon sit on the cold ground than that mess." Her hands worked her skirts into knots.

Gone was the lucid woman she'd walked in the garden with the night before. "Perhaps it will stop raining soon and tomorrow will be dry enough. Right now, there is simply too much mud. You'd get filthy."

She waved a hand. "Pah. Nothing wrong with getting a bit dirty. Mud never harmed anyone." She shook her head. "Your father, he's too protective. Always afraid I'm going to embarrass him."

"Oh, Mama, that's not it at all. Papa is never worried about being embarrassed." She, on the other hand, had certainly had those thoughts before, but she pushed the shame out of her mind. "He only cares for your well-being and wants you to be safe and healthy. You could catch a fever out in this weather. It is nicer to stay inside and keep warm and dry."

Her mother nodded, but her lips were pursed. There would be no convincing her. Not today.

So Willow went back to her embroidery. Her thoughts wandered to James and their night together. It had been nothing short of magical, but it was in the past now. She searched her heart for guilt or regret but found none. He had been there for her at the time she'd needed someone the most and she'd never forget him for that.

They would solve the case soon, and then she would probably never see him again. Or she'd see him in a crowded ballroom or at the theatre and she'd wonder how he was doing. And perhaps they'd exchange pleasantries and his wife would ask who she was and he'd say that she was simply a girl he'd known once. But their time together hadn't really meant anything. She knew that.

His desire was simply a product of their situation. The investigation kept them close and because of that, things that wouldn't have occurred otherwise had happened. Last night, it had been easy to see how women so frequently fancied themselves in love. When men showed their desire, no matter how chaste or passionate, it was a heady feeling. Powerful to know that you were desired, that a man wanted you.

She'd be a fool if she pretended that she had not developed some feelings for him. But they could be nothing save a memory for her aged years. She could say she did not have tender feelings for the man who was trying to prove her father guilty of murder, but that did not make it so.

But tender feelings and desire were not love. Her heart remained intact, carefully guarded in her chest. She might have let James touch her body, but she would never give him access to her heart. She could not afford to do so.

Her father's admission yesterday had shocked and terrified her and sent her running straight to James' arms.

Now, more than ever, her family needed her. What happened last night was in the past. They had shared a night together, and now she could shove her desire aside and pour her energy into the investigation.

Regardless of whether or not her father might be capable of murder, she refused to even consider it.

Chapter 17

Willow stepped out of the carriage with James' assistance and even through her gloves she could feel the warmth of his hands. Tonight might possibly be the biggest night in their investigation. Every woman who had sat for Malcolm Drummond was to be at the exhibit. Every woman but her mother.

Willow knew she should tell James about the truth of her mother's photographs, but she was too ashamed. If he happened to find some in that box they'd found, then so be it. Perhaps there had been mention of such photographs in the journal and James was keeping that a secret from her.

James leaned down to her ear. "Did I tell you that you look lovely tonight?"

The warmth of his breath sent chills down her spine. "Thank you." She looked down at her pale blue satin dress. It was simple in cut and did not contain many embellishments, but it was flattering. It was one of the few dresses she still had from the year she came out. The pattern was such that it had maintained its style for the past nine years. And since she had not worn it much, the fabric still had a new sheen to it.

The exhibit hall was abuzz as they entered. Immediately a footman took their cloaks and then they were greeted with a tray of champagne. Willow took a glass but was unsure if she wanted to sip any. She needed to keep all of her faculties in order tonight; she did not want to miss anything.

"Let us go meet our host," James said.

The Duke and Duchess of Argyle were standing in a receiving line greeting the guests. They had yet to open the doors to the exhibition and everyone milled about in the exhibit hall's lobby area.

Finally they had their turn and the duchess immediately grabbed Willow's hands. "How lovely to see you again," she said softly.

James and the duke were exchanging pleasantries and then it was her turn. The duke absently bent over her hand.

"Your Grace, I'd very much like to have a moment with you to discuss Mr. Drummond," James said.

The duke eyed him and then nodded. "You'll have to see my solicitor and see if he can schedule something. I am a very busy man." Then he turned away from James and directed his focus again to Willow. "Welcome to the exhibit," he said, and then she too was dismissed.

James pulled her away from the reception line into a relatively empty space by a closed doorway.

"He was rather dismissive," Willow said.

James scanned the room. "Not entirely surprising."

"May I have your attention." A voice was heard over the noise. "If you'll all look to your right, you'll see the doors open. Malcolm Drummond's 'Portraits of Ladies' is now officially open."

Many oohs and aahs escaped from the crowd as they began to file into the hall.

Willow waited for James' cue as to what they were going to do. They weren't really here for the exhibit; they had seen most of the photographs already. They were here to observe the crowd, to see if anyone might reveal any hidden secrets about a motive to kill Malcolm Drummond.

"What are we doing?" she finally asked James after a few moments of not moving.

"I'm looking for people," he said.

"Who?"

"Women. From the other photographs."

Her heart seemed to stop beating and she pressed her hand against her chest. So he had looked through those images, and tonight he would match faces with the nude bodies he had seen. She felt a twinge of jealousy. Would he still find her attractive if she stood before him without her clothes, now that he'd seen so many images of women?

"And there were women in those photographs whom you recognized?" she asked.

He nodded. "A few, but there are more here tonight. Let us get closer—perhaps you know some of their names."

No mention of her mother. Relief poured through her like hot water melting her bones, making it difficult to keep her footing. She grabbed on to his arm to steady herself, and then nodded as if she were merely allowing him to escort her into the next room.

They strolled through the exhibition, barely noting the lovely portraits hanging on the walls. The crowd around them conversed about the photographs and bent closely to see the details.

James leaned near to her ear. "Who is that woman? Over there with the pale blond hair."

She followed his glance. "That is Jane Portfield."

"You know her?" he asked.

"I do." She eyed his face for an explanation, but found none. "Do you recognize her?"

He nodded. "And there is mention of a Jane in the journal that meets her description. Is she married?"

"No. Not for lack of proposals, though. She has a bit of a reputation for declining them."

He smirked. "'Tis a game for her?"

"I'm not certain. I believe she simply enjoys her independence."

"And she has funds for such a lifestyle?"

"It seems I recall she was left a hefty sum by a favorite aunt."

"We will visit her tomorrow," he said.

They moved a little farther in and she wanted to ask him how long he'd had to examine those photographs in order to commit the women's faces to memory. She was curious to know how he felt about what he'd seen. But at the same time she didn't want to know. It was a cruel bit of curiosity and one she should not indulge. So she forced her lips to remain closed, the questions to go unformed in her mouth.

"And that one." He nodded toward a woman, perhaps her mother's age, whose red hair still shone. Evidently Malcolm Drummond's taste for women was wide in scope rather than focused on one specific look.

"Sophia Fulmer," Willow whispered.

"Do you know her?"

"Of her, but I've never even spoken to her."

"What do you know of her?" James asked.

"She's a widow. For the second time. Her most recent husband was the Earl of Craggmere." She swallowed, unsure if she wanted to share the next morsel of information.

James' eyebrows rose.

"There is talk that she is rather close to the new Earl of Craggmere."

"Her son?" James asked, clearly disgusted.

"Stepchild. I believe they are around the same age. She was the late earl's third wife."

James' lip curled. "That still is unpleasant, not to mention illegal."

"But you recognize her as well."

"Yes. So we will visit her tomorrow in addition to Miss Portfield."

They progressed into the next room of the exhibition. James stopped and casually visited with some of the women in the portraits, asking them basic questions about their interactions with Malcolm Drummond. Two of them were no more than girls and both of their mamas had been present at their sittings. Not one of them seemed to provide any new information or hints that there was more to their story beneath what they said.

Willow watched all the people around them. Dressed in their finery, women flirted with their fans, batting their eyelashes and occasionally daring to touch a gentleman's forearm. She located one specific couple, clearly not married but perhaps in the midst of a courtship.

The couple, while not stunning by Society's

standards, was handsome enough. He was not an overly tall man, but the girl gazed upon him with admiration. He assisted her as she walked and looked at her as she spoke, clearly expressing interest in what she had to say. He said something to her and she laughed genuinely. Perhaps that could have happened to Willow had she encouraged any of her young suitors the first few years after her debut.

She looked up at the man next to her. James was taller than most men in the room and as broad as some of the largest men. His black breeches and overcoat were well tailored to his muscular frame and his tie lay neatly in place.

However, there ended any similarities between him and the other men. While most of the men in the room had taken careful consideration with their appearance, smoothing their hair back with lotion and shaving any hint of stubble off their faces, James let his long blond hair hang seductively in his face, and while he might have run a blade across his face this morning, regrowth darkened his cheeks and chin. He might be dressed like a gentleman—he might even speak as one—but Willow knew he was far too dangerous to be a gentleman.

What was it about him that drew her in so inexplicably? Never before had she so much as looked twice at someone who so blatantly defied convention. Even knowing all of this about him, knowing he mocked propriety, she wanted him. Wanted to lean too close to him so that their arms brushed. Wanted to reach up and move that lock of hair out of his eyes. Wanted to press herself against him and feel his desire pour over her like a long-awaited rain.

But she could do none of those things. She'd had her one night and that was all she could enjoy. Now she had to focus on the investigation, clear her father's name, then return to her duties to her mother.

Everything was in place. James assisted Willow into the carriage. He'd already spoken to her father and received his blessing—now all he had to do was ask the question. He probably should have told his family he was getting married, but he wanted time to fairly warn Willow about what she was getting herself into.

He could already imagine the first dinner at his family's house. The seat across from him would finally be filled and his mother would chatter incessantly about tablecloths and draperies and other household nonsense. Yes, he needed time to forewarn his betrothed so she could prepare herself. He knew she'd know how to handle his mother. She'd be brilliant.

"That seemed successful," she said.

"What?"

"Finding three additional women to question. I feel certain that we're getting close to identifying the murderer."

"I think you might be right."

"Will you pick me up tomorrow?"

"Tomorrow afternoon. Around two o'clock," he said.

He probably should have purchased some sort of ring. A token that would represent their commitment. There hadn't been a lot of time, though, and he wasn't certain what to buy. Something simple, but elegant.

And then the carriage stopped, and he still hadn't asked her.

"James, is everything all right?" she asked, her forehead furrowed with concern.

"I have given it great consideration," he began, "and I believe the best and most appropriate option is for us to marry."

Her mouth fell open, but she promptly shut it. "Whatever are you talking about?"

"You are compromised, Willow, surely that fact has not escaped your attention."

"Well, of course it hasn't," she snapped. "But no one was going to marry me, and I certainly wasn't harboring any thoughts of you proposing." Her eyes widened and she pointed at him. "Is that why you think I came to your house the other night? To ensnare you? Do you believe that is the only way I could find a husband? I can assure you that if I did want a husband, I could find one. And I certainly have more pressing things to occupy my time other than plotting how to bring down bachelors such as yourself."

"Willow, I never said any of those things and I never thought them." Somehow he never managed to say the right thing to her. He sighed in frustration. "Calm down. I know you're not the sort of woman who would deliberately coerce someone into marriage. I would never suggest such a thing, let alone think it."

"You do?" she asked, clearly surprised but still angry.

"Yes, I do. This was my idea." He should have tried wooing her instead of appealing to her sensible side. Even a woman as proper as Willow wanted to be romanced, but it was a little late for that now. "I took liberties with you that only a husband has a right to take. So it is only right that I now become that husband."

"Honor," she said, furrows wrinkling her brow. "You're doing this out of honor?"

"Is it so difficult to believe that I know how to be honorable?"

Her lips pinched together. "You, who cares not a whit about what Society says? Why would you then allow them to dictate who you marry?"

"Because your reputation will be ruined."

"I will not be the first, or the last. Besides, no one knows I have been compromised—unless you have told someone."

"Of course not. But it being a secret doesn't make it any less true. You do not deserve to be used and discarded."

Her eyes met his. "I seduced you," she said matter-of-factly.

He had to smile. She thought she'd seduced him. In a way, he supposed she had. Over the time they'd known each other, each moment he'd spent with her had compounded his desire. And she had come to his home that night with the intention of making love with him.

Perhaps it had not been the sort of seduction to which he was accustomed, but it certainly had been the most effective. He smiled.

"I suppose you did. Even so, your reputation will remain intact. I've already spoken with your father. We have his blessing."

Her eyes rounded. "You did what?"

"I asked your father for your hand."

"Did you tell him?"

"No, Willow, I did not tell him. I only said I wished for you to be my wife."

"But that is not true. You wish to do the honorable thing. Well, rest assured no one will require you to fall onto the sword for this one. I shall endure any repercussions my own decisions may cause and you need not concern yourself with my well-being." With that she opened the carriage door and climbed down herself.

"Willow, wait." He stepped outside.

But she was already up the stairs to her house and opening the door. She stopped with her hand on the knob and turned. "I will still finish this investigation. But after that, you will be free of me." Then she slipped inside and closed the door behind her.

James watched her disappear into the house with a growing sense of frustration. Well, that had gone miraculously bad. But what had he expected, when he presented it like he was some sort of hero sent to save her? He was an ass.

Willow said nothing to anyone in her family, even though the lights were on and they were still awake. Instead she went straight to her room and closed and locked the door behind her. She leaned against the wooden frame and shut her eyes. Had that actually just happened?

Humiliation crept over her like a shameful blush and she wanted to scrub it away. She rubbed at her arms, but nothing inside her changed. He'd seen her as a duty and marriage to her as a way to ease his obviously guilty mind. Tomorrow she would have to look at him as if none of this had happened.

He had spoken to her father, telling him what, she was unsure. Now she would have to answer to her family as to why she had declined the only marriage offer she'd received in nine years. Not to mention gone back on a promise to her mother.

Perhaps if she said nothing they would simply believe he'd never asked. She'd rather have them believe she'd done something to prevent him from asking her than for them to know she'd passed up a perfectly good and honorable proposal.

Chapter 18

The first two women had not proved exactly helpful. While both admitted to sitting for the nude portraits, neither had men in their lives who knew of the images, and since in both cases they'd been taken years before, it seemed unlikely it would have caused someone to murder Drummond.

James and Willow waited in the parlor of the last woman. As they waited for Jane, Willow contemplated her new position and similarities to the lady in question. No, she hadn't received the number of proposals that Charlotte or Jane had, but Willow couldn't help but wonder if any of their proposals had been inspired by a sense of honor. She felt certain that Charlotte had not been compromised, but Jane had not been entirely discreet with her affairs.

Most discounted it to her eccentric nature, although it was Willow's experience that the woman wasn't particularly eccentric. She was bold and not shy, but that was not eccentric. Truth be told, she made other women nervous, and that was why people spoke unkindly about her. No one in London could understand why a woman would decline a perfectly decent marriage proposal, let alone more than one. It would be one thing if she'd been waiting for love, but that didn't appear to be the case.

No, it seemed as if Jane simply wanted to dally with whomever, whenever she chose, and she had plenty of money to ensure her security, so she never saw fit to saddle herself with an unwanted husband.

The woman stepped into the room and Willow smiled.

"Wilhelmina," Jane said with warmth in her voice. "What a lovely surprise. I did not realize you were accompanying the inspector."

Willow admitted she was surprised herself that Jane not only remembered her, but remembered her name. "Miss Portfield, it is a pleasure to see you again."

"Miss Mabson is assisting me with taking notes," James provided.

"Well, do sit. What is all this rigmarole about?" Jane asked.

"We're investigating the murder of Malcolm Drummond," James said.

"And you want to know about my connection with him," Jane filled in without being asked a question.

Willow watched the tall woman take a seat, then straighten her skirts. She wasn't exactly a beauty, although her features were striking. With her lithe body, pale blond hair and ice-blue eyes, she was exotic, and men found her irresistible. Willow looked to see if James had fallen prey to her spell, but he seemed unaffected.

"We were friends, I suppose," Jane said.

"Only friends?" James asked.

Jane gave him a sly smile "I knew him for many years and had sat for many photographs. I never took him for a lover, if that's what you're implying." She eyed Willow. "Is this too much for you, dear? I don't want my frank discussion to offend you."

Willow swallowed. "No, I'm all right, thank you."

Jane nodded. "Yes, well, we were never lovers, not because I chose not to be, you understand. I was certainly willing. He was a charming, handsome man who certainly knew how to be gentle with a lady. But I believe he was already involved. Or perhaps he preferred bedmates of the less feminine variety." Her eyes narrowed a bit. "I never could precisely decipher which. Of course I had my suspicions."

"We have reason to believe he was involved with another woman," James said.

"Ah," Jane said. "Well, that certainly seems right. So I suppose you want to know about specific photographs. The nudes," she said, her tone so casual it was as if she'd simply offered them a spot of tea, while the other women they'd questioned today had required considerable coaxing.

James didn't miss a beat. "Yes, what can you tell us about those? Did he approach you?"

"Yes," she nodded. "I'm trying to remember precisely when, but it has been a while." She waved a hand in front of her, her fingers long and graceful. "In any case, he discussed the prospect with me. Told me that they were fetching quite a handsome sum in some groups and that he thought I would be perfect for it. It seemed harmless enough." She shrugged.

"So he sold your photographs to someone?" James asked. "That means there must have been more than one."

"Unless you found the rest in his belongings, I suppose he did sell them. I never asked. He offered to give me a cut of the money, but he needed it more than I." A sly smile slid into place. "I've often wondered who purchased them and what they must think of me. I don't suppose it would be anything that hadn't already been said about me."

Willow eyed Jane with wonder. She couldn't

have been more than ten years her senior, but she carried herself in such a way—with such confidence—that she seemed older, worldly.

"Might I ask a question?" Willow asked.

James eyed her but said nothing.

"Certainly," Jane said.

"What made you agree to it? Why would you pose for such a picture without your clothes?" Then she swallowed. "Pardon my presumption."

"Not at all, my dear," she said as if she were old enough to be Willow's mother. "It's an excellent question. I'm not certain why I said yes that day, but after that first experience I knew I would agree to it again. It was the most liberating experience of my life." She crossed one leg over the other. "I've never been one to conform to convention, but even this was exceedingly bold for me. It wasn't so much being disrobed in front of him, a man who was not my lover, but more the unknown men who would see my image. It was exciting and exhilarating and powerful."

Willow let Jane's words fumble through her brain, and try as she might, none of them resonated. Was there something wrong with her? Something wrong with not wanting to be that liberated and not wanting unknown men to see her without her clothes?

"Do you have any idea of who might want to kill Mr. Drummond?" James asked.

"No, I really don't. He was an amiable fellow and everyone seemed to like him. Perhaps I wasn't the only woman, however, who would have welcomed an affair, only to be turned down. Pride is a fierce thing sometimes," she added.

James stood abruptly. "Thank you for your time. We appreciate your candor."

"Why did you ask her that question?" James asked Willow once they'd returned to the carriage.

She released a deep breath and looked out the window, but said nothing for a long while. Then she shook her head and met his gaze. "I simply can't comprehend it. I wanted to hear it from one of their mouths, why they would do such a thing. I'm not so prudish that I believe a woman should never be without clothing or that her husband should not be allowed to see her disrobed. But to intentionally pose for such a photograph that men you do not know will see." She frowned. "And a well-bred lady at that. I simply do not understand the desire."

"She said it was liberating," he reminded her.

"Yes, I heard her. A little too liberating if you ask me. There is no need for such a thing."

"She is comfortable with her body," he said.

"And I am not. I realize that," she snapped.

"I wasn't implying—"

"You don't need to imply anything, I can decipher all of this on my own." She sat back against the seat cushion and pressed her arms across her chest. "I have no such desires," she blurted out. "Does that mean something is wrong with me?"

He was unsure if she wanted him to actually answer her. "Willow," he said.

"Don't," she whispered. "I'm different. I realize that now."

"You're ashamed," he said, not even fully realizing he'd spoken aloud.

Her eyes widened and her face went white. "Ashamed," she whispered.

"Ashamed of your body," he said. He moved to sit next to her. "Do you know how many women in London would kill to have a body like yours?"

She still said nothing.

He pried her arms off of her chest and just looked at her. "You are so beautiful, Willow."

Tears filled her eyes and she shook her head. "No," she mouthed, but no sound came out.

"Yes, you are. You can't argue with me on this one. I've seen more women in my lifetime than you have. I'm an excellent judge of beauty." He traced a finger down her cheek and her eyes closed. She leaned into his touch as if she were starving for it.

His chest tightened and so did his groin. *His woman*. It was a thought he'd had on more than one occasion and he always shoved it out of his mind. He did not need a woman. Especially one as particular as Willow.

But when it came down to it, he recognized that after knowing her, every other woman in the world would seem lacking.

He cupped her face and bent in for a kiss. He didn't press his lips to hers, but moved his lips first to her right eyelid and then her left and then her forehead, down to the bridge of her nose and over to each cheek. Finally he pressed his mouth to hers.

It took little coaxing on his part to induce a response from her. Her hands wrapped around his neck and her fingers parted through his hair. Her touch was water to a thirsty man.

Their tongues molded and blended until it was difficult to tell where he began and she ended. The skin on her neck, where he gently stroked, was petal soft. He knew the rest of her was just as soft. He could close his eyes and see every inch of her flesh. Creamy and pale, except for the rosy peaks of her breasts. Desire surged through him. He deepened the kiss and she moaned into his mouth. Never had he wanted a woman the way he wanted Willow. It was indescribable, inexplicable, and terrifying.

Had the carriage not stopped when it did, he might have been able to make love to her again.

He held her close to his chest for a moment, both of them just breathing.

"Can we go to your townhome?" she asked.

He tapped the roof of the carriage, then went back to kissing her. He wanted to take her here, in the carriage, but thought better of it. This time they would share his bed. This time he would take his time. His mouth moved over hers, their tongues intertwined.

She was squirming on his lap, and her hands were tangled in his hair. He kept his mouth on hers, knowing full well she could come to her senses any moment and demand to be returned home.

And had he not been convinced that he could persuade her to marry him, he would have stopped it himself. He would not continue to take liberties with her if he knew she would never marry him. There was too much at stake. But she would agree. Eventually she would.

Finally they rolled to a stop and she looked dazed as she leaned back from him. He raised his eyebrows in a silent question and she nodded.

He helped her down and hurried up to his front stoop, pulling her gently behind him. His butler opened the door and he marched straight past him and up the stairs to the second floor. With his toe, he nudged his bedchamber door open then kicked it closed behind him.

Gently, he led her to the bed and shrugged out of his jacket. He loosened his tie and unbuttoned his shirt. She said nothing nor moved, but simply sat on the edge of his bed watching his every move. Before he completed undressing himself, he stood her up and turned her to begin unfastening her buttons.

His fingers moved quickly and before long they stood before each other nude.

"You would look stunning on one of those photographs. Your luscious body frozen in time. But I would hate for you to pose for such an image, as I could not bear it were I to know that another man had seen you this way."

"Only you have seen me," she whispered.

"I know." And he intended to keep it that way.

He laid her on the bed and crawled in next to her. Her hand smoothed the material beneath her—back and forth it rubbed. For once he was pleased he'd accepted the exotic bedcovers from his parents after their visit to India.

"I want you to know how beautiful you are," he said, leaning over her.

She shook her head.

"Yes, Willow."

"It's enough that you believe I am," she said.

"It's not enough for me. Give me your hand."

Reluctantly she slid her hand into his. Then he placed it on her opposite shoulder so that her hand covered her own flesh and his hand covered hers.

"Close your eyes, Willow."

She met his glance and held it for a moment before complying.

"Now, I want you to listen to my voice and just feel."

She nodded.

"You have the sexiest shoulders; they are so feminine and alluring. The first night I saw them, at the masque ball, I knew I would have to have you."

From there, they moved down to her left breast. With his hand he squeezed hers kneading her breast. Her breath caught. "You have perfect breasts," he said. He continued his attention to her breast, and then he moved their hands down her abdomen to settle at her waist. "Your skin is flawless, so soft. It is the skin men long to touch and women desire to have."

Her lips parted and her breathing tightened and was now coming in shorter spurts.

He slid their hands down to her rounded hips. "The way your hips flare, it's enough to drive me wild. Everything about your body declares you are a woman. Especially this," he said as he trailed their hands to the patch of hair between her legs.

She gasped.

"Have you ever touched yourself, Willow?"

She shook her head. "No," she whispered.

"What if I told you that I found it very enticing to watch your own hand move across your flesh?"

Her eyes popped open. "I—"

"Trust me," he interrupted. "I'll be right here with you." He pushed their fingers so that they parted through her crisp curls. "Do you feel that?"

She twitched beneath the touch, then nodded.

"Relax, love." With a slow and wide circle, he moved their fingers to rub against her hidden nub. He leaned close and feathered kisses against her cheek and then her ear. "I want you," he whispered.

She released a satisfied sigh.

He continued moving their fingers in a circular motion until she began to move beneath their hands. She was getting close. He leaned over and covered her breast with his mouth. The nipple hardened against his tongue and he moaned from the feel of it.

This would only work if he could keep himself together, keep himself controlled. He continued to suckle her breast and move their hands, and her body fidgeted against the bed. Her breathing was short and light and interspersed with small moans of pleasure.

Faster and faster he moved their hands and he

could feel her body get more and more rigid as her climax built. He leaned back up, not wanting to miss the sight of her release. He didn't have to wait long. Her body went still and then the waves of pleasure rocked her from her shoulders to her toes.

When she had subsided he moved their hands and placed a gentle kiss on her lips. Her eyes fluttered open and she gave him a tentative smile.

"So beautiful," he said. "Do not be embarrassed with me."

She nodded.

He laid back against the bed. "Come and sit on me, love."

She sat up and crawled across his body, straddling his legs and positioning herself against his erection. He bucked against her and she rubbed against him in return.

"Now, Willow, I need to be inside you now."

She leaned forward and kissed him passionately, almost fiercely, then she lowered herself onto him, taking all of him inside. She required no instructions, but followed her instincts and moved against him. Leaning forward so that she bent over him, giving him perfect access to her breasts. He cupped one and nipped at the other one.

She was so tight and so wet and she moved perfectly around his shaft. Pressure built inside him and he concentrated on her breasts. He suckled at her breast while she moved up and down.

And then he felt her tighten around him as another climax hit her. She tossed her head back and moaned loudly as she continued to ride him. The sound of her peak tipped him right over the edge as his own release overtook him and he yelled her name.

Chapter 19

Willow rolled over on her belly and set her head on James' chest. Absently, she raked her fingers through the mat of hair sprinkled across the plank of muscles.

"You're quite different from your family," she said.

His eyebrows raised slowly. "What makes you say that?"

"Well, for one, you're taller than all of them."

"Are you implying that I might not belong to my father? That's quite the accusation and from such a proper young miss." He gave her a playful swat on her bottom.

She laughed. "Young miss." She eyed the sheet draped loosely around them. "And not so proper anymore. I most certainly was not implying that. My brother and I look nothing alike. That does not mean he's not my brother." She raked her fingernails across his flesh. "It was merely an observation. You're just different."

"Yes, I am. I've always been different. Not interested in the same sorts of activities, less inclined to adhere to Society's rules." He shrugged. "Less impressed with myself than my brother and mother seem to be. My father follows the majority because it's easier. Which means allowing my mother to do and say as she pleases, because if she's displeased, she makes the most noise about it."

"So your father placates her to keep peace in the family," she said.

"Yes."

"And your brother?"

"Is the same as my mother. Only taller," he added with a smile.

"So you're probably more like your father—he just chooses not to antagonize them anymore."

"You," he touched her nose, "are very astute."

She kept her attention on his chest and the rippled contours of his body.

"How did an earl's son end up in the Scotland Yard?" she asked.

He smoothed her hair with his hand and was quiet for a long while. Perhaps deciding whether or not to share his story with her, she was unsure. She watched his eyes darken a shade while he continued to be silent.

"When I was a boy," he began, "my uncle committed a crime but never paid for it. That seemed rather wrong to me; so, when I grew up, I joined the Yard."

"That's it?" she said.

"That's it," he repeated.

There was more, though; she could sense it. More that he didn't want to share. "Hmm ... were you close to this uncle?"

"Yes. My mother's brother. He used to visit us and we'd often spend summers at his estate."

He continued to answer her questions. Perhaps he merely did not know how to talk about this particular subject. Family secrets were the most closely guarded of all. She knew all about that. "What did he do?"

"He killed a servant," he said flatly.

She propped herself up on her elbows. "You're certain of his guilt?"

He nodded, then sighed. "He claimed the girl tripped and fell down the stairs, but two other servants saw him push her. He's a marquess," James added with a smirk, "so what could the servants possibly know?" He did nothing to hide the sarcasm from his voice. "Those two servants were dismissed, probably never worked again, and nothing happened to my uncle."

"Nothing at all?" she asked.

"He wasn't even questioned officially. His peers all said he was a gentleman, that he could never do such a thing, but my brother and I knew better."

He paused a moment before continuing. "Uncle Felix was jolly fun to be around until he was in his cups, and then everything would change."

"Your mother?"

"I don't know if she believes him or not." His hand absently stroked her back. "I know we never spent another summer there, and he's only been to our home twice since then. He stays in the country now. Evidently he still writes my parents, as they just received word that he's ill. My mother is deciding whether or not to visit him."

"Sounds like she might be inclined to believe that he was guilty. She kept her children from visiting him again," Willow said.

"She did not want a scandal. So we never discussed what happened."

"His station in life saved him," she said.

"Yes."

So this was why. It wasn't arbitrary that he refused to follow rules. It was to segregate himself from a system he believed had failed. And he'd been trying to change that ever since, with each of his investigations. That's why he sometimes crossed lines. Because sometimes lines needed crossing.

"Enough about the miscreants in my family," he said. "What about your family? Which of your parents are you most like?"

She wanted to say more to him, to let him know

she understood—but she did not know how. He wanted to change the subject, wanted to talk about her family now. "I don't know. I suppose I am like my father as well. Edmond is very much like our mother. He's impulsive and full of life."

"You say that as if to imply you are not."

"I'm stodgy and bossy, that is not the same as being fun and impulsive," she said.

"You're not stodgy, and fun and impulsive are not the only definitions for being lively."

She poked him in the side. "I see you didn't object to my calling myself bossy."

"I try to be agreeable most of the time." He couldn't hide his smile.

"I'm more subdued, that's all," she said.

"Tell me about your mother."

"You mean the way she is?"

He nodded.

She frowned. "It started so long ago, it's hard to remember if it wasn't always a part of who she is. When I was a young girl, it was fun, her reckless behavior. She was exciting and childlike herself. But at some point, I recognized that tea parties in the rain and searching for gypsies in the forest at night were not safe or reasonable activities for mothers to engage in. She should have been chiding Edmond and me for such foolishness. Instead my father had to watch us constantly to make sure we came to no harm."

He said nothing, just continued to stroke her hair.

"She would never harm us, you understand, but she did leave us places a few times and she would get so distracted and upset about the silliest of things."

"And it's been getting worse," he said.

"Yes, as she ages, she slips further and further away, her behavior becoming more and more erratic. The doctor wants my father to drug her when she has an episode to calm her down until she comes out of it. But none of us can bear to do that. She looks so sad when she's medicated, like a shell of herself."

He kissed her head.

"My father is older than she is. By fifteen years. So I know he won't be here with her forever. It's my duty to care for her. Edmond needs to marry and produce an heir. He'll be viscount someday."

"So this is why you never married."

It wasn't a question. His green eyes bore into her and the intensity made her want to look away, but she found she could not. And why she'd declined his offer. It was unsaid, but it hung in the air, thick and impossible to ignore.

"Yes, this is why I never married. I don't think I could balance each responsibility equally. Someone would suffer. My husband, or children. I could never abandon her."

"No one would ask you to," James said.

Meaning him? "It matters not. I will not marry." She laid her head on his chest to look away from him. She couldn't deny she wished he'd ask her again. Perhaps this time she would be unable to say no. Now she wanted more, but she knew she simply could not have it.

James traced his fingers across Willow's forehead. Thick lashes rested against her cheek as she slept soundly, tucked against him. Without the worries of the world weighing on her, Willow's features were a picture of peace. So lovely, so beautiful.

Her naked body was warm and plush next to him. So many contrasts between them: she was so fair where his skin had seen too many days in the sun, her body was soft and pliant while his was rough and covered in crisp hair. And that was merely the physical differences. He couldn't ignore the obvious disagreements they had about following rules or ignoring them. Yet they both had their reasons, their scars.

Despite their differences, he'd never respected a woman more. And while she'd made it clear she would not marry him, he could only hope she would reconsider, that she simply needed time. Time to adjust to wanting something for herself. And to realize that she had every right to claim it.

Her eyes fluttered open. A shy smile slid into place. "How long have I been sleeping?"

"Not long," he said.

She burrowed her body closer to him. The citrus scent from her hair filled his nose.

"And you? You are not tired?" she asked.

"I didn't want you sneaking out of here without me knowing." He rubbed his thumb against her lip. "And you look lovely when you sleep."

She blushed and gave a slight eye roll.

He leaned forward and nuzzled the sweet flesh at her neck. "And so delectable. It's been a considerable challenge for me to lie here and keep my hands off of you. You look positively seductive wrapped in nothing but sheets."

Her gaze met his and he felt that familiar surge flow between them. Desire so thick, so hot, he nearly couldn't breathe. He might never persuade Willow to marry him, but he knew she was the only woman he'd make his bride, the only woman who could ever be his wife.

"Your restraint is showing promise," she said, dragging her hand down the side of his arm. "But I don't believe you've quite mastered it yet."

Her touch seemed to spark energy into every nerve in his body. He felt himself grow heavy again with arousal. It seemed his need for her was never satiated.

"I do know how to control myself," he said.

She braced herself on her elbows, bringing her face closer to his. Her nose nearly touched his own. "Are you quite certain?" she asked with a mock frown. "Because it seems to me that you make a practice of indulging yourself on every whim."

"I could interpret your remark as a challenge. And I could win said challenge by teasing your flesh for the rest of the evening. You would be writhing beneath my touch and begging me for more. But I would only tease you, and never indulge myself. I could endure, but I'm not certain you could withstand the torture." They both knew he was lying. He could no more deny his desire for her than he could take his next breath.

He pressed his erection against her hip, then slanted his mouth across hers. Hungrily, he kissed her. Their tongues met and melded, rolling against one another's in a lustful dance. Fire pounded his loins.

What had this woman done to him?

She turned her body toward him so that her full breasts pressed seductively against his chest. Her flesh was warm and soft and her peaked nipples brushed against his mat of hair. All the while, they kissed. Feverish, wanton, hot, wet and intense.

One of her hands slid down his torso, past his waist, then his hip until it rested at the top of his thigh. His erection pulsed with need. As if she'd sensed his want, she wrapped her hand around the length of him.

The tender touch of her fingers against him nearly shot him over the edge, but he managed to keep his control. There was no hesitancy in her touch. Willow faced lovemaking with the same fervor she had in every other aspect of her life.

Slowly she moved her hand along his shaft. Pleasure rippled through him.

"Willow, sweet Willow," he breathed. "Do you know what you do to me?"

She pumped her hand tighter and he rode the sensations until he could take no more. He clasped her wrist and pulled her hand away. Then he pushed her onto her back and leaning over her, he held her down at both wrists.

Her eyes widened with surprise, but he found no fear in the brown depths. Instead a devilish smile slid onto her face and she cocked one eyebrow. He moved against her, teasing her, but all the while, tormenting himself. Her flesh was so warm, so soft.

Desire had stained her skin in a lovely pink. In that moment he'd never seen a more beautiful woman and doubted he ever would. Entwining their fingers, he moved in for another kiss. With one swift movement he entered her. She was slick and hot and she cried out when he pulled back and then plunged back into her.

"James," she breathed.

His name, uttered from her lips and spoken with such pleasure, was a heady mixture.

Willow. His Willow.

With her legs wrapped around his waist and her nails biting into his back, he plunged into her. Over and over he moved within her and the hot, wet friction was so intense, he couldn't focus on anything else but the way her body felt. Beneath his own body, under his hands, the way she tasted, Willow surrounded him.

Her cries of pleasure poured over him like rain to the dry earth. Quenching. Bathing. Healing.

She bucked up to meet his movements. He knew she was nearing her climax, and he willed his own to wait until she slipped over the edge. Her heels dug into his back. And then her body tightened as her pleasure peaked.

He let his eyes take in her face as the last waves coursed through her. Her lips parted as she cried out and her eyes closed. And then his own orgasm rocketed through him.

After the sensations had subsided, he simply lay there, still inside her, their breath mingling, their hearts beating in perfect unison. She would leave soon, and he wanted to savor every moment until then.

James closed the door behind Willow and stepped back into his house. He leaned against the hard wood and closed his eyes. She'd made no additional mention of his proposal and he suspected that meant she still fully intended not to marry him. But she had allowed him another night of passion in her arms. She still wanted him.

He sighed, then couldn't help but smile.

He'd given it a valiant fight. Put on his armor and done battle as best he knew how. Yet still she had won. Had conquered him.

Not over the investigation, although that little wager they'd made had been lost somewhere along the journey. No, Willow had won his heart and he hadn't even noticed it was available for the taking.

He laughed at the irony as he pushed himself away from the door and headed up the stairs. His bare feet pattered against the wood floor once he hit the second landing. Here he'd spent his entire life bucking convention to prove a point, to prove that privilege and birth should not absolve someone of his actions. He'd rejected propriety because it stood for the very core of what he loathed most and yet he'd lost his heart to the very embodiment of propriety.

Warmth spread through him. She hadn't been so proper tonight as she'd clawed his back and screamed his name. She was a wanton as much as she was proper, and the intoxicating mixture had brought him to his knees.

She would never believe him if he told her now. She'd see it as a cruel way to trick her into marrying him. So his declaration of love would have to wait. Once she agreed to be his wife he'd tell her the truth.

Willow lay back in her bed, but could not close her eyes. She watched the shadows play across the ceiling. She might not understand Jane's extreme methods for experiencing liberation, but she certainly knew what it was like to need a modicum of freedom. For her, it was found with James.

It had started innocently enough with the anonymous letters she'd penned him. Inexplicably she'd written him, a stranger at the time, chastising him for taking drastic means to arrest people. People who no doubt deserved to be arrested. It had never been him she'd been angry with, she could see that now. She had only needed an outlet to express herself freely.

She thought of some of the things she'd written and wanted to apologize for her unacceptable behavior. But none of that mattered now. Perhaps because she'd already been so open with him before they met, it had been alarmingly simple to let go when she was near him. As if she'd opened her arms and released everything she'd stuffed inside.

With James she was free. In his embrace and in

his kiss. Every touch and caress and feathering of his lips across her skin pulled her more and more into liberation. At least for those moments. When all of her concerns passed away and nothing in the world mattered but how he made her feel. It wasn't right, she knew that. But after a lifetime of being tethered to the rules, losing control was incredible. And as much as she was terrified to admit it, she wanted more.

Chapter 20

Willow eyed her mother's sleeping form and sighed heavily.

"Why didn't you call for me earlier?" Edmond said.

Willow no longer could contain her tears. She had to have Edmond help her calm her mother down enough to get her to sleep. "It doesn't matter. Thank you for helping." With one last glance at her mother, she turned to walk away.

Her brother grabbed her by the elbow. "We're not finished here."

"Come out into the hallway, before you wake her," Willow whispered.

They stepped out into the hallway and Willow quietly closed the door.

"Willow, I'm serious," Edmond said. "You can't do this alone. And you shouldn't have to. She's my mother too."

"I know that. But you need to marry and have

a family. I don't have to bear that responsibility," she said. "So I'll bear this one."

"No, but you should get to have a family if you so choose, and you can't convince me you don't want one, so don't even try."

"Edmond, Papa is getting older and the years of caring for her are wearing on him. He won't be around forever and she needs constant care. How can I do that with children underfoot?" she said.

"You think we're the only people who've ever had a parent in this situation?"

She'd never thought of it before, but he was probably right. "Well, of course not. I know plenty of other people have struggles."

"Then why are you so damned special that you can sacrifice everything and play the martyr?"

"Why are you angry with me?" she asked.

He closed his eyes. "I'm not angry with you. I'm angry at the situation. All I'm saying is, stop pretending you're alone in this. She's my mother too."

"But you shouldn't have to—"

He held his hand up. "I want to. I've always understood Mother on a different level than you."

"You and she are much alike," Willow said.

He shrugged. "She's a free spirit. From here on, we share responsibility. Understood?"

"Yes." She turned to walk away.

"Oh, and you should marry that detective of yours."

She nearly tripped as she whirled around to face her brother. "I beg your pardon."

"You heard me."

"Did Papa tell you?" she asked.

"Tell me what?"

"That he'd asked."

Edmond smiled. "No, but I've seen the way he looks at you, dear sister. I knew the man would marry you. So when will you marry?"

She shook her head. "I declined."

"Willow, listen to me, do not walk away from your own happiness in some misguided attempt to take care of the rest of us. Marry him."

She couldn't argue with him, because she knew he would never understand. No one did. How did James look at her? She wanted to ask more questions, to know what he meant. But she forced herself to the climb the stairs to her room. There would be no getting sleep tonight. Her mind would be filled with thoughts of marriage and children.

Could she do it all? James had said no man would expect her to walk away from her mother, so perhaps he would help her do it all. Maybe, just maybe, if Willow's husband loved her enough, he could accept her and the duties she had to her mother. But James would never love her. He'd proposed out of a sense of honor. How could she be in a marriage where she provided the only love? Wouldn't that wear her down after a while? Make her resent him?

She might be willing to try a balance between her own family and caring for her mother, but she would only do so for love. And she knew that would never happen. Furthermore, James had seemed to ruin her for all other men. Both literally and emotionally. Even without his love, if she had to marry, he would be her only choice.

She didn't think she loved him. But there was a good chance she would. It was only a matter of time.

James had proposed once, but she'd foolishly declined. It was unlikely he'd ask her again.

James wiped a hand down his face.

Willow had come to see him so they could discuss the direction of the case, and he didn't know what to tell her. Neither could he pretend that her father wasn't a suspect. They had ignored that fact last night as they'd explored their mutual passion. But in the light of day, the truth could no longer hide.

She paced the room like a caged animal, her feet wearing a path into his rug. But she did not allow any of her control to slip. No tears, no angry outbursts, just restrained frustration.

There were times, though, when it seemed she was like a closed pot with the lid banging against the boiling liquid within and any moment, the lid would slide off and the contents would pour to the floor. He'd seen her lose control. But never in a situation like this one.

Not today.

"So I have no way to prove my father's innocence?" She stopped pacing. "James, I know my father didn't do this. I know he's not capable of such a thing. Why should he be punished because Drummond was obsessed with my mother?"

"What are you asking me to do, Willow?" Because right now, he was willing to do anything for her. Anything to clear her eyes and get her to smile.

She covered her mouth. "I don't know," she said through her fingers.

"You want me to remove any mention of your father or mother from the investigation? Do you want me to hide the evidence?" While he might have always followed his own guidelines in this job, he'd never once cheated evidence. Yes, he went by his gut more than he ought, but it was the way he worked. But for her . . . for her he would put his job on the line.

She shook her head in horror. "I could never ask you to do such a thing."

"You can't or you won't?"

"Both."

"Because, you must know, I would do that for you."

She stopped and looked at him. Emotion filled her eyes and he swore he saw love looking back at him.

They had questioned everyone on their list and still had not solved the case. James leaned back in his chair, his bare feet stretching out in front of him.

"Do we have any other suspects?" Willow asked.

James cracked his knuckles. "No."

"Only my father, that's it?" her voice rose.

"Willow, I don't believe he did this any more than you do, but I can't ignore evidence."

"What evidence?"

"All of the things Drummond wrote about her in his journal. Your mother obviously had some relationship with Drummond."

"What about all the other women he wrote about?" she asked. "Are they not suspects as well?" She pointed at him. "Did they pose nude for him?"

"As best I can tell, yes, with the exception of two," he said.

"My mother," she said.

"Yes. And Camille, or 'Millie,' as he called her. She even told me of that nickname and that they

had been lovers, when she came to visit me, but—"
He shook his head and then rose to his feet. "I
just didn't make the connection."

"The duchess?"

"Yes, I found one picture of each of the other
women in that box. Except your mother and the
duchess." He opened his mouth to say something,
but Willow's face stopped him.

Concern crossed her features. She sat down.
"There is something you should know."

"What?"

Her hands fidgeted in front of her, clearly por-
traying her nerves. "My mother did pose for him.
It was many years ago. My father told me." Her
words came out in rapid bursts.

"Your father knew?"

"Yes, he said he was furious with Drummond
for taking advantage of my mother's illness." She
shook her head. "He did not know what happened to the actual photograph. I'm sure Drummond sold it."

"You did not want to tell me this, did you?"

"No," she whispered.

"Because it makes your father look even guilt-
ier?"

She nodded.

He grabbed her firmly and pulled her to him
for an abrupt kiss. "I do believe, however, that
you may have just solved the case."

"How?"

"I think your mother's pictures aren't the only ones that are missing," James said.

Realization lit her eyes. "You believe the duchess also posed?" she asked.

He nodded. "A few days ago Duchess Argyle came to visit me at the office. She wanted to let me know that she and Drummond had been lovers. She never said anything about nude photographs, and she said there was no way her husband knew of the affair. It should have occurred to me earlier." But he'd been fixated on Willow and he'd lost sight of the investigation and had nearly missed the biggest clue.

"If the duke knew of the affair, then that would certainly give him the motivation to kill the photographer," Willow said.

"Precisely. Destruction and deception, all because of loving one woman. And this man—he's so cold, he'd be perfectly capable."

"Can you arrest him?" she asked.

"Not yet, but I can question him. Perhaps persuade him to confess and then arrest him. But we should get Camille out of the house first." He pulled out his pocket watch. "Parliament is still in session so he should be there for a few more hours."

"I'll go," Willow said, coming to her feet. "I'll bring her here."

"No, it's too dangerous."

"But you said yourself he won't be home." She put her hand on his chest. "I'll bring her here."

He eyed her cautiously. Telling her he loved her was right on the edge of his tongue.

"All will be well. You wait an hour; then you can go over there and wait for his return. When you're done, the duchess and I will be safely here, waiting."

"Get in and get out of there as quickly as you can," he said.

"I shall. Do not worry, I can take care of myself." She tentatively rose up on her toes and pressed her mouth against his.

"Of that, I have no doubt," he assured her. It was himself he was worried about, as he didn't think he could live with himself if anything happened to her. He still needed to convince her to marry him, because only after she agreed could he tell her he loved her. He wanted to say it aloud to her. To watch her eyes widen in disbelief. To feel her melt into his arms as she admitted she loved him too.

Willow took a seat in the duchess's parlor but declined the tea offered her. "There's really no delicate way to say this, so I'm simply going to come right out with it. James and I believe it's possible that your husband is the one responsible for Malcolm Drummond's death," Willow said.

Camille frowned and shook her head. "Are you certain?"

"No, we're not positive, but the evidence is certainly pointing that way. You and Mr. Drummond had an affair?"

"Yes, but I don't think my husband ever knew about it."

"It's quite likely he did know," Willow said.

"I simply can't believe it."

"Do you not believe he's capable of murder?" Willow asked.

"No," she said with a shaky laugh, "it's not that. He's quite capable of violence. He yells at our staff all the time and he's pushed me a few times, but I never thought . . ." her voice trailed off.

"James is coming over to speak with your husband." Willow stood and tried to gather Camille. "I'd like for you to leave with me so that you'll be safe," Willow said.

"She's not going anywhere with you."

Willow turned at the sound of the voice and found the duke standing in the doorway. His looming figure seemed to darken the entire room. He nudged the door shut with his foot and walked toward them, his eyes narrowing.

It was then that Willow spotted the metal in his hand. A pistol. Her heart sped to a racing tempo.

"Randall," Camille said. "Miss Mabson was just leaving."

"No, she isn't," the duke said. "Stand up!" he yelled at his wife. Then he leveled the pistol on her. "Both of you, over there." He motioned to a spot in front of the fireplace. "Now, what was it you were telling my wife? That you wanted to remove her from our home for her safety?"

Willow steeled herself, trying to feign as much bravery as she could muster.

"We know you killed Malcolm Drummond," Willow said. She was amazed at how she managed to keep her voice steady.

The duke sneered at her. "You don't know anything."

"Why did you do it?" Camille said.

"Quiet," the duke said.

Willow stood next to Camille, and the woman huddled against her while the duke aimed the pistol at them.

"I will shoot both of you," he said calmly.

"Darling," Camille said, her voice shaking. "Miss Mabson has nothing to do with this. She only came by for tea. Please allow her to leave."

"Do not call me such names," his voice raised to a higher pitch. "And do not presume to think I will let this . . . this *woman* go, so she can then bring help to save you. Do you think me a fool?" His lips tilted into a slight smile. "Of course you do, or you would not have been cavorting with that bastard behind my back."

Willow's heart was beating so loudly she could scarcely hear anything else. She was not so much afraid for her safety, but she knew James would be there any moment. The large clock standing in the corner declared it was ten minutes after the hour.

If James burst into the room, it would startle the Duke enough that he might shoot. In her mind she could imagine James clutching his chest as blood pooled on his shirt. She squeezed her eyes shut. She could not allow him to die.

Not now. She wanted to marry him. She could endure their marriage without his love. Her love for him would be more than enough for both of them. Her love. She loved him. Why had she not realized this before? And he had to care for her to some degree, else he would never have proposed.

Knowing what she knew of him now, of his uncle and James' feelings about decorum—there had to be more than honor spurring him to propose to her. Without some affection for her, he would have walked away.

She could take affection. Affection was a start. Besides, his smile and his touch were all she needed. Perhaps now she'd never have the opportunity to tell him. Tell him she loved him. Tell him how much he'd taught her. About life, about love, and about herself.

The duke's eyes moved from her to Camille. The stiffly restrained nature of his demeanor chilled Willow to her core. This was a man who believed he could control his emotions even though they ran dangerously close to the surface. Willow had lived much of her life trying to be that controlled. Foolishly believing that if she kept her feelings at bay she could prevent herself from becoming like her mother. Thinking that if she tried hard enough, she could banish any desire she had to fall in love and even more so her desire to be loved.

James had changed everything, though. He'd opened her eyes and her heart, and now she might not ever get the chance to thank him or tell him how she felt.

Out of the corner of her eye she saw the door move slightly. "Talk to him," she whispered to Camille. "Keep him focused on you." If they could keep him distracted, perhaps he would not notice when James stepped into the room.

"Randall, think of what you're doing," Camille pled with her husband.

"Shut up, Camille," he yelled. "I have no further use for your lies." He took two steps toward them and Willow saw the door behind the duke open even further. James peeked into the room, but was careful to remain unseen.

"I went over there that night to cut off his funding," the duke explained. "I had heard he'd been taking unsavory photographs and selling them. Chester Fields bought several of them, but then he was always an offensive man. But I didn't want our good name sullied with the likes of Drummond's activities." Then he released a humorless laugh.

James stepped all the way into the room and crept along the wall behind the duke. Willow squeezed Camille's hand, hoping the woman would do nothing to alert her husband to James' presence. The woman gasped.

"You know what I found, don't you?" the duke asked, his features lined with disgust.

"Yes," she blurted out, tears streaking down her face, "my photographs." Her voice was no more than a whimper. She was doing well at keeping her husband distracted.

He nodded. "You can save those tears of yours, my dear, I can assure you I am rather unaffected."

Although Willow was not so certain that was the truth. He might not feel compassion for his young wife, but he was not unaffected.

"Yes, I found those filthy photographs of you," he continued. "And there he was, sleeping on the damned chaise lounge, where your naked body had been in those pictures." He shook his head.

"I couldn't allow that. Not my wife. Not my good name. What was he going to do with those images, Camille? Was he going to sell them for the highest price? Come and buy a picture of the Duke of Argyle's whore wife."

"You never spoke to him?" she asked, clearly surprised.

James inched closer to the duke and Willow kept reminding herself to breathe. She didn't want to do anything to alert the duke to James' presence behind him. She continued squeezing Camille's hand, hoping the woman would continue doing what she'd been doing.

"No. I simply picked up the nearest thing I could find and I killed him," his tone remained as even as if he'd only announced that he was retiring for the evening.

"So you never knew," Camille said softly.

James kicked hard, hitting the duke behind the knees and buckling his legs so that he fell to the ground. The gun went off, shooting the wall behind them. Camille screamed. James put his knee in the duke's back, then pulled his arms back to place the manacles on him.

"Never knew what, Camille?" the duke yelled, lifting his head.

"That we were having an affair. That I loved him." She put her hand on her heart, then shook her head. "You killed him for some silly pictures."

"You will pay for this," he told her.

"No, I believe you'll be the one paying," James told him. "Your Grace, the Metropolitan Police will be filing charges against you for murdering Malcolm Drummond and for attempting to murder your wife and Miss Willow Mabson." He pulled the man to his feet and then called for the constables waiting in the hallway. James stepped over to Willow. "Are you all right?" He ran his hand down her cheek and looked her up and down.

"Yes."

"Let me help them bring him outside to the wagon. I have some papers I have to sign. You ladies wait right here."

James hauled the duke out of the room and Willow heard Camille sigh deeply.

"What will you do now?"

Camille gave her a shaky smile. "I'm not certain. Spend his money, perhaps."

"Will you be all right here tonight, alone?"

She took a deep breath, then moved to sit on the edge of the sofa, her hands constantly wringing the fabric of her dress. "Probably not." She gave a shallow laugh. "My sister does not live far from here, and she's always itching to rid herself of my pesky nephews for a few hours. I believe I'll stay with them for a few days, and then see how I feel." She rose and embraced Willow. "Thank you for this. I'm certain he would have killed me," her voice choked on the last word.

Willow squeezed her tightly, then pushed back to look Camille in the face. "You're welcome, and you send for James if you need anything at all."

Camille nodded. "Go." She smiled. "I know love when I see it. Don't ever let anything stand in the way of love. I should have done that when I had the chance. Go. Get your inspector."

Willow smiled in return, and then raced out of the room. She nearly ran straight into James as she stepped out onto the front stoop.

"You worried the hell out of me, woman," he said, pulling her tightly to him. He held her for several long moments before loosening his hold on her. Then he frowned and cupped her face. "What is it? Willow, what's the matter? Why are you crying?"

She swiped at her tears. Infernal things simply wouldn't stop. "I love you," she said, her voice sounding rather annoyed. Then she released a nervous laugh. "I know it doesn't mean anything to you, but I just wanted to be able to tell you. I can't believe I only just realized it today. I'm sure you've known for quite some time now." Like her tears, her words came in a swift flow she couldn't seem to control. "I can't imagine I've been all that discreet. Oh, all the things I've said to you, I feel like such a fool. Well, aren't you going to say anything?"

He smiled and grabbed both of her hands. "You were talking and I didn't want to interrupt you."

"Oh, right. Sorry."

"So you discovered today that you love me?" He seemed amused, his lips lifted in that devastating smile of his.

"Yes. You think I'm a silly schoolgirl, don't you?"

"Why would I think that? Willow, I love you, have loved you probably from that first night at Colin and Amelia's house. That sharp tongue of yours entranced me from the very beginning." He shrugged. "I was simply waiting for you to come around."

"You knew I would fall in love with you?"

"Of course. How could you not? I am dashing and intelligent and—"

She popped him on the arm. "Of all the arrogant . . ."

He laughed and pulled her into his arms. "I know I'm a lowly detective, but I was hoping you had reconsidered and would agree to become my wife."

She frowned. "My brother said I should marry you."

"Did he, now? Smart man, your brother."

"I was rather hoping you would ask me again, since I said no the first time."

"Yes, you did and I must admit, my pride is

still rather bruised. You might have some making up to do on that account."

"I have not even agreed to be your wife yet."

"Well," he asked.

"Yes, of course I'll marry you." Then she smiled. "On one condition."

"I should have known that with you, there will always be conditions."

"Yes, you should have known that."

"What is it?"

"Even if I am not an official employee of the Metropolitan Police, I shall assist you in all of your investigations."

"I think that's asking a bit much." He kissed her on the forehead. "You are going to be the most difficult wife in London," he said.

"I suspect I might be," she agreed.

"I wouldn't want it any other way."

Epilogue

She was married.

Willow stood in a crowded parlor awaiting the grand feast in celebration of her nuptials. She and her three friends huddled together as they'd done at countless balls and soirees, but today it was different.

She was a married woman. Not only that, but she loved her husband, and he loved her. She shook her head in disbelief, it still seemed so far-fetched, yet it was true nonetheless.

Willow knew she had a foolish grin on her face, but it would not seem to fade. And at the end of the day, she'd spent so much of her life not smiling that it felt amazingly good to feel giddy with love. Her friends chatted around her, but she heard none of their words.

"I feel certain that we can still catch him, uncover his identity," Charlotte said.

The Jack of Hearts, Willow realized. So often their

talk turned to him. He'd been their ongoing investigation for almost two years, and still they had been unable to uncover any decent information on him. Granted the police hadn't fared much better.

"We might never catch him," Meg said, rubbing her hand across her large belly.

"Perhaps it is past time we let go of this particular mystery," Willow agreed.

Amelia cleared her throat. "We cannot relent yet, ladies. There are still clues to uncover, and I have a feeling that when it comes to this case, we will prevail."

Charlotte sighed in relief.

James appeared behind her. "Might I borrow my wife for a moment?"

The word "wife" sent a fresh wave of shivers through her. She had spent much of her life believing that marriage was not to be for her, and for once she'd been glad to be proven wrong. Through the crowd they walked and out the parlor, into a darkened study.

Once the door was closed behind them, he pressed his body against hers. "Do you know how badly I want you right now?"

Desire poured over her limbs. "I think I might have a small inkling."

"There is a perfectly good rug in this very room," he said, then nibbled his way down her neck.

She enjoyed the torment for a while, before

popping him on the arm. "James, honestly, we cannot do this here. Right now."

"Why not?"

"Because everyone will know what we're doing. Besides." She walked her fingers down the center of his torso. "I want to take my time with you tonight." She went up on her toes and gave him a fiery kiss.

"Saucy wench. When you put it that way, you know I cannot deny you." He linked her arm with his as he led her out of the room. "Indeed. So what is the Ladies' Amateur Sleuth Society scheming tonight?"

"We were discussing whether or not we should cease our chase of the Jack of Hearts," she said.

"And what was the consensus?"

"We'll keep hunting. We'll find that bandit, sooner or later."

"Of that, I have no doubt, my love. As much as I'm loathe to admit it, you are quite the detective," he said with a smile.

"Loathe?"

He squeezed her to him. "Okay, perhaps not loathe, but I will not concede that your detecting skills rival mine. But I love you, nonetheless."

"How positively generous of you," she said.

"And." He nudged her.

"And I love you." She could not help but laugh. "Even though you are completely insufferable."